"It's over and done with," Miguel

Adriana stated emphatically.

"It doesn't have to be," James said quietly.

"It does!" She whirled around, her eyes blazing with the emotions that bubbled inside her. "There wasn't anything between us, and there won't ever be. There can't."

He shrugged. "Why not?"

"Because I don't want it! Whatever we felt was something removed from reality. The only reality is the trial. I can't say, 'Let's start over fresh, as if nothing ever happened.' I'm not that generous. I could never feel anything for the man who sent my father to prison."

Dear Reader,

Once again, Silhouette Intimate Moments has prepared a stellar list of books for your reading pleasure. So go ahead, sit in the sun (or the shade, if you prefer) and treat yourself to a few hours of enjoyment.

First up, Kristin James finishes her trilogy called "The Marshalls" with *The Letter of the Law,* featuring James Marshall, the last of the brothers to have his story told. And don't forget—if you missed *A Very Special Favor,* the first of the series, you'll be able to find it in bookstores in September. Rachel Lee made her first appearance as part of the "February Frolics" new-author promotion, and you won't want to miss her second novel, *Serious Risks.* It's a wonderful blend of romance and white-knuckle suspense. I think you'll love it. Dee Holmes spins a warm tale (despite its wintry setting) in *Maybe This Time,* a story proving that love can, indeed, conquer all. Finally, one of your favorite authors, Kathleen Korbel, is back with *A Rose for Maggie.* I don't want to give anything away about this one, so I'll satisfy myself with saying that this is truly one of those books that will bring tears to your eyes as you share the very special love of this family in the making.

As usual, we're keeping an eye on the future as well as the present, and you can count on seeing more of your favorite writers in months to come. To name only a few, look for Nora Roberts (next month!), Emilie Richards and Marilyn Pappano. And also next month, look for Judith Duncan—a name that many of you may recognize—to make her first (but not her last) appearance in the line.

As always—enjoy!

Leslie Wainger
Senior Editor and Editorial Coordinator

KRISTIN JAMES

The Letter of the Law

SILHOUETTE·INTIMATE·MOMENTS®

Published by Silhouette Books New York

America's Publisher of Contemporary Romance

SILHOUETTE BOOKS
300 East 42nd St., New York, N.Y. 10017

THE LETTER OF THE LAW

ISBN: 0-373-07393-3

First Silhouette Books printing August 1991

Printed in the U.S.A.

KRISTIN JAMES,

a former attorney, is married to a family counselor, and they have a young daughter. Her family and her writing keep her busy, but when she does have free time, she loves to read. In addition to her contemporary romances, she has written a number of historicals.

Chapter 1

Adriana Cummings picked up her bag from the luggage carousel and walked out the door of the airport. Even though it was late in September and no longer extremely hot, the humidity of North Carolina was a surprise to her after the high, dry air of Taos. It was that way every time she came back for a visit. She had lived in New Mexico for almost seven years, and gradually it had grown to seem normal, whereas the dampness and lush growth of her native Winston-Salem were strange to her now. She set down her bag and glanced around. Suzanne had said she would pick her up at the airport. Adriana hadn't been surprised that her sister wasn't there to meet her when she stepped off the plane. After all, Suze was not known for her promptness. But she had expected her to show up by the time she had claimed her baggage.

A horn tooted, and a white van pulled over to the curb and jerked to a stop. The driver, a tall slender woman with light red hair, jumped out and came around the van, arms outspread. "Dree! You old thing, you!"

Suzanne might be thirty-four and the mother of three children now, but her voice still sounded like a Homecoming Queen and Tri-Delt, drenched with enthusiasm and sweetness. Adriana smiled. She and her older sister had never been much alike, Suzanne the model debutante and Adriana the quiet, artistic loner, but there was a strong bond of affection between them. "Hi, Suze, how are you?"

Adriana stepped forward to meet Suzanne's embrace. Suzanne squeezed her tightly and said, sotto voce, "Damned relieved, that's how I am." She stepped back, giving her sister the small wry smile that was much more a part of her personality than the bright beauty pageant grin she presented to the world. "I've been with Mama for three days, and I tell you what, even those three screaming little darlin's at home are looking mighty good. Ted most of all."

"That bad, huh?"

"Yes. The closer the trial gets, the more antsy Mama is. And the more determined to put up a brave front. By now she's talking nonstop and laughing in that phony way. My nerves are in shreds, honey. Absolute shreds. And I have to come back next Monday when jury selection begins. I can't *not* show up the very first day of the trial. But at least you'll be here, too, and that'll make it easier. You have a calming effect on her, just like Daddy." A subtle change touched her features, then was gone as she pulled a comic face. "What's worst of all is knowing she's so much like *me*."

Though she had said it in a funny manner, it was the truth. Their mother, Millie, and Suzanne were both high-strung women possessed of great nervous energy and a flirtatious, talkative charm. Either one of them could irritate a person to death, but they were also hard to resist. Adriana, on the other hand, had always been much more like her father, quieter and calmer, with more stamina and practicality. Ever since she could remember, the family had fallen along those lines, Adriana being closer to her father and Suzanne closer to their mother.

"Well, I'll see what I can do this week. We can't have her all wrought-up when the trial begins. That won't help Daddy any."

Suzanne grimaced. "What will?"

She picked up Adriana's smaller bag and walked to the back of the van to set it inside. Frowning, Adriana grabbed the large suitcase and followed her.

"What did you mean by that?" she asked in a worried voice as she swung the suitcase into the van.

"Oh . . . you know." Suzanne shrugged and slammed the door shut. "There's lots of talk. Lots of rumors."

She walked around to the driver's side, cutting off the conversation, and Adriana had no choice but to go around to the passenger side. She climbed inside and glanced around the luxurious interior. "Hey, talk about a suburban mom!" she teased.

Suzanne giggled. "I know. Isn't it a scream? Remember how I always used to say I'd have a chauffeur and a limousine to drive my children around? *I* was going to spend all my time at the club." She expertly wheeled the big vehicle out into the traffic, chattering away. "Now look at me. I do spend my time at the club—taking Jory for swimming lessons and Kayla to play tennis and watching Kimmy in the baby pool half the afternoon. I think the kid's part fish. Thank God summer's over. Of course, now all the dance lessons and karate lessons and soccer practice have started. I should have gone to driving school, not Sweet Briar.''

"It's hard to imagine." Adriana looked over at her older sister. All the time Adriana was growing up, Suzanne had lived for her looks, her appeal to the opposite sex. She had practiced walking, flirting, putting on makeup. She had dated first this boy and then that, testing her skills. She had talked of little except dating and clothes. Now, looking at her, it was hard to believe she was the same person. She was still pretty, of course. Her beauty was natural, and her vivacious charm deeply ingrained. But she wore a casual pair of blue jeans and a T-shirt, tied on one side at the waist, with plain brown sandals on her feet. Her fingernails were cut short and sported only clear polish. The red-gold hair was pulled up into a simple ponytail atop her head, and her face was devoid of any makeup except lipstick. There was a sprinkling of cinnamon-colored freckles across her nose and cheeks.

She had married a very successful doctor and lived in an enormous house with a part-time maid to care for it, as well as a live-in helper for the children. But, even so, her life was filled with school and after-school activities, and she was so busy with her volunteer work at the school and the hospital, as well as the kids, that her life was too hectic for her to spend hours each day on looking good.

Suzanne felt Adriana's eyes on her and turned toward her, smiling. "You look really good, you know."

"Thank you." Adriana smiled, pleased by the compliment. Somehow, it was especially gratifying when Suzanne complimented her. She had grown up thinking that Suzanne was the beauty of the family, and she still felt that way. Even though she knew that she herself was attractive, she had never realized that her deep auburn hair and classic features were actually more beautiful than Suzanne's carroty-colored hair and cute face.

"New Mexico must agree with you."

Adriana nodded. "I like it. Although sometimes nowadays I find that I get homesick. Isn't that odd? I never did when I was young. I thought that was when you were supposed to be homesick." She sighed. "Maybe that's because of the divorce. When I was married, I always wanted to put as many miles as possible between us and Mama and Daddy. They disliked Alan so."

"With good reason."

"That makes it even worse. I guess I always suspected they were right, and that only made me more stubborn and determined to make things work. It was like beating a dead horse, though."

"Mm. Probably about as pleasant." Suzanne cut her a sidelong glance.

Adriana had to chuckle. "Yeah. You're right. Alan was weak."

"And critical."

"And jealous."

"And an utter Philistine, to boot."

The chuckle turned into a laugh. "Lord, but he hated my art."

"He knew it would take you away from him. Everything about you that meant growing up, expanding, exploring, meant you'd leave him. He wasn't capable of any of those things."

"Isn't it amazing how clearly you can see the mistakes you made in the past? Four years ago I never would have admitted any of that. Now we've been divorced two years, and I look back at him and think, why in the world did I marry him?"

"I think because Daddy disliked him so much."

"I was into rebellion back then." Adriana had been twenty years old when she married Alan and determined not to let her father or anyone else tell her what to do. She had adored her father when she was younger, depended on him, trusted him, followed his advice. Yet when it came to love and marriage, she had set herself fiercely against him, almost as though she had to break with him to love another man. For a few years things had been strained between them, until at last she admitted to herself how right Jack Larson had been about Alan. Since then, though, she and her father hadn't quite recaptured the special closeness they'd once had, but the awkwardness and restraint were gone—and so was the need to oppose him.

They were silent for a moment. Adriana glanced over at Suzanne thoughtfully. "Okay. Now tell me what it was you didn't want to say when we were putting my bags in the car."

"What do you mean?" Suzanne didn't look at her.

"Come on. You know what I mean. When you asked what would help Daddy, as if nothing would. Then, when I asked, you made some vague remark about rumors. What rumors? What were you saying?"

Suzanne sighed. "Oh . . . I don't think this town has to try Daddy. I think they've already convicted him."

"Everybody thinks he's guilty?" Adriana was shocked. "But so many people know Daddy, know what he's like. How could they believe those charges?"

"Well, not *everybody*. There are a few friends of Mother's who insist he didn't do anything wrong. But in general . . . yeah, that's what I've heard. I mean, think about it. When you see someone going into the police station and courtroom on TV and hear how they've been charged with this or that, don't you pretty much assume that they're guilty? You don't sit there and say, 'Why, he could be innocent. I want to hear his side of the story.'"

"I guess that's true. But Daddy's so well-known, so prominent—"

"That's reason enough for some people to hate him. You know the kind of mentality that thinks all rich people are bastards and crooks and deserve the worst. Besides, the media has crucified him."

"Poor Daddy." Adriana sighed. "And poor Mama. What does she say about the rumors?"

"You know her. She doesn't admit they exist. She likes to pretend that nothing is wrong and everyone is standing by Daddy."

"But they're not?"

Suzanne shook her head. "Not by a long shot. Suddenly he doesn't have any friends in government anymore. Or anywhere else, for that matter."

"Oh, Suzanne, this is awful."

"You don't know the half of it. Wait until you get jumped on by reporters a few times, or have people stop you in the grocery and tell you they think your father's a crook."

"Suzanne! That's happened to you?"

Her sister nodded. "It hasn't been a pleasant time."

"Why didn't anyone tell me how bad it was? I could have come home sooner. I didn't *have* to wait until the trial. But Mama kept telling me how well everything was going and assuring me that Daddy was out on bail and doing fine. All of his friends rallied around, she said, and everybody was telling her they were sure he was innocent." When her mother had first called a few months ago, sobbing out the story of her father's arrest for insider trading, Adriana had offered to fly home at once, but her mother had convinced her that it wasn't necessary.

"Dree—" Suzanne's voice sounded pained at her naiveté "—you know our mother rearranges the facts to fit with what she wants them to be. This is the woman who insisted that Marie Hemmings is simply a little moody when everybody knows that Marie spends at least three months a year locked up in some private sanitarium or other."

Adriana looked at her. Suze was right. To say that Millie Larson was optimistic was to be kind. Naturally she would pretend that everything was going better than it was. Why had she believed Mama when she had said they were getting along fine and that Adriana needn't bother about coming out before the trial? The answer to that was obvious: because she had wanted to believe it. She didn't want to have to face the thought of her family being devastated by the trial, or the possibility of people turning against her father, believing that he had committed the crimes they'd accused him of.

"How bad is it really?" Adriana asked flatly.

"How good is the prosecution's case?" Suzanne shook her head. "I haven't any idea. But I figure they wouldn't have brought it to trial if they hadn't been pretty sure of themselves."

"That's not necessarily true. Once they'd arrested Dad and made such a big to-do over it, they might have figured they had to go through with it, no matter what. They couldn't have said, 'Sorry, we don't have enough evidence after all,' and let him go. They'd have to save face."

"That's what Mama says, too. Maybe it's true. I hope so. But I keep thinking, how much face can they save if the defense is able to tear their case apart in a public trial? Why wouldn't they have plea-bargained?''

''The prosecutors are using a famous case to make their careers. If it hadn't involved someone well-known and wealthy, they probably would have dropped it a long time ago.''

''Again, how is it going to make their careers if they don't get a conviction? If they look like ill-prepared fools who came to court without enough evidence?''

Adriana stared at her sister in horror. ''Suzanne! What are you saying? That you think Daddy's guilty?''

''No. No, I'm not saying that. But I find it hard to believe that they don't have a good case.''

''But he didn't do it. Surely that counts for something. And he's got a good lawyer. There are bound to be holes in the other side's case. Like motive. Why would Daddy risk doing something like that? He hardly needs the money, not with the kind of salary he makes—and with Mama's money, too.''

''What I've read doesn't say anything about money. The stockbroker who used the inside information is a woman. A rather attractive one. The papers are implying that she and Daddy were having an affair. They're saying he did it for love.'' She stated the last words in a mockingly melodramatic voice.

Adriana was shocked. Her mother had never breathed a word of this to her. ''Daddy? Oh, Suzie, no, that couldn't be.''

Suzanne shrugged. ''I don't know. All I know is that he's not living at the house.''

''What?''

''Mama says it's because of the trial, that his attorney wants to keep him hidden where the press can't get to him, instead of at home.''

"That makes sense."

"Yeah."

"You don't seriously believe . . . ?"

"I don't know what I believe anymore!" Suzanne scowled, gripping the steering wheel so hard that her knuckles turned white. "It's all so confusing. Surely Daddy couldn't have done anything criminal. But on the other hand, I wonder, then why did they arrest him? They must have some evidence against him." She glanced at her sister, and her eyes were pained and puzzled.

"It's those glory hog prosecutors," Adriana said, firmly. "I'm sure Mama's right about that. They've brought in hotshot attorneys from D.C., and they're playing it up for all it's worth. They want to get their names in the newspapers and on TV. People will remember who they are, even if they don't win the case. Innocent people do get caught in things like this. Remember that case in Texas where they got the wrong guy, and he even got convicted, when all the time he couldn't possibly have done it because there were eyewitnesses who said he was somewhere else at the time? And I know I read just recently about a man who'd been in prison for years and was finally released because some other man confessed to the crime. Things like that do happen. That has to be the way this is. You know Daddy couldn't have done anything like that!"

"I know. I guess it's just that seeing it in the newspapers and on TV all the time, it sort of shakes you." Suzanne smiled at Adriana. "I'm glad you're here. You'll help bolster me and Mama up. You really have faith. You believe. Sometimes I think Mama says all those things just because she's trying to convince herself." Suzanne sighed. "Oh, let's stop talking about this. I'm going to drive myself crazy. How would you like to hear about your nieces and nephew?''

Adriana smiled. ''I'd love to.''

They chattered about other things the rest of the way to the house. It was a long drive, for the regional airport was closer to Greensboro than to Winston-Salem, but finally Suzanne pulled the van into the driveway of their parents' house, a large white Southern colonial in the ''old money'' section of town.

Adriana smiled at the house. It looked belovedly familiar. She had grown up here; they had moved in when she was eight years old. It was an imposing house, but she had never thought of it that way. To her it was simply home.

She and Suzanne pulled her bags out of the van and started toward the entrance, but before they had even reached it, the door flew open and their mother rushed out. Millie Sedlow Larson was a slim, wiry woman with graying blond hair that she had never tried to dye to a more youthful color. Her skin, though pale, had the slightly leathery look of someone who had spent hours in the sun, and her face and arms were liberally sprinkled with freckles. A socialite, she was not the sort who spent her time on volunteering and clothes, but a country club woman who spent most of her time at the pool and on the golf course.

''Oh, Adriana!'' she cried, smiling hugely, and threw her arms around her.

''Hi, Mama.'' Adriana hugged her back.

Millie stepped back and smiled into Adriana's face. ''You look absolutely beautiful. Your father will be so happy to see you. I know it will give him a real lift just knowing you're here. He depends on you, you know.''

Adriana wasn't sure about that. Much as she loved her father, he had never been someone who depended on anyone else. He had always been his own man, quiet and capable. "Well, I hope my being here helps him."

"It'll help me, that's for sure. Suzie's going home tomorrow, and I dread the thought of waiting for Monday all alone." She sighed and linked her arm through Adriana's. "Come inside, dear, and fill me in on everything you've been doing."

Adriana proceeded to comply with her request, dredging up anything of any interest that she had seen or done in the past year. It didn't really matter what she said, she thought; it was obvious that her mother was listening with only half an ear. Adriana was sure that her mother's mind was on her husband and the trial. Adriana talked until she had run completely out of things to say, and then a silence fell over them. Adriana didn't know where Suzanne had disappeared to. She was probably upstairs packing to go home and tactfully giving Adriana and her mother some time alone.

Adriana spoke up. "I hope I'll get to see Daddy soon."

A faint frown touched her mother's forehead. "I don't know, dear. His attorney's trying to keep his whereabouts a secret, I think. So he can have some rest from the press. They've hounded him to death."

"But surely he calls home. You must talk to him."

"Oh, yes, I'm sure he'll call to say hello to you. You'll get to speak to him."

"It seems so odd to think of him not being here with us."

"There's nothing about our lives anymore that isn't odd." Bitterness tinged her voice. "Strange people calling us. Reporters camped out on our lawn. Living everything by what the attorneys say. Why, do you know that

Jack's attorney even told me very specifically what to wear to the trial? You, too. Conservative dresses and suits, neutral tones. Nothing that looks too expensive or flashy. As if *I* would wear anything flashy. I felt like telling him that my mother taught me how to dress, and she was a far better judge of propriety than he.'' She paused, studying her fingernails. ''But, of course, I didn't.''

Millie chewed on her lower lip for a moment, not looking at Adriana. Then she jumped up and crossed the room to the bar, busying herself with taking a soft drink out of the refrigerator and pouring it into a glass. She took a couple of sips, set it down on the marble-topped counter and walked over to the window to look out. Adriana watched her rapid, aimless movements. She had been jumping up and down and walking around like that ever since they'd begun talking. She was obviously as nervous as a cat, however much she tried to hide it with bright smiles and talk.

''Mama, are you okay?''

''Okay?'' Millie turned, flashing one of those quick, false smiles. ''Of course I'm okay.''

''You seem awfully nervous.''

''Well, you know how I am. Jack always tells me I'm too much of a worrier. 'Things will take care of themselves,' he'd tell me, 'and your worrying about it won't change it one bit.' He's right, of course. But sometimes it's awfully difficult not to...'' Her voice trailed off, and she drew a shaky breath. Tears glinted in her eyes. ''Oh, Lord, Dree, I'm scared to death. What am I going to do?''

Adriana rose and went to her, curling a comforting arm around her shoulders. ''Of course you're worried and scared. It's only natural. But I'll be here to help you, and Suze'll come back for the trial, too.''

"Suzanne has been a great comfort to me. I shouldn't depend on you girls like this, but I can't help it." She wiped tears from her cheeks with the edge of her hand. "Your father's the strong one, not me."

"You'll do fine. I know you will." She gave her mother's shoulders an encouraging squeeze.

"Thank you, dear. I'm so glad you're here." Millie managed a tremulous smile and patted Adriana's arm. "Well, it does no good to dwell on that. Let's talk of something else, shall we?"

But though they turned to another topic, Millie was still restless, and before long the conversation had drifted back to her worries about her husband and the trial. As the next few days passed, Adriana found that that was the pattern of her mother's life. She was nervous, anxious, worried, and though she tried to hide it with smiles and conversation about other things, it was impossible to mask it completely.

Adriana was worried, too—about her mother. Millie seemed almost at the breaking point, and Adriana was afraid that at some point she might snap. The thought of the trial was enough to make anyone nervous, and Millie had never been a calm person. But to make it worse, there were always people calling, sometimes almost total strangers, wanting to know about the trial or to give their opinion as to Jack Larson's guilt. Reporters tried to contact Millie for a story, not only on the phone but even coming up to the door and knocking. There was often a reporter outside waiting for them to leave, and he would come hurrying up to ask them a question. Once when Adriana stepped outside for a peaceful walk around the grounds, a photographer popped up, seemingly from nowhere, and took her picture. It was infuriating, but it was also rather intimidating. It made her feel a little nervous, almost claustrophobic, afraid to go out of the house because she would have to face one of *them*. She wondered how her mother had managed to stand it this long. It was no wonder she was overwrought.

The day after she'd arrived, her father had called her. "How's my girl?"

"Oh, Daddy! I'm so glad to hear you. It seems so strange being home and you not being here."

"I know. Hopefully it won't be for too long."

"I want to see you. How can I see you?"

"I want to see you, too, sweetheart. That's why I called. Why don't we set up a meeting?" His chuckle had little humor in it. "This trial's turned us into secret agents, huh? You sneak out and give the press the slip, and I'll meet you at—say, the square in Old Salem. It's mostly tourists there, less chance of my being recognized."

Tears sprang into Adriana's eyes. It was so horrible to think of her father having to hide out, like a hunted animal. "Of course. When? Tomorrow?"

"Yeah. Let's make it morning. We'll get some of that sugar cake and sit in the square and have breakfast. How does that sound?"

"Great."

The next morning he was standing waiting for her beside the pump in the town square of the original Moravian community, a white bakery sack in his hand. He was still a handsome man, the silver streaks at his temples lending dignity to his rich auburn hair, and he was as impeccably dressed as ever, but Adriana saw that he looked older and more tired. He smiled when he saw her and enfolded her in his arms, but much of the old familiar vitality was missing from his voice.

They sat down on a bench and ate the sugar cake that he'd bought down the street at the Moravian bakery, licking the stickiness from their fingers. Adriana thought of how many times, all through her life, her father had brought home the hot sweet bread on a Saturday morning, and she and he shared it, sitting at the small table in the breakfast room, laughing and talking about anything and everything. It had been something of a ritual, their casual Saturday breakfasts together, treasured moments of closeness with her busy father. She had even gotten up early when she was a teenager and had been out late on a date the night before just so she could spend those few minutes alone with him, before Mama and Suzanne got up.

"Thinking about Saturday mornings?" he asked, a small, wistful smile on his face.

"Yeah. How did you know?"

"I was, too. You were such a bright, funny, inquisitive kid. I always enjoyed those mornings so much." He sighed. "Oh, Dree... the way life messes you up."

His arm went around her, and she turned her face into his shoulder, squeezing him tightly. She didn't ask him if he had done what he was accused of. He didn't try to explain his innocence. Either would have been an insult to their relationship. With the love of years, she trusted him, and he knew it.

"I love you, Daddy."

"I love you, too, sweetheart."

The next morning, the Carters, a couple who were among her mother's best friends, came over for a visit. The real purpose of their visit, Adriana suspected, was the subject they brought up right before they left, almost as an afterthought. "Say, there's a dance at the club tonight—the last one before the warm weather ends. It's by the pool, a luau or something." Mr. Carter beamed at Millie. "Why don't you two come with us?"

"Oh, no, I couldn't," Millie protested immediately.

"Sure you could. Why not?"

"Well, it just...I couldn't..." She turned toward Adriana. "But why don't you go, sweetheart? It'd be nice for you to see some of your old friends."

Adriana doubted that there would be many of her old friends there tonight, but the thought of getting out of the house for a while was rather appealing. It would be wonderful to hear something except talk about the trial for a change, and music, food and idle chatter would be soothing to her psyche after several days around her mother's nerves. Much as she sympathized with Millie, it was difficult not to get irritated—and even more difficult not to show it.

"I'd like to go," she admitted. "But I can't just leave you here alone. You come, too."

Millie shook her head. "Oh, no. I hardly ever go to the club anymore. I know I'm weak. I ought to hold my head up and just go on, for pride's sake. Jack says when I stay away it looks like I'm embarrassed and that he's guilty. That's not what I mean at all, but...well, it's just so hard. I can't stand the stares and the whispers. I'm just sure that everyone's talking about me."

"It's merely your imagination," Mr. Carter said robustly. "The people at the club love you. You know that."

Adriana couldn't imagine her mother staying away from the country club. In the past it had been her second home. In decent weather hardly a day went by when she wasn't out there doing something—golf, tennis, bridge, or at least having lunch. It must be terribly hard on her to be cut off from her friends and her normal life. Anger rose in Adriana at the thought of whispers and looks and sly innuendoes her mother must have intercepted to make her dread the club.

"Daddy's right," she said, squaring her jaw. "You shouldn't let them run you off like that. You love the club. You ought to go ahead, and to hell with what they think."

Her mother smiled ruefully. "I wish I could. But I'm not like you, Dree. I'm not that strong."

"Nonsense," Mrs. Carter contradicted softly. "You're a very strong person. And you'd like the party once you got there. I'm sure. We'd stick with you the whole time."

"No." Millie shook her head. She was adamant. "I can't handle it. Not yet. After the trial, when everyone's learned how wrong they were, well, then I'll go. But not now. Please, don't ask me."

Mr. Carter looked at her for a moment, then sighed and said, "Okay, Millie, if that's what you want. We won't try to argue." He turned toward Adriana. "What about you, young lady? Would you be willing to go with a couple of old fogies?"

Adriana hesitated. She would like to get out. Of course, she didn't relish the thought of having to put up with whispers and sidelong looks all evening. But surely it couldn't be all that bad. Mama was probably exaggerating; she was very sensitive to any kind of snub. Adriana thought she could handle a few looks. Besides, her father was right. She ought to face down the gossips for pride's sake, let them see that she was convinced of her father's innocence, show them how unconcerned she was by their gossip. Mama's embarrassment probably had made everyone believe even more that Daddy really was guilty.

She lifted her chin a little. "All right. I'll go. What time should I be ready?"

Chapter 2

James Marshall wound his way through the crowd, balancing a plate of food in one hand and carrying a drink in the other. It was no mean feat, considering the crush of people around the pool. A woman stepped back, knocking into his arm and almost sending his plate flying, and, not for the first time, he wondered what in the world he was doing here. The case opened Monday, and he should be back at his house or the office, making last-minute preparations, instead of mingling with a crowd at the country club's Farewell to Summer party. He didn't even like such parties—or most of the people here, for that matter. How had he ever let Adam talk him into coming?

He reached the round metal table where his brother Adam sat and laid down the plate and drink with a sigh of relief. "I must be crazy."

Emily, Adam's wife, looked up at him and smiled. As always, she looked cool, comfortable and very pretty.

There was a serenity about Emily that was soothing, and James had to smile back. Though he generally preferred a more vivid beauty in women than Emily's pale blond prettiness, he could understand how she had woven a spell around Adam. There was a sweetness and calm about her, a gentleness, that must have been a relief after Adam's troubled first marriage. Obviously Adam was still very much in love with Emily after a year of marriage. If for no other reason, James would have liked her for the happiness and tranquillity she had brought his brother, but the longer he was around her, the more he had come to appreciate her for herself.

"Bad day?" she asked.

James shook his head and sighed, stretching out some of the kinks of tension. Until this moment he hadn't realized how knotted up he was. "No worse than usual. It's just this case."

"Contelco?" Adam asked knowledgeably.

"Yeah. We're going to court Monday. It's kind of frustrating, doing all this work, but knowing that it's mainly going to be the boys from Washington who'll be handling the trial."

"It's tough," Adam commiserated. Nobody enjoyed doing a great deal of work on a case and not being the one to actually try it. "But you know the Feds."

"Yeah. This is too important for them to let a local yokel prosecute it." James grimaced.

"You won't get to do any of it?" Emily asked sympathetically.

"Oh, I'll make the opening statement. That'll sit better with the jury, they think. They're afraid their Yankee accents will put the jury off right at the beginning."

Emily smiled again. "They're probably right about that."

"Yeah," Adam agreed. "Nothing worse than a gang from 'Up North,' Feds yet, going after a native son."

James shrugged as he dug into his food. He'd been so busy today that he'd completely forgotten about lunch, and it wasn't until he'd seen the buffet table that he had realized how hungry he was. "They won't have any problem, anyway," he said confidently. "We've got Larson cold." He glanced at Adam. "You know that."

Adam nodded. Contelco was one of Marshall, Pierson's biggest clients, and Adam had been working on a civil suit against Larson almost as long as James had been preparing the criminal case.

"You look awfully thin, James," Emily put in, frowning. "I think you've been working too hard on this case."

"Sometimes I forget to eat lunch," he admitted. It wasn't uncommon for him to lose fifteen pounds when he was deeply involved in a trial. Whatever James got involved in, he did it with such concentration and commitment that he excluded almost everything else. It had made him a very successful prosecutor, but there were times when it played havoc with his life outside the office.

"I knew it." Emily looked exasperated. "You ought to eat more. It won't help your case any if you get sick, you know."

"Yes, Mother." James shot her a teasing glance, then looked at Adam. "How do you put up with it?"

Adam grinned. "I'm used to it—from all those years she bullied me at the office. Now she bullies me at home, too."

Emily rolled her eyes and groaned expressively. All three of them knew that she was one of the gentlest and most compliant people around, unlikely to bully anyone. It was only when it came to the well-being of some-one she loved that she would put her foot down, but when that happened she was as immovable as a rock. She had been Adam's secretary for years before they fell in love, and she had taken care of him at the office, not only keeping track of his appointments and having whatever file he wanted at his fingertips, but also bringing him a sandwich at noon when he was immersed in a case as James was now—and making sure that he ate it.

"Right. That's why every attorney in Winston-Salem would kill to get her for his secretary," James commented dryly.

"Don't remind me." Adam smiled at his wife, and his face was suddenly very warm and loving. Something seemed to pass between them in the look.

James, watching them, felt a slight pang. He could only guess at the love and closeness that made two peo-ple capable of communicating so easily without words. He had certainly never felt it with a woman, and he doubted that he ever would. As more than one woman had reminded him, he was too caught up in his career to have room for a woman in his life, except in a peripheral way. With his typical Marshall good looks, he had no trouble attracting women, but he had managed few long-term relationships with any of them. There were times when he had wished he could, when coming home to his austere bachelor house made him feel cold and empty, and he longed for a touch of regenerating love. Seeing Adam and Emily, he could almost believe such love was possible, but he was afraid it was something he was in-capable of feeling. In dark moments, he had wondered if he was like his father and love would never be more than a mild emotion for him, while his heart and pas-sion were given to work.

"I'm going to lose my secretary soon, I'm afraid," Adam went on, his hand covering Emily's on the table.

James's eyebrows went up. He couldn't imagine Emily abandoning her job, not the way she loved both it and Adam. "What? Why?"

Emily's smile was dazzling. "I'm pregnant."

"What? Why, that's terrific!" James grinned and jumped to his feet, shaking Adam's hand and leaning across the table to plant a kiss on Emily's cheek. "Congratulations. When's it due?"

"The end of March. I'm going to quit work in January."

"Or the first icy day this winter," Adam put in firmly.

"He thinks I'm such a klutz I'd fall down and injure the baby." Emily looked a little aggravated, but there was a warmth at his concern in her voice, too.

"I bet our father is bursting with pride," James commented. Leith Marshall was a great believer in family traditions and old values, but until this moment, despite having three sons, he had had no grandchildren to pass things on to.

"Of course. Even Mother's excited."

James found that hard to believe. Joyce Marshall was not given to excitement; she was always cool and collected, every well-groomed hair in place, no matter what kind of storm was breaking around her. "And Tag, no doubt," James said, referring to their youngest brother. "He'll spoil the baby rotten, I feel sure."

"He'll have to get in line behind its father, then," Emily chuckled. She cast a wry look at James. "And I suspect its other uncle will give Tag a good run for his money."

James grinned. "Oh, I might have some fondness for the child."

For the next few minutes they chatted about the first grandchild in the Marshall family and all the joy and wonder that involved. Then James happened to glance across the pool, and his eyes fell on a woman standing beside a table, leaning down a little to talk to an older woman sitting there. James tightened involuntarily, and whatever Adam and Emily were saying faded into the background. At that moment his only focus was on the woman.

She was a stunner.

Her hair was red—no, not red exactly, but a deep, rich auburn—and it fell to her shoulders in thick, gentle waves. Her skin, in contrast, was milky white. She was turned sideways to him, and he could see only her profile, but it was elegant, the line of her throat long and graceful. She wore a dark sundress splotched with big white flowers, and she had tucked a matching creamy white camellia in her hair above one ear. On another woman it might have looked too theatrical, but nestled against her thick, burnished hair, it looked exactly right. More than right. It was enticing, a subtle sensual lure. The dress was high-necked in the front, covering full, firm breasts, and a wide belt ran around her waist, emphasizing her voluptuous hour-glass figure. But when she turned, he could see that the back of the dress was cut down almost to the waist, revealing a long expanse of smooth white skin, and a fierce stab of desire shot through him. It was not an overtly provocative dress, yet somehow the surprise of the sexy low back after the almost prim neckline of the front was incredibly stirring.

James couldn't look away from her. She straightened and turned toward him, her eyes moving over the crowd as though looking for someone, and for the first time he could see her full face. The sun was sinking, but it was still bright enough for him to see that the woman was beautiful. He couldn't tell, or even guess, the color of her eyes from this distance, but they were large and lovely. Her face was oval, her nose straight, her mouth wide, with a sensually full lower lip. James wanted to see that face close up. He wanted, quite frankly, to whisk her back to his home and take her straight to bed. He might doubt his ability to love any woman deeply, but he was still a man of strong sexual appetites, and this woman aroused them immediately and intensely.

His brother noticed his lack of attention to the conversation and glanced in the direction of James's gaze. When he saw the woman James was staring at, he grinned and shot is wife an amused glance. "I think we've lost him," he joked.

"I'd say you're right," Emily agreed dryly. She, too, looked at the redhead, intrigued. She had never seen James react so strongly to any woman.

James ignored their teasing remarks. "Who is she? Do you know her?"

"No. I can't recall ever seeing her before. Emily?"

"No. But, then, you know me. I don't hang around the country club much."

"Tag would probably know her."

"No doubt," James responded dryly. No one who looked like that would have escaped Tag's attention for long. Handsome and frivolous, Tag was an inveterate flirt and was far more a member of the country club set than either of his brothers, especially James.

"Too bad he's gone to the ranch in Texas." Tag, in disgrace with his father, as was often the case, had left a few days ago to spend some time at the ranch the Marshall family had bought as a tax write-off a few years ago.

"We can ask around," Emily offered. "I'm sure someone here knows her."

"I'll manage." James pushed back his chair and stood up. "If you two will excuse me...?"

"Of course."

He was already on his way, weaving his way purposefully through the crowd around the pool. Adam and Emily glanced at each other and grinned.

"And you said James wasn't impulsive," Emily teased.

"Apparently he is." Adam looked again at the striking auburn-haired woman, now strolling alongside the pool. "Given the right stimulus."

Adriana Cummings tried to ignore him, but she was very aware of the man staring at her from across the pool. She had been bending down talking to Mrs. Van Poole, one of her mother's friends, when she had gotten a funny feeling that someone was watching her. She had straightened and glanced around, trying to look as if she were casually searching for a friend. She had seen at once who had been watching her; he didn't even look away or try to hide it. He was sitting at a table with another man and a woman across the pool from her. He was dark-haired and handsome, and she knew that once she would have been vaguely pleased to catch him gazing at her. Once she would have assumed that it was simply an expression of frank male approval.

But not now. Now it made her feel conspicuous, as she had all evening. Why in the world had she agreed to come to this thing? She must have been crazy to let the Carters talk her into it.

Now the other two people at the table with him were turning their heads to look at her, and Adriana felt a blush rising in her cheeks. Turning away, she began to walk down the length of the pool, doing her best to appear as if she were casually sauntering along, admiring the sparkling turquoise water, not trying to outrun yet another curious stare.

There had been lots of them, beginning the moment she walked in with the Carters, and there had been a sizable number of whispers, too. She was aware of every sidelong glance, every turned head, every whispered word. There had been questions, too, from Mrs. Van Poole's sympathetic, "How is your poor mother taking this?" to the blunt, boorish, "Did your father really do it?" It seemed as if there was no other topic of conversation in Winston-Salem society except the trial of Jack Larson. At least, not around her. Everyone wanted to pump her for the last juicy bit of gossip. Within five minutes of her arrival, Adriana had been wishing she hadn't come.

She had tried to maintain her calm and dignity, to ward off offensive questions or comments with a cool smile and a noncommittal response. After all, she shouldn't gain any more bad publicity for her father by bursting out with an angry answer. It would only further convince everyone that he was guilty. And she couldn't leave, either, for her father's sake. She had to stay and face down the gossip.

It wasn't easy. In fact, it was growing more difficult by the moment. When she had seen that man staring at her from across the pool, she hadn't been able to gaze coolly back. His expression was too intense; she was too drained by her efforts this evening to protect herself from the looks and rumors.

Casually she glanced back across the pool. He was no longer there. Her eyes flickered over the crowd, trying to find him, but she couldn't. Then she realized what she was doing and how silly it was. What did it matter where he had gone, as long as he was no longer scrutinizing her?

She continued heading toward the end of the pool. Perhaps she could walk out onto the lawn and keep going. There must be some place where she could sit alone for a few minutes to recover some of her shredded nerves. She glanced toward the clubhouse, where couples danced on the patio and light streamed out of the elegant French doors. It certainly didn't look like a refuge. She pivoted slowly, taking in the darkened expanse of grassy lawn and the mass of trees beyond, until finally she was once again facing the pool.

"Adriana!" A short, stocky man was walking toward her, flashing a toothy grin and waving. It was Mike Stedman, whom she'd known since she was in elementary school and who was just as obnoxious now as he'd been then. Even worse, beside him, headed straight for her, was the dark-haired man who'd been staring at her earlier from across the pool.

James was determined to meet the unknown woman with the auburn hair, even if it meant walking up to her and introducing himself. However, it would be better if he could find someone to introduce him to her. In general he preferred a straightforward, even blunt, way, but in this case he was afraid it might come across as if he was just trying to pick her up, and the lady obviously had too much class for that. As he rounded the corner of the pool, his eyes fell on Mike Stedman. He would be perfect. As far as James was concerned, Mike was something of an idiot and not too likable, either, but he was younger than James, more in the age category of the redhead, and he was also the sort of person who made it a point to know everyone and everything that went on at

the country club. James was willing to put up with Mike
for a few moments in order to get an introduction to his
mystery woman.

"Mike," he said, reaching out to shake the other man's
hand.

Mike stared at him, surprised by the pleased note in
James's voice. "James. Hello. How are you?"

"Fine. In need of your expertise, though."

"My expertise!" Stedman repeated in a voice that was
so stunned it almost made James laugh.

"Yeah. I need a name."

"Oh. Who?" The other man glanced around interestedly.

"Her." James pointed toward the redhead's back. She
had reached the end of the pool and was looking around
indecisively.

"You don't know her?" An odd expression crossed
Mike's face.

"No. I've never see her before."

Mike grinned slyly. James suppressed his irritation.
Obviously Mike liked thinking he had knowledge James
Marshall didn't. "Her name's Adriana Cummings."

"Adriana." James savored the name. It fit her—
smooth and lovely, a trifle exotic.

"You want me to introduce you to her?"

Looking at Mike's smug face, James would have liked
to say no. But this woman was too special for him to
louse things up just because he disliked Mike Stedman.
"Sure."

"Come on, then. Let's catch her before she gets away."
Mike started after her, and James quickly followed him.

When she saw the two men approaching, Adriana
suppressed an immediate, panicked urge to flee. Much as

she didn't want to talk to Mike Stedman or the other man right now, it would be too obvious if she turned tail and ran. She had to paste a smile on her face and greet them.

She returned Mike's wave with a certain lack of enthusiasm and waited for them to reach her. They would be full of questions about her father and the trial, and she didn't feel up to answering them. Besides, for some reason she couldn't put her finger on, she didn't want to see the avid curiosity on the stranger's face that she had seen on so many others tonight.

"Adriana! How are you?" Mike greeted her as if they were the best of friends, reaching out as though to hug her.

Adriana quickly grasped his hands in hers, keeping her arms stiff to hold him at a distance and moving back a little. She saw a faint grin touch the other man's face, and she thought he must have guessed that she was holding Mike off more than greeting him. She glanced away, surprised to find that her lips wanted to twitch up in a return grin. It was the first time she'd had the urge to smile all evening.

She also noticed that, up close, the stranger's hair was as black as it appeared at a distance and his eyes were a bright, light blue. He was handsome, but there was something more, too. He had charisma. Power. She couldn't deny the funny tingly feeling she got inside when he looked at her. That surprised her, too. Lately she hadn't thought or felt much about anything except the trial.

"It's been so long," Mike went on, squeezing Adriana's hands. "Have you decided to move back?"

"No." He must know why she was here, but she refused to give him the satisfaction of explaining. Mike had always been one of the world's worst gossips, eager to know the dirt on everybody, even people he didn't know.

He looked a trifle chagrined at her short answer, but plowed on steadily. "How's you mother?"

"She's doing well. And how is yours?" She knew Mike's mother about as well as he knew hers, which was to say hardly at all, but she was determined to block his curiosity if she could. He was going to have to get blunter than this to dig anything out of her.

"Divorced again. You know Sally. Ah, well." Mike shrugged. "Addy, I wanted to introduce you to someone." Mike's eyes went from Adriana to the man beside him and back again.

Adriana braced herself. Mike looked too pleased with himself. She suspected that this was going to be bad.

"This is James Marshall," Mike went on. "James, Adriana . . . Cummings. Isn't that your name now?"

Marshall looked startled, then quickly suppressed it. "Mrs. Cummings," he said, reaching out to shake the hand she extended.

Adriana smiled. "Not Mrs. I kept the last name after the divorce because it was what I had used professionally."

There was no mistaking the relief in James Marshall's eyes at her statement. Could it be that he was actually interested in *her,* not in her father's trial? But if so, what game was Mike playing? And why was he standing there watching them with such a gleeful expression?

"Professionally? What do you do?" Marshall moved forward and to the side, subtly disconnecting them from Mike.

"I weave. Hangings, rugs, that sort of thing."

James smiled, his eyes staring deeply into hers in a way that had nothing to do with their casual words. There was an intensity in him that was almost disconcerting. Yet Adriana found that it stirred her as well. It was as if whatever he was concentrating on was the only thing that existed for him at that moment, and there was something alluring about being the focus of his very masculine attention. James glanced up and over at Mike, and his expression was a dismissal so clear that even Mike couldn't ignore it.

"Well, I guess I'd better be going," Mike said, moving back reluctantly.

"Yeah. Good-bye," James told him cheerfully and turned back to Adriana. "I'm afraid I'm a Philistine. I didn't realize that people still made a living weaving."

Adriana chuckled. She was always happy to talk about her work, which she loved, and she felt more at ease now that Mike was gone. Her face and voice were animated as she said, "I'm not sure you can really call it making a living. But I make enough to get by." Aided by money from her trust fund, she thought, but she didn't add that. Actually, nowadays she was making enough money to live on, for her works were becoming well known, at least in the Southwest and California. But for the first few years, she would not have been able to concentrate fulltime on her craft if she hadn't had the fund from her grandfather. "There are other people who do it, too, especially where I've been living the last few years. When we moved to Taos I was more into other kinds of fabric art, but as soon as I tried weaving, that was it for me."

"I knew as soon as I saw you that you were different." James smiled a little sheepishly. "I guess you caught me staring."

Adriana nodded, not sure what to say. She was hoping fiercely that he wasn't about to tell her that he had stared at her because she was Jack Larson's daughter.

"I'm not usually so lacking in finesse," he went on. His eyes were serious as he looked down into hers. "But I have to tell you, you threw me for a loop."

"Why?" Her voice was breathless. The look in his eyes made her feel a trifle weak in the knees.

"Why do you think? Because you're beautiful. You must have had plenty of male stares before now."

Adriana lowered her eyes to mask the sudden delight in them. He didn't know who she was. He didn't know about her father. He had wanted to meet her simply because he was attracted to her. She couldn't imagine why Mike hadn't told him about her, but she wasn't about to question it.

"Modest, as well?" He chuckled. He glanced toward the clubhouse. "Would you care to dance?"

"No. Not really." Adriana shook her head. "I'm sorry. That was ungracious."

"Don't worry about that. There are those who would say I don't know the meaning of the word 'gracious.'"

Adriana chuckled. "I doubt that."

He raised his eyebrows. "Then you obviously haven't spoken with certain members of this club. My mother likes to call it being 'too outspoken.'"

"Are you trying to tell me that you're an outcast with the local social set?"

"You might say that. I'm too inclined to tell people what I think."

"I can understand that. I've raised a few eyebrows myself. Being an artist, you know. People either think I'm a dabbler or that I'm a little bizarre."

"Not bizarre," he protested. "Unique. Maybe even a little exotic. I think you're very intriguing."

Once again, Adriana wasn't sure quite how to respond to him. He *was* awfully direct. But there was something she liked about his straightforward manner, a sense that she could trust this man, that people always knew where they stood with him. Besides, she wasn't sure whether it mattered that she liked or didn't like his bluntness; the response he stirred in her was deep, immediate and physical. At that moment, she didn't think she could have walked away from him.

"Would you like to take a walk, then?" James went on. "Get away from this crowd?"

"Yes, I'd love that." The relief in her voice was unmistakable. It would be heavenly to escape from the stares and whispers. Besides, the longer they stayed here, the more likely it was that someone would come up and start talking about her father, and the last thing she wanted right now was for James to realize who she was. She didn't want to face his reaction.

He took her arm, and they climbed the shallow steps from the pool to the lawn, then strolled along the sidewalk, dimly lit by the glow from the pool and clubhouse.

"Have you been living in New Mexico for a while? I don't frequent the club, but surely I would have noticed you."

"Yes, I've lived there for several years."

"Taos is something of an artists' colony, isn't it?"

Adriana shrugged. "Sometimes it seems like more of a tourist town, but it's still lovely. I try to get away in the summer to avoid the mobs."

"Are you thinking about coming back here to live or is this just a visit?"

"I'm just visiting my mother." That was a subject she wanted to avoid, so she went on quickly, "What about you? Do you live in Winston-Salem?"

"Yeah," he admitted. "All my life, except when I was in college."

"What do *you* do for a living?" She wanted to keep the focus on him for a while.

"I'm an attorney." James didn't go on to say where he worked. For weeks, everyone had been plaguing him for word about the upcoming trial, and he had no desire to get into another discussion about it, particularly not now, not with this woman.

"Oh. That Marshall. Marshall, Pierson, etc."

"Yeah, that's my father's firm."

"I think I've met your brother, Tag."

James smiled a little. "Probably. Most people have, it seems."

Adriana remembered Tag as a handsome man, quick-witted and charming, but she preferred James's looks. There was power in James—perhaps leashed now, but still there, nonetheless—and she found that exciting. Her ex-husband had been a handsome man, but weak, and she had quickly lost all respect for him. Only her stubbornness had made her stay in the marriage as long as she did.

They reached the edge of the trees and stopped. Adriana turned, leaning against the thick trunk of one of the trees, to look back at the pool. From this distance the noise was muted, and the lights cast a soft glow over everything. The scene looked so lovely and genteel, so much the same as she had seen it many times before. It was almost possible to believe that life was normal, that things were as they had always been, that her family's world hadn't gone spinning wildly out of its orbit.

She glanced up and found that James was watching her silently, and though his eyes were dark and his face shadowed in the dim light, there was a tension, a hunger, there that made her catch her breath. He reached out a hand and lightly brushed his knuckles down her cheek.

"I suppose a million men have told you how beautiful you are," he said.

Adriana shook her head a little, summoning up a shaky smile. "Not quite that many."

"When I saw you tonight, it hit me like a ton of bricks." His thumb touched the corner of her mouth, then gently traced her lower lip. "I don't usually act so impulsively."

"Really?" Her voice was shaky. Just the touch of his skin on her lips sent shivers of excitement through her. She knew that she was attractive, and over the years many men had made passes at her, some with finesse and others crudely. But no man before had ever raised such an immediate and intense response in her. She found that she wanted to lean into his touch, wanted to feel his hand drift down her face, onto her throat, and lower...

James saw her eyes darken in arousal, and it shook him. He didn't quite understand what hold this woman had over him, why he wanted her so suddenly and fiercely. But he knew that her skin felt like velvet against his fingers, that her eyes were huge and mysterious in the darkness, pulling him in, that his body was already pulsing with desire for her.

He bent toward her. Almost imperceptibly, she moved upward to meet him. Desire shot through him like a white-hot spear. He wrapped an arm around her, pulling her up into him, and his mouth came down to cover hers.

His kiss was long and slow and thorough. Adriana went weak all over, and she dug her hands into his shoulders, holding on as though she might simply sink to the ground without his support. An ache started deep within her. His mouth was as soft and dark as the night around her, as hot and full of promise. His body was tough and hard, pressing into her gentler flesh. She was aware of a wild urge to rub herself against him, to test her power over him and feel his answering strength.

Alan had often told her that she was too strong, too willful, that she intimidated a man, but Adriana sensed that this was a man who would not be intimidated, who could meet her will and strength with an even greater power. She did not think that there could be tears or anger—or passion—that James Marshall could not take.

Lost in his kiss, Adriana let all thoughts of the present, of the trial, of her family's problems, fly away. In this moment there was nothing but him and her and the enveloping darkness, nothing but the heart-stopping sensuality of his mouth on hers. Her lips moved against his, kissing him back, and her tongue twined around his, testing and exploring. His breath shuddered out against her cheek, and his hands slid down her back and over the smooth curve of her derriere, lifting her up into him.

His skin was like fire. She could feel the heavy rise and fall of his chest against her own. His mouth left hers and moved down, trailing kisses down her throat. Adriana let her head fall back, shivering with delight at the velvet nibblings of his lips on her skin. Restlessly, her hands moved over his shoulders and back.

James's mouth reached the material of her dress and stopped at the barrier; he groaned softly in frustration. He lifted his head and looked down into her face. Adriana could see the glitter of passion in his eyes.

''Come home with me,'' he said.

Chapter 3

Adriana almost said yes. She wanted to. But even as she stood looking up into James's mesmerizing eyes, her body thrumming and heated, she knew she couldn't. She simply was not the kind of person to engage in sex lightly. In fact, never before had she even kissed a man she had met only minutes earlier in the way she had just been kissing James. It wasn't at all like her. The only explanation she could think of was that she was so upset over what was happening to her mother and father that her emotions were simmering just below the surface, easily spilling over at the slightest provocation.

But then, looking at James, she knew that this was not the reason. It was him. She could think of a dozen other men whom she had dated and liked who could have been here with her this evening, and she wouldn't have responded in this way at all. There was just something about this particular man. She had felt a special chemistry with him from the very instant they met—or even earlier, from the moment she had glanced across the pool and found him watching her.

Even so, that was no excuse for acting irresponsibly. She could not jump into an affair with a complete stranger, and especially not now, when her family was in such turmoil. She already felt ashamed for so completely forgetting her parents and the agony they were going through just because she had been swept away by a momentary passion. It was unthinkable that she would let it go any further, ignoring both her principles and her family's situation in order to share a night with a handsome, compelling man.

"No." Adriana shook her head and stepped back from James. She was surprised by the depth of the regret she experienced at saying the word. "I can't. I'm sorry. It's just . . . well, I don't usually . . . jump into things so fast." Her words came out stiffly and awkwardly. She flushed. He must think she was foolish.

James sighed. "I can't say I'm not sorry." He had outwardly recovered his composure by now, though his eyes still glowed with desire. "But I understand." He knew somehow that she wasn't the kind of woman who gave her love or her passion easily, no matter how hungrily she had kissed him back this evening. It was better for him, too, he reasoned. He had too many last-minute trial preparations to make; he couldn't spend the weekend in bed—and he knew that was exactly what would happen if they made love tonight. Still, reason didn't hold much sway against the desire churning inside him.

"Do you?" She had looked away from him as she talked, and now her eyes came back to his face hopefully. "Really?"

"Sure." He couldn't keep from smiling at her. "You're not the type for a one-night stand. Not that that's all it would be. But . . . it was simply wishful thinking on my part.''

He took her hand, laying it flat against his, palm to palm, and with his other hand he traced each finger to its end. His eyes on their hands, he said softly, "I'd like to see you again, though. Is that possible?''

A grin broke across her face. Possible? Absolutely!

"Yes, I'd like that.''

He raised his head and smiled at her. "Good. I'll call you.''

He searched his pockets for something to write on and finally came up with a scrap of paper, and Adriana wrote down her mother's telephone number for him. He took the paper back and folded it up carefully, then stuck it in his pocket. They stood looking at each other for a moment; then James bent and kissed her lightly on the lips. They linked hands and strolled back toward the lights of the clubhouse.

James managed to bury himself in the case for the rest of the weekend, but he found it much harder to do than it normally was. His thoughts kept straying to Adriana Cummings—the rich gleam of her dark auburn hair in the soft glow of the pool lights, the appeal of her light silvery gray eyes looking up at him, the sleek perfection of her legs and the smooth curves of her body. He couldn't remember when a woman had attracted him as much and as instantly; certainly one had never interfered with his work as much.

He called her twice. Once an older woman answered and said Adriana wasn't at home. The second time Adriana herself picked it up. James knew instantly that it was her voice, though he was surprised he recognized it so surely. His heart began to slam in his chest, and his palm turned sweaty on the telephone receiver. It was crazy, he told himself. You'd think he was a teenage boy calling the prom queen for a date, not a successful thirty-four-year-old man who had dated any number of attractive women without ever really losing his heart.

"Hi. It's James. James Marshall."

"Hi. How are you?"

He could hear the smile in her voice, and he realized that he was grinning back idiotically. "I'm great. Doing fine." Except for feeling like a tongue-tied fool. "How about you?"

"I'm okay."

"Just okay? Is something wrong?"

"No. I feel better now, anyway."

"Good." He hoped he was right in assuming that his call had something to do with her feeling better. He held the phone tightly to his ear, unconsciously hunching his shoulders and lowering his head as if there were someone around listening to the conversation. "I keep thinking about you."

"Do you?" She sounded a little breathless.

"Yeah." His hand tightened around the pen he'd been holding, and his thumb began to rub slowly up and down it. "It's played hell with my work."

Her chuckle sounded not at all displeased. James wanted to see her now. Immediately. He wanted to forget the stack of files on his desk and drive like a bat out of hell from Greensboro, where the federal offices were, all the way back to Winston-Salem. He estimated that it would take forty-five minutes to get there. Another forty-five to get back, because he had to finish his work here. And God knows how long he'd let himself stay there— once he was with her, he knew he wouldn't want to leave.

It was crazy, irresponsible. Particularly with a case as important as this one coming up.

Still, he had to clench his teeth to keep from asking her if she'd see him tonight. Finally he said, "I want to see you again."

"I'd like that."

James remembered the warmth of her lips beneath his, the taste, the way her mouth had opened up eagerly to him. Inwardly he cursed; it was stupid to let such arousing thoughts into his head when she was over thirty miles away and there was nothing he could do about it. "When?"

"Whenever you'd like."

James thought of the usual eighteen-hour days he put in during an important trial. But the Feds were running this show, he reminded himself; surely he could slip away for a few hours one evening. "How about Wednesday?"

"Fine."

"I'll call you and we'll make plans." He didn't want to hang up, but he knew that if he didn't, he would start talking about seeing her sooner, even tonight, and before he knew it, he would have talked himself into running over there this evening. Where had all his much-vaunted discipline fled to?

"Okay."

"Good-bye."

"Good-bye."

Reluctantly he lowered the receiver and placed it back on the hook. He tilted back in his chair, lacing his hands behind his head, and stared dreamily off into space. He paid no attention to the small, spare, efficient office, largely bare of any personal mementos or photographs.

Instead he saw Adriana Cummings, stunning in the low-backed sundress, standing beside the pool.

James Marshall didn't believe in love at first sight. There was such a thing as immediate attraction, he would admit that, an instant lust; he'd felt it before. It was shallow and meaningless, of course, but there were times when shallow and meaningless were precisely what he wanted. What was puzzling him was the fact that what he'd felt when he saw Adriana didn't fit into that category. It hadn't been just that piercing lust in his gut, though that had been there, too, only fiercer and harder than he'd ever known it before. There had been more, a heat and excitement that had burst in his chest as well as his loins and sizzled along his nerves. He had wanted to talk to her, to be with her, not just go to bed with her.

James had known instinctively when he saw her that there couldn't be anything shallow and meaningless with this woman, and talking with her had only confirmed it. She had quality and depth; it was obvious in her eyes, in her manner, in her speech. He wanted to know her, to sit with her and explore each layer of her being, to feel those wide, intelligent eyes penetrating his innermost secrets. He wanted her to know him, and, knowing him, like him, and that was the strangest of all. He had always been a confident person, complete in himself. It didn't bother him that there were those who disliked him, who thought him hard or unemotional. He was what he was, and others could take him or leave him, as they chose. But with Adriana, it mattered very much what she thought of him.

She wasn't the type of woman to whom he was normally attracted. A society beauty, a country club girl. He hadn't gone out with a woman he'd met at the club since he was in high school; in fact, it was rare that he even visited the club at all. A tiny smile touched his lips. *It must have been fate.* And that sort of romantic thinking wasn't his style, either.

She was an artist—a weaver, of all bizarre things!—and that wasn't his sort of woman, either. He thought of artists as being overly emotional and probably a little strange, given to flights of fancy and outre clothes, mercurial and irresponsible. The women with whom he'd had serious relationships had by and large been professionals or business women, the kind who understood his commitment to his career and were equally committed to theirs. They had been intelligent and realistic, the kind of women he could talk to, who approached life in a similar way to him. Brains and a strong will, even toughness, drew him, for they were a challenge, a match.

Yet there she was, a society woman, a sensitive, artistic type, and she made him feel eager, aroused, excited. His feelings amazed him, and yet . . . there was something quite pleasant about feeling this way.

The fizzy rush of excitement stayed with him through the weekend, and even early Monday morning, when he headed for court, he could feel it still bubbling deep inside his chest. He didn't show it, of course, or even allow it to surface, for he was much too disciplined an attorney to let his feelings take over. But he was aware it was there.

He went in the side door of the Federal building, leaving the crowds and reporters out front to the D.C. attorneys, who were much more interested in making a public statement than he was, anyway. James didn't pursue publicity; he wasn't in this line of work for the glory. All that mattered to him was the case, each case, and his only interest was in putting criminals away.

He made his way to the courtroom and went inside, walking past the spectators' seats and inside the bar. He settled himself at the prosecution table, opening his briefcase and pulling out a file and a pad of paper. Jury selection would begin today, and he would do much of the questioning for the government. The prosecution team had agreed that it would be best to start out on the best foot with prospective jurors and not set up any feelings of sympathy in them for the local boy being hounded by prosecutors from Washington, D.C.

The doors opened, and the other prosecutors walked in, followed only moments later by Jack Larson and his defense counsel. James glanced at them and nodded slightly to Roger Manning, Larson's attorney. Manning was one of the best criminal lawyers in the state, with a good, detail-oriented staff working for him. James had met him in court before and respected his ability; Roger had once gotten a not-guilty verdict on one of James's cases that still rankled.

There was more noise at the door, and James cast a look at the door. A slight, middle-aged woman was entering the courtroom. Though she maintained a composed look, the strain on her face was obvious. James recognized her as Jack Larson's wife. He had seen her several times on television and in person during the earlier proceedings when Larson had first been arrested and arraigned. On one side of her was a younger woman, Larson's daughter; she usually accompanied the mother. But it wasn't either of those women that sent a shock running through him like electricity. It was the woman on the other side of Mrs. Larson, her hand beneath the older woman's arm. She wore a trim navy blue suit, conservative and subdued, and her hair was caught up in a neat knot at the base of her neck. But nothing could hide the beauty of her face and form, or the vibrant auburn of her hair. It was Adriana Cummings!

She looked toward the prosecution table and noticed him, and he saw the same shock he felt reflected on her face. She missed a stride, then recovered, following the other two women into the front row of seats behind the defense table. Her face was white, and she glanced at him again and then down at her hands, clasped together in her lap.

For a moment James was too stunned even to think. He struggled to absorb the fact that Adriana, the woman who'd disturbed his thoughts far too much over the past couple of days, was actually in this courtroom—and sitting with Jack Larson's wife! What was she doing here? What connection did she have with Larson?

He remembered the sly grin on Mike Stedman's face when he'd asked about Adriana and again when he had introduced them. He had known Adriana was connected to Larson. No doubt he had thought it hilarious to bring James, all unknowing, face to face with her. Perhaps he had even hoped that one of them would realize who the other was, and there would be fireworks.

Who was she?

A vague memory stirred in the back of his mind. He swung around and thumbed through the files in his briefcase. He pulled one out and opened it, scanning the pages until he found the information he wanted. There it was: personal data on Larson—wife, daughters. There were two of them; one didn't live here. Only one of them had ever accompanied the Larsons to court, and the existence of the other one, immaterial to the case, had slipped from his mind.

The name leaped out at him from the print: Adriana. The younger Larson daughter was named Adriana. She had said that Cummings was her married name. James slumped back in his seat. He felt as if someone had punched him in the stomach. Adriana Cummings was the daughter of the man he was about to prosecute!

Adriana went cold inside when she saw James sitting at the prosecutors' table, and she almost stopped in midstride. It took every ounce of self-discipline she possessed to continue down the aisle and follow her mother into the row of seats. She sat down heavily, her mind and emotions in turmoil, and looked at him again as though to convince herself that what she had seen was true. James Marshall was sitting at the table with the men who were trying her father. He must be one of them.

It couldn't be true. It couldn't.

She leaned over and whispered to her mother, "Who's that dark-haired man at the far end of the table?"

"Who? Where?"

"The prosecution."

"Oh." Millie Larson's mouth tightened. "That's Leith Marshall's son. Not the oldest one, although *he's* trying to destroy us, too."

"James." Adriana supplied the name weakly.

"That's right. James. I'd always heard he was cold and hard as nails, and I believe it. He has eyes like ice. I heard him at one of those early hearings. He talked as if your father were some kind of thief. I couldn't believe it—turning against his own kind like that. Though I guess that's what you can expect from someone who goes into the U.S. Attorney's office instead of joining the family firm." She sighed and added, as if it were the crowning blow, "And I went to school with his mother."

Adriana drew a shaky breath and looked down at her hands to hide her expression. She was sure that her face must reveal the shock that she felt inside. James Marshall—the man she had kissed the other night, the man who had awakened her senses so quickly and dazzlingly, the man whom she had been thinking about all weekend, feeling a little guilty in her secret excitement—that man was trying to send her father to prison. She had been acting as giddy as a schoolgirl about one of her father's enemies!

She looked across at James again. He had turned away from her and was reading a file. All business, of course. He wouldn't be feeling the pain and stunned surprise that she was. It wouldn't be any surprise to him; he must have known who she was. It was obvious, now that she thought about it. No wonder he had been staring at her so intently. He had probably seen pictures of her with her father. Then he had gotten Mike Stedman to introduce him to her. She had been flattered by the intensity and openness of his pursuit of her. And she—she had fallen like an idiot for his ruse. Adriana's cheeks flamed with belated humiliation. Rage surged through her, replacing the numbness and shock. What a snake he was!

She thought of the way she had floated through the weekend, daydreaming about him, hugging the thought of him to her whenever the anxiety and sorrow about the trial had become too much. She had listened to her mother and comforted her, tried to bolster her, and half the time her mind had been happily on James Marshall, remembering his kiss and the feel of his arms around her.

It had been such a long time since she had felt like that about anyone, since before her divorce two years ago. She had been devastated by the failure of her marriage, which she had sailed into with such blissful certainty that it would be the same kind of loving, happy marriage that her parents had. Instead, it had turned out to be a mistake from the very beginning. After she had finally admitted that it was over, she had had no interest in men.

She had dated a few times, but more for form's sake than out of any real desire. Gradually it had gotten better, but she still hadn't met anyone who made her feel alive and glowing... until James Marshall.

Did she have spectacularly bad taste in men? Was she for some reason drawn only to the worst possible choices? First Alan, and now this man who wanted only to use her! Thank God she had had enough sense and restraint to pull back from him the other night when he had wanted to take her to his home.

The morning crawled by. Prospective jurors were called and interviewed, and the lawyers questioned and wrangled over them. Adriana watched James as he asked his questions, calm and cool, usually serious, but now and then flashing that unexpectedly charming smile. But she couldn't have told anyone what he had said or asked. She heard his voice but not his words. Her mind was unable to concentrate on anything except James's deception and her own anger and hurt.

When the noon recess came, Adriana stood up to leave the courtroom. At that moment James turned around, and for an instant they looked at each other. His face was unreadable. Adriana swung back toward her mother.

"Why don't you and Suzanne go on and eat?" she said, hoping that her smile didn't look as false as it felt. "I—I'm not very hungry." She was certain that food would choke her, the way she felt right now. But more than that, she didn't want to have to make conversation with Suze and Mama, trying to be bright and cheerful, when all the while she was consumed inside with this anger and hurt.

"Oh. Well..." Her mother hesitated, glancing at Suzanne and then back at Adriana. "If you're sure... Are you feeling all right?"

"I'm fine. Really. I just—it's the stress. I'm not used to the reporters and everything."

Suzanne grimaced. "I don't think you ever get used to them. You just learn to live with it eventually, I guess."

Her older sister looked tired, and Adriana was swept with guilt. Suzanne had had to struggle with all this for months, while she had been safely out in New Mexico, hearing about it secondhand.

"I'm sorry," she said swiftly, reaching out to put a hand on Suzanne's arm. "I'll be better tomorrow, I promise. It'll just take me a little while to get used to all this. Right now I need to sit and be alone."

"Sure. I understand." Suzanne put an arm around her and gave her shoulders a squeeze. "It'll be okay."

Someday, Adriana added mentally. She watched her mother and sister file out of the courtroom with the others, and she sank down with a sigh into her seat, resting her head in her hands. She wanted to burst into tears, and she would have given anything not to be in such a public place.

The noise receded, and the courtroom fell into utter stillness. Then a voice spoke in front of her, startling her. "Adriana..."

Her head snapped up. James Marshall was standing two feet away from her, inside the low wooden railing that separated the spectators from the participants in the trial, his briefcase in front of him, resting on the railing.

Adriana's eyes widened in amazement, and she jumped to her feet in a swift surge of rage. "I can't believe you actually have the gall to come up and speak to me!"

"I'm sorry. I know that it's impossible for us now." He sighed and raked a hand back through his hair. "Lord. Nothing like this has ever happened to me. I never even dreamed of it happening. I'm sure I'm not your favorite person right now."

"Not my favorite person! That's the understatement of the century." Angry tears came to her eyes. "I think you're the lowest person I've ever met."

His mouth tightened. "It's my job. I have to prosecute people who break the law. I understand your loyalty to your father, but—"

"It's your job? It's your job to try and seduce the daughter of the man you're railroading into prison? What did you think? That I'd be so utterly enthralled with you that I'd tell you anything you wanted to know?"

James stared at her. "You think I was trying to seduce you? To worm the secrets of the defense out of you? My God, Adriana, I didn't have the slightest idea who you were! If I had, I would never have come near you, no matter how attracted to you I was. Why, it's probably unethical for me to even be talking to you here." He glanced around the empty courtroom. "But I couldn't bear to walk off and never say another word to you, not even good-bye."

Adriana crossed her arms defensively across her chest. "You're claiming that you had no idea who I was? That our meeting was a coincidence?" She invested the word with the deepest scorn.

"I had no idea who you were. What I told you Friday night was the simple truth. I saw you, and I wanted to meet you. Not because you were Jack Larson's daughter. Because I thought you were the most beautiful woman I'd ever seen."

"Mike Stedman knows who I am."

"Well, he didn't see fit to inform me of your identity. If you'll remember, he didn't tell you that I was a member of the prosecution team, either. No doubt he thought it was a wonderful joke on us both." As Adriana continued to regard him stonily, he burst out, "Come on, Adriana, be reasonable. Why the hell would I jeopardize my career and this case by trying to sneak information out of you? What possible good could it do me? What could you tell me that would be of any help? We already have everything we need to convict. It wouldn't make sense."

He was right about that, Adriana admitted reluctantly to herself. She knew nothing about the case except what she had heard secondhand from her mother. Why, her father's own attorney had never even contacted her. She'd been living in New Mexico when the whole thing took place, and certainly her father had never confided any secrets to her. *Not that he had any secrets to hide, of course.*

James could see the doubt touch her face, and she glanced away. "I don't know what to think. Given what you're doing to my father, you must be capable of anything."

There was sympathy, even pity in his eyes. "I'm sure you'd like to believe that. Sometimes it's awfully hard to accept the truth."

Her chin came up, and she met his eyes defiantly. "It's not the truth. You found a victim, and you went after him. Once you'd arrested him, you couldn't back down and admit that you'd gotten the wrong man. You're railroading him."

James looked down for a moment, then back up. "Look, I'm not here to argue with you. I'm sure it would be hopeless anyway. I just—I want you to know how much I regret the circumstances."

Her mouth twisted. "The circumstances. That's a nice way to put it. But then, no doubt you're very good with words. It's your job, as you say."

Adriana couldn't keep the bitterness out of her voice. Maybe he was telling the truth when he said he hadn't arranged his meeting with her. Perhaps he hadn't had any idea who she was. Mike Stedman had always had a bizarre sense of humor, and he might very well have thought it would be funny to introduce them and see what happened. Besides, as James had said, there was no reason for him to try to get information out of her. Still, she found herself reluctant to let go of her anger. She felt betrayed. He was the enemy, and she had been vulnerable to him, and even if it was only a quirk of fate, with no one to blame, it left her feeling empty and sick inside. She had melted in his arms, and now he was after her father.

She turned without another word and walked out of the courtroom, leaving James there alone, looking after her.

Chapter 4

Adriana had brought one of her frame looms with her when she flew back to North Carolina, as she usually did wherever she went, since it was small enough that she could carry it on the plane with her. She disliked being anywhere without at least a small loom to weave on. There were times when she felt as if she simply had to weave an idea that had come into her mind, and she never knew when such a compelling idea or pattern would come. Even when she wasn't struck by inspiration, she had always found the act of weaving so soothing that she sometimes wove simple things in order to calm her tension or to give herself a chance to think.

Tonight was one of those nights when she needed something to calm her nerves, to free her mind of its present turmoil by concentrating on her work. When she and her mother returned from the trial's opening day, she pulled out her loom and went to work, not even pausing to eat supper. She set the loom on a small table, propping it sideways against the wall. Then she picked up two spools of cotton warp yarn and tied them to the first nails at the top of the frame on the left-hand side. She pulled the double thread across the yarn to the first nail on the other side and looped the threads around it, carrying them back to the second nail on the left. She continued warping up the loom all the way down, keeping an even tension. She had done this so many times that it was second nature to her, and the mere repetition and familiarity began to calm her.

When she was finished, she taped the "cartoon," a full-size drawing of the pattern she was creating, blacked in with a felt-tip pen in one-inch squares, to the back of the loom, where she would be able to copy it exactly as she wove. She had drawn the cartoon several days earlier, but had had no time to start the sampler yet. When she was finished, she set the frame up lengthwise on a small table, leaning it back against the wall, and picked up her tapestry bobbin. She wound it tightly with black weft yarn, then began to slip the bobbin through the warp threads, thrusting her left hand between the threads to make a "shed," so that the bobbin could be passed behind. She passed the bobbin through to her left hand, leaving a small loop and pressing it down with the point of the bobbin.

As her hands moved across the frame with quick skill, taking one small section after another all the way across, then back again, her nerves relaxed more and more. She concentrated only on the movement of her fingers, and as she did, her mind let loose of the problems that had been racing around inside it and let them drift away. There was an almost hypnotic quality to the work, yet it was so precise that it required a concentration that excluded everything else, even problems. By the time she had finished the solid selvedge at the end of the piece and beaten down the weft with a heavy, tined tapestry beater, she felt almost herself again, no longer wound as tightly as a spring. She set aside the loom and rose, stretching to get out the kinks in her back and arms that long sessions at the loom always caused.

She walked to the window and gazed out at the dark lawn in back of the house. Now at last she thought she would be able to go up to bed and fall asleep, untroubled by thoughts of James Marshall. She certainly hoped so. The last thing she wanted was to go into court tomorrow looking weary or worried. She had to appear confident for her father's sake and to bolster Millie's courage, as well. And she certainly didn't want James suspecting that seeing him in the courtroom today had had such an effect on her. She had to look and act as if she had dealt with his perfidy and put it aside.

It wasn't the truth, of course, at least not yet. But it would be. She was determined to make it the truth. She would forget all that she had felt for James Marshall the other night. Before long he would be nothing more to her than one of the prosecutors, and she would be able to look at him without feeling a twinge of hurt.

It was a long trial. They moved slowly through jury selection and into the opening statements. Adriana attended every day with her mother, watching James work, her face carefully blank. He was good. There was no doubt about that. He was crisp and efficient, incisive, but he tempered his almost too well-ordered competence with an occasional smile or a good-humored, self-effacing remark that would endear him to the jury. Watching him, listening to him outline what the prosecution would prove, Adriana felt the first cold pangs of doubt begin to settle around her heart. How could her father ever get out of this? If the state could prove what they were contending—and looking at the cool, rational, expert way James handled the case in the courtroom, it was hard to believe that he didn't have the proof to back him up—it didn't seem possible that a jury wouldn't convict Jack Larson.

As the trial wore on and the requisite proof was added bit by bit, even Adriana's faith in her father was shaken. The icy, empty doubt inside her grew, and each day she returned home from the ordeal of the trial feeling heavier and sadder. Much of the government's evidence was dry and boring; there were few flashes of drama. But it mounted up toward the inevitable conclusion, no matter how hard she tried to deny it. Witnesses testified that Jack Larson was one of only seven people within Contelco who knew of the proposed buy-out of a small company in Virginia. Documents proved the sudden and large purchase of the Virginia company's stock by clients of a particular stockbroker, Patricia Dayton. One buyer, who had negotiated a deal with the government, testified that Dayton had suggested that he purchase the stock, stating that she had "reliable" information from "within the company" that Contelco was about to purchase it. A tape recording of a conversation between the government witness and Patricia Dayton was introduced in which the witness pressed her for the identity of the informant. Finally Ms. Dayton answered by giving the position of the informant within the company. It was Jack Larson's title.

"She was making that up," Millie Larson declared staunchly the evening after the tape was played. "Why, she wasn't even Jack's broker. She probably didn't know him. She just used someone else's title to avoid implicating the real criminal."

Adriana couldn't keep from glancing over at her sister. Suzanne shrugged. Adriana knew that Suzanne wasn't buying her mother's explanation. The realization that she herself didn't believe it either lay like a hard lump in Adriana's chest.

Later, after their mother went to bed, Suzanne looked over at Adriana and said, "He's guilty, isn't he?"

Tears sprang into Adriana's eyes. "We don't know that."

"It doesn't take a lot of brains to figure it out."

"Maybe Mother's right. Maybe she was covering up for the real crook. Maybe she doesn't know Dad. She *wasn't* his broker. I know that."

"That doesn't mean he didn't know her."

"No. But he didn't make any money off the deal. Even the government admits that. There wasn't anything in it for him."

"Sex is a powerful motivator sometimes," Suzanne commented dryly.

"We don't know he was having an affair with her! There's nothing but rumors. He loves Mama." Adriana looked to Suzanne for reassurance. "I mean, doesn't he? They always seem happy together. All those times when I'd see them go out to a dance at the club, or to a play or something, they always looked happy. Like they were still in love. Remember the presents he'd buy her?"

"Guilt."

"Don't be cynical. It wasn't guilt. He loves her."

"That was years ago, when we were kids. What do we really know about their relationship for the past few years? You've been away in New Mexico. I've been wrapped up in my own family. We see them at Christmas or for a weekend here and there. But how closely do you ever observe them? I didn't. I never look to see if they're still happy. I just assume...I mean, they're our parents. You don't expect them to change."

"Or to be something other than what you've always thought they were." Adriana's voice was thoughtful and slow. "What if we were wrong about Dad all these years? What if he *was* different from what we thought?"

"I don't know." Suzanne jumped up and began to pace, rubbing her arms as if she were cold. "I don't want to think about it. Maybe he didn't know her. Maybe they didn't have an affair."

But in the days that followed, the prosecution laid out, time and again, proof that Larson did indeed know Patricia Dayton. Knew her very well. Most damning of all were a long series of motel registrations over the course of months, in the name of Mr. and Mrs. John Porter. Adriana stiffened when she heard the last name. It was her father's cousin's name. The couple had used the same motel over and over, always in midday, and the clerk who had checked them in every time without hesitation identified Patricia Dayton and Jack Larson as the couple known to him as Mr. and Mrs. John Porter.

Adriana felt her mother sag slightly against her, and she put an arm around Millie's shoulders. She burned inside with humiliation, and she knew that the shame her mother felt must be many times worse. It would be public knowledge now, spread all over the newspapers and TV by tonight, that her husband had carried on an affair with a younger woman for months. She knew that for pride's sake, if nothing else, Millie was struggling to look unperturbed by the news, and in that moment she hated the press. Most of all, she hated the prosecution for shaming her mother in the most public of forums. Millie Larson had committed no crime, yet, in a way, she was suffering the most.

Millie made it through the rest of the afternoon without letting her hurt show, and when the day was over, Adriana and Suzanne hustled her past the reporters in the hallway, protecting her on either side. The reporters trailed after them for a moment, then turned back to question the prosecutors who had just emerged from the courtroom. Glancing back, Adriana saw that James had not stopped to answer questions with the other two prosecutors but was walking down the hall in her direction. Adriana turned back sharply and quickened her pace. Their lives, especially her mother's, were lying in shards around them, destroyed by the prosecutors, and she could feel nothing but a sharp, hot fury for James Marshall. At that moment all her hurt and embarrassment, her sense of betrayal, her vast disappointment, were focused into a hatred of him, and she would have liked to fly at him, fists swinging, until the venom had left her soul.

"Oh, no!" Suzanne, slightly in the lead, stopped abruptly at the front doors.

"What?" Adriana looked out through the glass upper portion of the doors, where her sister was staring, and let out a groan.

There were more reporters and photographers waiting on the front steps. Several cameramen held minicams on their shoulders, ready for them the minute they stepped outside. Adriana glanced at her mother. Millie had been leaning more and more heavily against her as they walked down the hall, and now Adriana saw that there were tears on her cheeks and her face was ravaged by despair and sorrow. Pain squeezed her heart. She couldn't let them see her mother like this! She couldn't let them plaster her mother's tortured countenance all over the evening news. She glanced around desperately, wishing there were some way out. But the reporters outside had already seen them and were surging up the steps toward the doors.

"Adriana!" A man's voice spoke sharply behind them, and Adriana turned. It was James Marshall, and he was holding open a door to one of the offices along the main hallway. "In here."

Suzanne looked at Adriana in surprise. Millie was past surprise about anything; she merely exuded dull resignation. Adriana hesitated. The last person in the world she wanted to go near at the moment was James Marshall. She glanced back out the door; the crowd was almost upon them.

"Come on," she muttered to her sister and pulled Millie unresistingly into the room where James stood.

Quickly he closed the door behind them and locked it. "You're safe in here," he said. He looked at Mrs. Larson, and his face softened, regret flickering briefly in his eyes. "You can sit down here and wait, or I can take you out a side entrance."

"I want to get out of here." Adriana faced him almost pugnaciously, as if she was prepared to fight her way past him—or through him.

A faint smile touched his lips. "Okay. Follow me."

He wound his way through a series of connecting offices and into a private back hallway. They emerged finally in a legal library. James crossed between the stacks and opened another door. He stuck his head out, and Adriana saw that it opened onto another hallway. But this one was quiet and almost deserted. He held the door for them to pass through.

"I'm sorry about the reporters."

If it weren't for him and his cohorts they wouldn't have to be running from reporters, Adriana thought bitterly. There was nothing she could say that would adequately express her anger, so she simply gave him a hard, contemptuous look and swept past him.

"Go down those stairs to your left," he said calmly. "There's an outside door at the bottom. No one's ever there."

"Thank you," Suzanne said a little hesitantly. Adriana said nothing and didn't even glance back at him.

They took their mother down the stairs and made it outside to her car without incident. Millie climbed into the back seat of the Jaguar, handing the keys to Suzanne. Suzanne and Adriana looked at each other worriedly, then Suzanne shrugged and walked around to the driver's side. Adriana got into the front seat, too, and Suzanne pulled into traffic. Adriana glanced back at her mother. Millie was slumped in the seat, her head against the butter-soft leather. Her eyes were closed, and tears were streaming down her face.

The two special prosecutors from D.C. came into the U.S. Attorney's office chuckling and talking. James could hear them from his office. They were obviously high on excitement and self-congratulation. As they walked down the hall, they paused at James's door, leaning against either side of the jamb. Heckel and Jeckyll, James thought sourly—though they probably resembled vultures more than the pair of cartoon crows.

"It was great, wasn't it?" Don Berg, the taller and balder of the two, asked in tones rich with triumph.

"Yeah." James's voice was less than enthusiastic, but the other two were too happy to notice.

"I thought today would be the kill," added Stan Kolinsky, the other bookend.

"It was," Berg assured him. "They're dead in the water now," he went on.

"You could tell as soon as you looked in the jurors' eyes."

They were like a vaudeville team, James thought, tossing lines to each other. But he knew what they were talking about, and they were right. Sometimes there was a moment in a trial when the evidence really hit hard, and from then on the verdict was yours. He had seen that look in jurors' faces before, an expression of dislike or anger or disgust that said that the juror had chosen sides and was now against the defendant. From then on it was a matter of not screwing up. They had reached that moment in the Larson case today. The jury had seen the proof of Larson's infidelity, and they had been convinced.

Normally James would have felt as up and happy as Berg and Kolinsky. He would probably have joined in their mutual backslapping and gone out for a celebratory drink. But tonight he didn't feel a sense of victory. He just felt tired.

Usually he paid little or no attention to the families of the defendants he tried. His entire focus was on the case, on bringing another criminal to justice, on winning. If he thought of people, he thought of the victims and their families, not of the family on the other side. But this time he had been very aware of Larson's family, and he had seen the effect the trial was having on them. Larson's wife was at the breaking point. He couldn't stop thinking about the look on Millie Larson's face, the wounded animal pain in her eyes.

Nor could he forget the animosity in the eyes of her daughter. There was no doubt about it. Adriana Cummings's attitude toward him hadn't softened as the trial went on. She despised him. He had known that it would turn out that way; there wasn't any hope for anything else. But it was tough to see it so clearly, to feel the depth of her contempt when those luminous gray eyes shot through him as if he were a worm.

"You want to knock back a few cold ones with us?" Berg asked.

"No. I have to go through my messages." James indicated the stack on his desk. "And shuffle some other cases. I'll stay here."

"Okay." Kolinsky shrugged, bafflement at James's lukewarm attitude showing on his face. "Well, see you tomorrow, then."

"Yeah. So long." He turned his attention back to his desk, pulling the first message off the spindle. But he found it difficult to concentrate. All he could think about was Adriana.

He leaned back in his seat and closed his eyes wearily. What a mess this was. Not the case itself—that was going beautifully. No, it was himself personally that was a mess.

At first he had considered withdrawing from the case. His encounter with Adriana had cast a shadow on his objectivity. But they were so far along in the proceedings, and he had done so much work on the case, that it would be extremely damaging for him to pull out now. James had been certain that he would not let his attraction for Larson's daughter lead him to do anything that would harm their case. He had always been single-minded in his pursuit of justice; he never let emotions interfere with prosecuting a criminal. He would simply put her out of his mind and move on.

And he had managed to operate in his usual crisp, efficient manner, concentrating on his job. He had questioned the jurors and given the opening statement as competently as always. Watching him, no one would have guessed his inner disturbance. No one would have known that half the time his mind was not on the case but on the row behind him, where Jack Larson's daughter sat.

It would have been impossible for him not to think about Adriana. He saw her all the time. Every day she was in the courtroom looking calm and lovely sitting beside her mother, absorbing each new blow of the prosecution's case. Often she reached over to take her mother's hand when some especially troubling evidence was presented, but her own composure never cracked. He saw her once or twice leaving the courtroom, shielding Millie Larson as best she could from the inquisition of the reporters, turning questions aside with a pleasant smile. In the evening her photogenic face was often on the news as she answered the reporters, reiterating her belief in her father's innocence.

James had been struck by Adriana's beauty from the moment he saw her, but now he saw, over and over, the strength of her character, as well. This woman was no weak reed. What she heard in the courtroom had to shake her, but she handled it well, and even though James was sure that the facts the prosecution had presented must have her doubting her father's innocence by now, she continued to stand staunchly behind him. James understood and appreciated family loyalty.

And that was what made it difficult. If there had been nothing to her but good looks, he could have put her out of his mind. But he could see daily the courage in her, the loyalty, the quiet love in the way she clasped her father's hand or placed herself in front of her mother as reporters and photographers moved in. And the strength and love he witnessed in her only made her physical beauty even more desirable.

Surreptitiously he watched her throughout the trial. He couldn't seem to stop himself. He never entered the courtroom without his eyes being drawn immediately to the spot where she sat. He became adept at glancing at her out of the corner of his eye as he sat at the prosecution table. He was always aware of what she wore, and though she wore nothing that wasn't plain and conservative, it was impossible for her to completely hide the luscious curve of her hips or the fullness of her breasts. All too often, when his head was bent over his notepad, his elbow resting on the table and his hand bracing his forehead, he was merely pretending to take notes or be lost in thought. In reality his eyes were turned so that he could see, unobserved, the shapely curve of Adriana's legs. The best thing was to come upon her unexpectedly in the hall, for then he could watch her walk away from or toward him, and either view was equally stirring.

He told himself he was crazy for even thinking about her. There could never be anything between them. The positions this trial had placed them in made her as unreachable for him as a faraway star. He could not possibly approach the daughter of the defendant and talk to her, much less ask her out.

He had become her enemy, and even after the trial was over, he was sure that she would continue to regard him as such. To her he would always be one of the men who had sent her father to prison. Worse than that, he would be responsible for shattering her illusions about her father—unless she refused to accept the truth, and then she would have to believe that he was even more of a villain for having sent an innocent man to prison. They would probably never meet again, and if they did, she would doubtless turn and walk away. The proof of that was the way she had reacted to him today.

But for the first time he could remember, James couldn't control his thoughts; his reason and dedication couldn't overcome his unruly emotions. No matter how much he told himself to forget her, to ignore her, to concentrate on the case to the exclusion of everything else, he was unable to do it. It was troubling, unsettling. Never before had he had to struggle to keep his mind on a case while he was sitting right there in the middle of the trial.

His mouth twisted in a grimace. Damn. As if to prove his point, here he was again, sitting thinking about her instead of doing his work. With an effort he pulled his mind back to the stack of notes in front of him and began to work. Quickly he ran through the messages, separating them into those he had to return the next morning before going to court, those that could wait, and those he didn't recognize. He was able to catch a few late workers at their offices, but the majority of them would have to be taken care of tomorrow. Next he tackled the files, scribbling notes to his secretary and paralegal assistant as he went along so that they could work on some of the problems the next day without him.

He worked late, as he usually did. When he was in the middle of a long trial and trying to juggle other cases in progress as well, he often stayed at the office until eleven or twelve o'clock. Tonight was no exception. But the late night, following a string of others, took its toll on him, and by ten o'clock he was having to struggle to stifle his yawns. The words began to blur in front of his eyes, and he could not seem to keep his lids from closing. Twice he dozed off, head on hand, and came to with a start a few moments later. Finally, with a jaw-cracking yawn, he stretched and laid his head down on top of the files, pillowing his head on his arm. Almost immediately he slid down into the dark, deep well of sleep.

He dreamed of Adriana.

He was in the courtroom, and it was filled with people. He was questioning a witness, but he kept forgetting what he wanted to say, kept backtracking and searching helplessly through his notes. Then the witness changed, and it was Adriana on the stand. She wore a sheer blouse, with no bra beneath it, and he could see the dark circles of her nipples through the fabric. Her skirt was unbelievably short and tight, and she crossed her legs as she sat on the witness stand, casually swinging one foot. He couldn't keep his eyes off the smooth line of her legs where the skirt cut across them. The room was suddenly stiflingly hot, and he was aware that everyone in the court was staring at him.

He was supposed to ask her something, but he couldn't remember what. All he could think of were her legs and her shadowed breasts beneath the thin material. Adriana looked at him with a mocking smile, fully aware of her power over him, and somehow that smile only made his desire more fierce.

"You have to answer the question," he told her sternly.

"What question?" Her voice was as insolent as her expression, and she continued to swing her leg idly.

Then suddenly she was no longer sitting in the witness chair but was standing right in front of him. Staring at him, she unbuttoned her blouse and pulled it off. He knew that he should tell her she couldn't do that here, but his tongue was frozen. She sauntered away, swinging her hips provocatively.

She turned and faced him, leaning back against the jury box, hands on her hips, completely unconcerned by her nakedness. "What question?" she repeated.

He was hot and throbbing with passion, unable to think. He wanted her, had to have her.

Adriana strolled back to him lazily, stopping only inches from him. Desire exploded in him, and he reached out and ripped off her brief skirt. She was utterly naked beneath it, and she held out her hands to him, inviting him. With a growl, he bent her back over the prosecution table, burying his face between her breasts. He took her on the table, thrusting into her deep and hard. His hands cupped her breasts, fingers pressing into the pillowy softness. He drove into her again and again, and she moaned and writhed beneath him.

And around them everyone watched. He knew they were there, knew he was ruining his career, yet he could not stop. He could do nothing except race toward the explosion of fulfillment waiting for him within her. She grasped his hands with hers, fingernails digging into the backs of his hands, almost sobbing as she arched up into him.

James awakened with a start. There was pain in his hands, and he looked at them and saw that his hands were clasped, the nails of each one digging fiercely into the back of the other. He sat up abruptly. His body was burning up, and he was hard and aching.

He muttered an expletive and rubbed his hands over his face, trying to clear his mind. It was laughable—having adolescent wet dreams in the midst of his legal files. At least, he knew it would have been laughable if he had been able to consider it with any objectivity. But he couldn't dismiss the dream; it hit too close to the truth for comfort.

He couldn't remember when, if ever, he had met a woman who intrigued him, *aroused* him, as much as Adriana Cummings. But the undeniable, awful fact of the matter was that there probably wasn't another woman in the world with whom there was less of a chance of anything ever happening. He couldn't stop thinking about her. Yet he knew that it was utterly futile. Adriana hated him. There was no hope that she would ever even come near him.

James slammed his fist down on the desk in front of him. Damn it! Why couldn't he get that woman out of his mind? Where was his usual calm? His celebrated cool? Adriana was driving him crazy. And for the first time in his life, he felt helplessly out of control.

Chapter 5

After the evidence of her father's affair with Patricia Dayton, Adriana could no longer pretend to herself that she believed he was innocent of the charges. She felt as if the foundation of her life had shifted, leaving her sad and uneasy. She had spent her whole life thinking her father was a certain kind of man—honest, honorable, clear-thinking, faithful—and now she had been forced to realize that he was not. He had broken the law, betrayed his wife, cheated his company, all to follow a mindless impulse of passion. If she had been so wrong about him in those things, how wrong had she been about him in other ways? If he had lived the lie of the loving husband and the devoted employee, how many other pretenses had he carried on? What was he like? Did she really know him at all?

And if her father was not who she thought him, then how much of her own life was based on false ground? He was an integral part of her childhood, her life; she had grown up adoring him. Her father had been the rock of her life; her mother had been the weak reed. She had wanted to be strong, calm and reasonable like Jack; she had prided herself on being her father's daughter. Much as she loved her mother, she had always known that her mother had to have someone like her father to cling to or she wouldn't survive. Millie was sweet, but indecisive, overly emotional and dependent; the life she lived seemed purposeless and lazy to Adriana. It was her father who went out and accomplished things, who knew where he was going and what he was doing. He was strong.

If the part of her life that was her father was false, where did that leave her? If what she had adored, tried to be like, had been an illusion, then what exactly was she? Adriana told herself that her life and what she was weren't changed because she had found out that her father had not been exactly what he'd seemed. But she couldn't drive out the emotional disturbance within her with such rational arguments. She felt saddened and betrayed and somehow adrift.

What was worse was the fact that she was in the public eye all day long and had to present an optimistic, supportive front. Whatever her father had done, she still loved him. And she had to support her mother through this ordeal. For the sake of her family and her pride, she couldn't let it show that she had lost faith in her father. She had to keep the defeat and sorrow out of her face. The family had to appear united and certain. She had never been good at deception; Adriana tended to be forthright and open about her feelings, and it was difficult for her to pretend something so at odds with her feelings. It was a constant strain not to let her inner turmoil show.

Hope flickered within her that somehow her father's attorney would restore her faith, that he would prove the prosecution false or explain away the facts they had presented, but every day that hope grew fainter and fainter as the government's case piled·up. Their final bombshell was the testimony of Patricia Dayton herself, who admitted that Jack Larson had given her the information in order to help her in her business. Adriana held her mother's hand and watched the woman on the stand. She was far younger than her mother, probably no more than five years older than Suzanne, Jack's own daughter, and she was attractive in a sleek, polished style though her looks were hurt this day by the tenseness of her body and the tired lines around her eyes and mouth. Adriana would have liked to disbelieve her, to have thought that her statements didn't ring true, but she found that she couldn't help but believe the woman's flat dispassionate statements.

The defense case seemed to consist primarily of legal maneuvering over the admittance of the prosecution's evidence and the issue of Jack Larson's intent. Her father was the primary defense witness and contended that while he had had an affair with Patricia Dayton and might, in the course of "pillow talk," have let slip some vital information from which she figured out the upcoming merger, he had not intentionally given her inside information with the understanding that she would use it to benefit her clients. It was, perhaps, a valid legal argument; Adriana didn't know enough about the law to judge that. But she knew that it made little difference in her heart. Jack Larson had still betrayed his family and given up the secrets that he was honor-bound to hold. Besides, she knew deep inside that, much as she hated to admit it, it was Jack Larson's words that didn't ring true.

She believed the woman who had been his mistress; she couldn't believe her father.

The day of his testimony was the hardest day of all for Adriana. She had to fight to keep from breaking down and crying, and it was impossible to turn a calm, cheerful face to the cameras as they left the courtroom. As soon as they reached the privacy of their house, she left her mother and sister and went upstairs to her bedroom, preserved as it had been when she was a teenager, and threw herself across her bed, giving in to a storm of tears.

Later she tried to wash the ravages of her tears from her face before she went downstairs to join Millie and Suzanne, but nothing could erase the mottled look from her usually creamy white skin or the puffiness from her eyes. She found them on the sunporch, sitting amidst the cool floral prints and white wicker, sipping drinks and gazing out across the still-green back lawn. They greeted her but made no mention of the state of her eyes. Adriana noticed that their own eyes looked little better. It had been a hard day for them all. She wondered, a trifle bitterly, if it had been nearly as hard on her father as it had been on the rest of them.

"I'm sure your father's testimony will turn the tide," Millie said, the confidence in her voice ringing false.

Suzanne shot Adriana a look and grimaced. "Oh, Mama, give it up."

"Suzanne..." Adriana warned.

Millie turned wide, innocent eyes on her older daughter. "I don't know what you mean, dear."

"You know as well as I do. As well as Dree does. Daddy was lying through his teeth today on the witness stand, which I guess makes him guilty of perjury, as well." Suzanne's voice dripped bitterness.

"I don't want to hear you talking that way about your father," Millie flashed, and the ring on her hand began a nervous tattoo against her drinking glass.

"How long are you going to keep up this pretense? How long are you going to play the faithful little wife?" Suzanne's voice rose almost hysterically.

"Suze, come on." Adriana crossed the room and put a hand on her sister's arm. "This isn't doing any good. Not for anybody."

"I just wish she'd face up to it! I wish she'd stop lying to herself."

Millie rose to her feet and faced her daughter with dignity. "You think that I would actually abandon your father now? When he needs me the most?"

"Yeah, needs you to get sympathy. He hasn't even been living with you! What do you owe him?"

"I owe him for thirty-five years of marriage," Millie retorted. "Your father is a good man. He has always been a wonderful father and husband."

"Well, I only hope that my husband doesn't turn out to be that wonderful!"

"Suzie!" Adriana gripped her sister's arm hard. "You're overwrought. You haven't thought about what you're saying."

"So you're still on his side, too?"

"I'm not taking sides. He's my father. She's my mother. They both need us. You're not helping Mama this way. You know that." Firmly, she steered Suzanne toward the door. "Why don't you go up and lie down? It'll calm you down. I'll tell Lannie to bring you up a tray."

When they reached the doorway, Suzanne twisted her arm out of Adriana's grasp. "Are you sending me to my room?"

"For Pete's sake, Suzanne!" Adriana hissed. "What are you trying to do? Make Mama crack up? She doesn't need you badgering her, as well as having to put up with this trial!"

Suzanne glared at her for a moment, then sagged, the anger draining out of her face. Tears sprang to her eyes. "I know. I'm sorry." She pushed her hand back into her red-gold hair, usually so perfectly tended, but today hanging limp and uncurled. "I don't know what's the matter with me."

"You're tired and upset, just like the rest of us. Take a nap. You'll feel better."

Suzanne nodded. She looked over at her mother. "I'm sorry, Mama."

She left the room, and Adriana turned back to her mother. Millie looked at her for a moment. Then her face began to crumple. "Oh, God." She raised her hand to cover her sudden tears.

Adriana's heart ached for her mother. She went to her and put her arms around her. Almost desperately Millie clutched her and broke into sobs. Adriana patted her back.

"Shh, Mama. It's all right. It'll be okay."

"No!" Millie's voice was choked by tears. "It's not all right. It will never be okay again. Everything's destroyed."

Adriana hugged her mother tighter. "It seems that way now, but it'll get better. It has to."

Millie only cried harder, as though her heart was breaking. Adriana guessed that it was. Poor Mama. Nothing in her life had prepared her for this. She wasn't sure anything could prepare someone for this, but certainly a pampered existence as the pretty daughter of one of the wealthiest landowners in the state, and then as the wife of a top executive with Contelco, hadn't done so. She had always been sought-after, popular, well-liked. Her father and her husband had taken care of all business matters, and she had spent most of her time doing the gardening and playing the sports she loved.

Finally Millie's sobs quieted, and then she moved away, taking a long shuddering breath, and reached for a tissue. "I'm sorry."

"Don't apologize. There's no reason to. It's only natural for you to cry. You're under a great deal of strain. Heavens, I was just up in my room crying my eyes out."

Her mother gave her a little smile. "I'm sorry. I know it's been hard on you and Suzanne, too. I shouldn't have barked at her."

"It's okay. She understands. She shouldn't have said what she did to you, either."

Millie wiped her eyes. She pushed the hair back from her face and stood there for a moment, eyes closed, hands pressing against either side of her head, as though she could hold something in, keep it under control.

"I'm so afraid," she whispered hoarsely. "What am I going to do?"

"Oh, Mama..." Adriana's throat closed with tears. She felt unutterably sorry for her.

"I always thought my life was perfect, or close to it." She took her hands down and opened her eyes, plopping dispiritedly back down into her chair. "I had a beautiful home, two lovely daughters, a wonderful husband. I did pretty much what I pleased when I pleased. The worst I had to do was go to some boring business parties at other executives' houses—or give an equally boring one here. I thought—I thought Jack loved me. Even after all this time. Silly, I guess, to be so deluded. I didn't see it. I never guessed he was having an affair. I must have been blind.''

"No. You're a loving and trusting person. There's nothing wrong with that.''

Millie made a hoarse noise, not quite a laugh. "Yeah. Until you get hit in the face with it.'' She rubbed her hands tiredly over her face. "Ahh, Dree...he did it, didn't he? He's guilty.''

Adriana shifted uncomfortably. Somehow she couldn't bring herself to say that her father was guilty.

"You don't have to say it,'' Millie went on. "I know it. I didn't want to. I fought it all the way. I pretended I believed Jack, every word he said. I couldn't let myself think he did it, because then I'd have to think about *why* he did it. But you can't stick your head in the sand forever. They're going to convict him. I'm sure of it. And you know the worst thing—I'm more scared for *me* than I am for him. What am I going to do without him?''

"It won't be that long. You don't know that he's going to be convicted, and even if he is, there's always parole. Just a couple of years, maybe.''

Millie shook her head. "No. He won't be coming back to me. I have to face that, too. He doesn't love me anymore. I don't know when he stopped, or if he ever loved me. Do you know what's awful? I wonder sometimes if he married me for my money and my father's connections to half the businesses in the state.''

"Of course he loved you! Don't think this way. You don't know that he doesn't still love you. A husband can stray, you know, without necessarily falling out of love with his wife. Maybe it was just a physical thing.''

"No. He loved that other woman. I could see it in his face when she testified. He feels betrayed, just like I do.'' She made a wry face. "That's not much for us to base a marriage on, don't you think?'' She paused. "He won't come back. He hasn't lived here for weeks, months really, almost since this whole mess began. He says it's on his attorney's advice.'' She shrugged. "Maybe. But I doubt it. He doesn't want to be near me. He just doesn't want the bad publicity of a divorce. Suzanne's right. He needs me for sympathy. 'The wronged and loyal wife.'''

Adriana didn't know what to say. How could she offer advice or sympathy to her mother? It seemed so inadequate. Her mother's life had been ripped apart, devastated. Adriana knew that the confusion and pain she felt were only a fraction of what her mother must feel. She reached out and took Millie's hand silently. Millie gave her a faint smile and squeezed it.

"I don't know who I am anymore,'' Millie said softly. "I don't know what to do, where to go. For thirty-five years my life has been tied up with Jack's. How do I live all by myself now? I don't even have the club or my friends anymore. I'm too embarrassed to go there. I'm too ashamed to visit my friends. Sometimes at night I wake up, and I feel terrified. I'm so alone now.''

"No, you're not. You have me. And Suzanne.''

"Suzanne will go back to Charlotte. I can't expect her to continue spending half her time with me, away from her family. And you'll fly off to New Mexico. What am I going to do then?''

"No,'' Adriana said impulsively. "I won't.''

"What are you talking about?''

"I won't go back to New Mexico. I just decided. There's no reason why I have to live there. I can do my work anywhere. I could move all my things back to Winston-Salem. I could live here again.''

Millie stared at her. "Oh, no,'' she said half-heartedly. "I couldn't let you uproot your life for me. You shouldn't have to come home and baby-sit your feeble-minded old mother.''

''It's not a question of baby-sitting,'' Adriana retorted. ''Maybe I'd like to come home. I've found myself missing North Carolina more and more the past couple of years. I think I'll enjoy living here again.''

Her mother looked doubtful, but she didn't point out that now would be the least enjoyable time for a daughter of Jack Larson to live in Winston-Salem. ''I ought to protest. I ought to insist you stay out there. You're happy in New Mexico.''

''It's not New Mexico. I could be happy anywhere. And there's no point in trying to dissuade me. The more I think about it, the more I like the idea. I'm moving back.''

The trial came to a close. Both prosecution and defense rested, and the jury withdrew to deliberate. It didn't take them long to return with a guilty verdict. The verdict was no surprise to Adriana and her family—or anyone else, for that matter. Two days later Jack was sentenced to five years in a minimum security federal prison. He would be eligible for parole within eighteen months. Adriana listened to the verdict and the subsequent sentencing almost emotionlessly. She had been so battered by her stormy feelings during the weeks of the trial that it seemed as if she had nothing left inside her to feel. She hugged her father, listened to his attorney promising an appeal on several issues of evidence, and took her mother home, all in the same listless state. If she felt anything, she thought, it was closest to relief that the whole thing was finally over, and then she felt guilty for feeling that way.

She went to visit her father in jail before his transfer, but she had difficulty talking to him. It was so strange and uncomfortable to be sitting with him in this weird, sterile place. What he had done and the destruction of her faith in him lay like a huge barrier between them, far more impenetrable than any screen the jail had erected to keep inmates and visitors apart. They talked briefly of commonplaces, avoiding all mention of the trial or his future, and Adriana soon left.

She flew back to New Mexico to gather up her belongings and materials and leave the small house she had been renting. She shipped her things home, then drove her car back to Winston-Salem. The long drive was a calming time for her, a few days of mindless activity and slowly changing scenery that allowed her frazzled nerves and emotions to begin the process of healing. She wasn't sure if she would ever completely recover from the awful experience of the trial and her shocking disappointment in her father, but by the time she reached Winston-Salem, she was at least functioning normally again, out of the state of semi-shock that she had been living in for the past weeks.

At first she moved into the house with her mother. Millie needed her companionship, she knew, and for that Adriana was willing to give up her prized independence for a few months. The trial had stretched on for so long that it was now November, with the holiday season looming before them, and she knew she couldn't leave her mother in the house by herself during that time. Desultorily she looked around for places to live, taking the time to find exactly what she wanted.

In the meantime she set up her studio in the unused servants' quarters out back and began to work again. It was wonderful to be able to bury herself in the craft she loved, blocking out all her shadows and problems. When she wasn't working she spent as much time as she could with her mother. Adriana couldn't remember when she and Millie had done so much together—gone shopping, seen movies, traveled to the beach or the mountains for a long weekend of relaxation. She found that she enjoyed it. She was rediscovering her mother, finding in her qualities that she hadn't even known existed when she was younger.

Millie was doing better all the time, too. Adriana had been shocked during the trial to find out that her mother was taking tranquilizers all the time. After the trial, she was able to cut back to taking them only at night and finally got rid of them altogether. Her nerves gradually calmed and she began to take an interest in things outside her life again. It was a triumph for Adriana when she persuaded her mother to accompany her to the club for lunch one day. Adriana was relieved when no one stopped to question Millie about the trial or Jack. Two women stopped by to tell Millie how happy they were to see her back and how much she had been missed around the club. It seemed to Adriana as they drove home that there was more color in her mother's face and a hint of a sparkle in her eyes.

They got through Thanksgiving, then Christmas, and though there was a certain sadness in the atmosphere because of Jack's absence, Adriana was glad to see that her mother didn't fall into a full-scale depression. Gradually Millie began to pick up the pieces of her life again, going shopping, visiting with her friends, spending an afternoon at the club playing cards.

Adriana realized that it was time that she set up a life of her own. Her mother didn't need the baby-sitting Adriana had been providing for the last couple of months; in fact, it would probably be better for Millie to start living on her own. And, Adriana was forced to admit, she had been depending on her mother's companionship, as well. She, too, needed to build a separate life. She didn't want to move back to Taos. Her mother still needed her here, she thought, and, besides, she was enjoying living in her old home town again. She found a small house with a large room at the back that was perfect for a studio and moved into it not long after the start of the new year. Once she was settled and busy again with her work, she decided to get back into the charity work in which she had been active in New Mexico.

A few years earlier, during the time immediately following her divorce, she had gotten involved with an organization that provided a shelter for battered wives and children. As time went on, she had become more and more active, both in volunteer work at the shelter and in fund-raising. By the time she left New Mexico, she was on the board of directors, and it had become a cause dear to her heart. She wanted to continue that work here, so she found a local group that operated such a facility, known as the Women's Center, and volunteered her time and energy.

The facility's director was Lynn Muller, an absolute fireball of enthusiasm and energy, and she was delighted to accept Adriana's offer of help. "I can't tell you how thrilled I am," she told Adriana after she had explained the work she had done in Taos. "We're always in desperate need of volunteers. And someone with your experience! You came at just the right time, too. We're beginning a massive effort to raise money for a new facility. Right now we have one safe house, a big old place, and these little offices. We want to build a new center with meeting rooms, a playroom for the children and expanded facilities for short-term stays. An interim sort of place where we can take care of a woman immediately and give her a little breathing room while we arrange for her to move in with relatives or go to the safe house."

"It sounds marvelous," Adriana agreed.

"It will be. Once we get it finished, of course. Right now we haven't even gotten to the blueprint stage. We're forming a building committee, and I think it would be super if you would be on it."

"Sure. I'd love to." It would be an interesting project, something she could really sink her teeth into, something that would occupy a lot of the free time she had on her hands these days.

"Great. We're having a board of directors meeting this Thursday evening at 7:30. Why don't you come and let me introduce you to our board members? We're a small group, just struggling to get going, and our board is very actively involved in the organization. We'll be setting up the committee that night, too."

"Okay. If you want me to, I'll be happy to come."

That Thursday, Adriana arrived at the cramped offices of the Women's Center, which seemed even smaller than usual with about ten people jammed into the tiny conference room. Lynn rushed over to greet Adriana with a cry of delight and insisted on getting her a cup of coffee, then introducing her around to all the board members. Adriana knew one of the women, Kelly Pressler, who was about her sister's age and was one of those society women who had her finger in a dozen charity pies. Adriana had never particularly liked Kelly and was far more interested in talking to Milt Cohen, a freelance writer, a lively, witty middle-aged man with an engaging twinkle in his eye. He was in the midst of a funny story about his dealings with a national magazine when Lynn interrupted, putting her hand on Adriana's arm.

"Oh, Adriana. Sorry to interrupt, but I have someone here I'd like you to meet. He's volunteered to be on the building committee, too, and he's one of our most active board members. I'm afraid he arrived late, so I couldn't introduce you earlier."

Adriana murmured a polite apology and good-bye to Milt and turned, following Lynn. She glanced across the conference table, which Lynn was circling, and stopped. But Lynn had retained her grip on Adriana's arm, and she tugged her forward; Adriana followed, too numb to resist.

"Here he is. Adriana, I want you to meet one of our board members. James Marshall."

Chapter 6

Adriana couldn't speak. She felt as if she had been hit in the stomach. She had never expected to see James Marshall again, let alone meet him face to face—and in such a public place! She couldn't turn around and simply walk off. Lynn would be horrified, especially since she'd been so happy to introduce her to James.

James smiled. "Hello, Adriana. It's nice to see you again."

"You two know each other!" Lynn crowed. "Isn't that nice? And now you'll be working on the same committee together."

"We will?" James cocked an eyebrow and glanced at Adriana in surprise.

"Yes. Adriana has been kind enough to offer to help on the building committee. She has a lot of experience with a women's shelter like this where she used to live, so I'm sure she'll add a great deal to the committee."

"I agree." James looked straight at Adriana. "Adriana will be invaluable, I'm sure. I look forward to working with her."

Adriana wanted to grind her teeth in frustration. Here they were, deciding her future for her. Worse, she had been standing there like an idiot, unable to put together a coherent enough sentence to tell them that she had no intention of being on the building committee. Not as long as James Marshall was on it!

She could never work with him in any way, no matter how little time they might spend on the project or how many other people would be there with them. She simply refused to be around him. Perhaps he hadn't intentionally gotten to know her that evening at the country club so that he could pump her for information about her father, but he was still a snake. He was one of the men who had sent her father to prison, who had broken up her family and put them through the hellish misery of the trial. He, like the other two, had seized on the publicity Jack Larson's trial offered. Hadn't her mother said she'd heard that James Marshall had political ambitions? The trial had been the perfect stepping-stone. No doubt next year she would hear that he was running for some office, probably carrying "law and order" as his banner. The ordeal her family had suffered would help propel him into office.

She hated that. She hated him. Most of all, she hated herself because she had melted like butter in his arms. What was wrong with her, that she seemed invariably to be attracted to the wrong men?

Adriana tried to collect her thoughts to speak, to explain that she couldn't possibly work on the building committee, after all. Then out of the corner of her eye, she spotted Kelly Pressler watching them interestedly.

Kelly, of course, would know all about the trial and what part James Marshall had played in it. She would love to witness a juicy scene between the two of them that she could take back to the club and gossip about. However Adriana felt about James Marshall, it was overridden by her determination to do nothing that would cause her family any further embarrassment or stir up the trial again. There was no way that she was going to give Kelly even the slightest bit of gossip.

Sternly Adriana pulled herself together and forced a brittle smile to her face. "I really don't have that much experience. But, of course, I'm happy to help wherever I can." Well, that was mealymouthed enough. But it would have to do for the moment. She would tell Lynn later that she had changed her mind about the building committee. Maybe by then she would have worked up a decent excuse.

"I'm sure you're being modest." It was a common enough rejoinder to what she had said, but because it was James, Adriana couldn't help but examine his words for sarcasm or some ulterior purpose. He turned toward Lynn. "Adriana is a weaver. Did she tell you?"

"No! Why, how fascinating! Would you be willing to teach a class here at the center? Or, rather, at the new center when we get it built and have room enough for classes."

"I'm sure I wouldn't mind," Adriana murmured. She glanced away, searching for an excuse to leave the conversation. She hated being this close to James. It made her nervous. Already her palms were perspiring and her stomach was jumping.

She glanced at James again and found him watching her. There was a faintly amused look in his eyes that told her that he knew what she was doing, and why. She didn't understand him. She didn't know why he was content to remain in the conversation, either.

"Oh, there's Chester Winkman," Lynn said, waving to a man who had just entered the room. "If you all will excuse me, I have to talk to him."

She walked away, leaving Adriana and James alone together. There was a moment of awkward silence. Adriana wondered why she didn't simply leave, too. She had no reason to be polite to James. She supposed it was a reflex for her ladylike Southern upbringing. Well, she wasn't going to stand there like a dope, pretending out of politeness that she was friendly with the man. She had trained herself to be honest and open, and now was no time to take a step backward.

She drew a breath. "I won't be on the building committee, so you needn't worry. I'll tell Lynn after the meeting that I've changed my mind."

"I wasn't worrying. Why should I? I meant what I said. I'm sure you'll be a valuable asset to the group. After all, you do have some experience in the matter, which is more than you can say for quite a few of us."

"If I'm so valuable to the committee, then why don't you remove yourself from it?"

"Because I want it to succeed. If I'm there, I'll see that things get done. That's my contribution, efficiency and persistence."

The arrogance of the man! As if no one else could push a project through to completion! Adriana's mouth drew even tighter.

"Anyway," he went on, "I don't see why it's necessary for one of us to withdraw from the committee."

"Why pretend? It would be an uncomfortable situation, certainly for me, and I would think for you, too."

James sighed and looked down, as though searching for the right words. "Adriana... I know it's probably difficult for you to understand because of the way you feel about the trial and your father's conviction. But I have no personal animosity even toward him, and certainly not toward his family. Just because he committed a crime and got sent to jail for it doesn't mean that his wife and children are outcasts from society. I tried your father, not you."

"And you feel no guilt for the pain you inflicted on my family? No discomfort at being around someone who despises you?"

"No, I don't feel guilty. It was your father who inflicted the pain on your family, not me. As for being around people who despise me, I've been in the courtroom with too many defendants to be bothered by that. Believe me, your animosity couldn't begin to compare to some of the venom I've gotten from prisoners. Besides, I see no reason to let a little awkwardness between us personally to sabotage an important project. Surely you and I are capable of rising above our personal feelings for the sake of the new shelter."

He had touched her pride, as well as some of her prized beliefs, and Adriana's chin came up pugnaciously. "I'm certainly capable of ignoring my personal feelings if it's necessary."

"Good. I don't think it will be that great a strain on us, anyway, to sit at the same table with other people and discuss the new building."

He was right. It wasn't as if they would be alone together, and the conversation wouldn't touch on anything personal. It would be no more bother than having to see him a few times over the next few months. Surely she could put up with that. After all, she had endured his presence in the courtroom for weeks, hadn't she?

"That's true." She wasn't about to admit to him—or even to herself—that merely seeing him caused an ache inside her, a swirling, chaotic blend of pain, anger and regret. "I suppose it wouldn't be too difficult to deal with each other."

"I'm sure not." There was a rough quality to his voice that made her glance at him, but his face was devoid of emotion.

"Excuse me, everybody!" Lynn's voice rose above the babble of voices. "We'd better get started now. If everyone would just sit down . . ."

Adriana seized the opportunity to walk away from James, finding a spot at the end of the table beside Milt Cohen, which guaranteed that she wouldn't be unlucky enough to have James sit down beside her. Unfortunately, she had a clear view of him across the table. Having to sit there watching him made her wonder whether it would really be all that easy to endure those committee meetings.

There was an awful, traitorous part of her that couldn't keep from noticing how handsome he was, how attractive his voice was, how clear and incisive his contributions to the conversation were. Her mind went back to the night they had met, and she remembered how quickly and deeply she had wanted him. Her heart picked up its beat as she felt again the remembered excitement. She could almost taste the sweetness of his kisses, feel the ripple of desire shoot down through her when he touched her, hear the thrumming of her own blood in her ears. She had never felt such an instantaneous response to a man, such an immediate, overwhelming physical attraction. Why did it have to be him? And why couldn't she root all the vestiges of that desire out of her system?

It was humiliating to admit that even while she hated him, even during the trial when all day long she had focused all of her anger and pain on his dark head, inside her there had always been a still-burning spark of that desire. How was it possible to dislike someone as thoroughly as she disliked him, to know that he was the enemy, the man who had brought about the destruction of her parents' lives, and yet still feel a surreptitious tingle when she looked at him? The conflict he caused within her made her dislike him all the more.

Adriana looked away, pushing him out of her mind, and tried to concentrate on the discussion going on around her. It was difficult, especially since she knew none of the people involved, and the evening passed slowly. It was a great relief to her when the meeting finally ended and she was able to get up and leave.

Lynn shook her hand warmly, thanking her for coming and telling her how much she was looking forward to working with her. "I'll give you a call about the first building committee meeting, okay?"

Adriana nodded faintly. "Yeah. Thanks." Would she really be able to pull it off? Doubt nagged at her. This evening hadn't been easy. What made her think that the smaller committee meetings would be any better? It would be a lot better for her emotional state if she took herself off the committee, as she had planned. Why had she let James talk her into it? Or, more accurately, goad her into it. It had been his contention that he could handle it, with the implication that only she might be too weak to, that had really prompted her to say she would do it.

She walked out of the building and toward her car, deep in thought. There were footsteps behind her, hurrying to catch up, and James came up beside her. Adriana glanced at him and grimaced. "What do you want?"

"I thought I'd walk you to your car. You shouldn't walk alone in the dark, you know."

"Alone?" Adriana cast a sardonic glance around at the other board members in front of and behind them, all walking toward their cars in the parking lot behind the building.

"I wanted to ask you something," he admitted.

"What?"

"I want to know how your mother is."

Adriana's head snapped around toward him and her eyes shot sparks. How dare he inquire after her mother! "I don't see that that's any of your business."

"Pardon me." His voice was tinged with sarcasm. "I hadn't realized that being concerned for someone's health wasn't permissible for anyone besides family and friends. Or is it that prosecutors can't be concerned? Or perhaps it's only me."

The resentment and anger in her eyes flared higher, and her voice was chipped. "I find it hypocritical for you to ask after her as if you cared what happened to her, when you are the one responsible for her being a nervous wreck."

His eyebrows rose. When she had met him she had thought the expression charming. Now she found it vastly irritating. "*I'm* responsible? If you'll remember, it was your father who broke the law. I think he's the one who's responsible for your mother's heartbreak, not me."

"Oh, right. The law. It doesn't matter who gets hurt, does it, as long as the letter of the law is enforced!"

"The law doesn't deal in emotions. It deals in facts."

"That's obvious. The law is cold-blooded, and so are you."

A spark flared in his eyes and was quickly brought under control. "I'm rational, if that's what you mean."

"Self-serving is more like it. You used my family's tragedy to gain publicity for yourself—"

His mouth hardened. "You're way out-of-bounds, lady. I have never used a case, any case, least of all that one, to gain publicity for myself."

"No?" Adriana let contempt color her voice. "It certainly wouldn't hurt a future political career, would it?"

They had reached her car by now and stopped walking, but she was too involved in their argument to unlock the door and get in. Instead, they faced each other beside the driver's door, voices low but charged with anger, oblivious to the other people getting into their cars around them and driving away.

"Look. Number one," James ticked his points off on his fingers in a thoroughly lawyerlike way that raised Adriana's hackles "I have never said that I'm running for office. Rumors about my political career are simply that, rumors. Number two, even if I did plan to seek office in the future, I do *not* use my cases to manipulate the public or pump up my popularity. I am not a publicity hound, and I don't do what I do for the sake of getting my face on the six o'clock news."

"No?"

"No. I bring a case to trial and I do my very best to win it because I believe in bringing criminals to justice. Perhaps it sounds corny to you. I'm not an artsy type or a society lawyer, just a guy with pretty basic beliefs about right and wrong. The way I see it, I'm an advocate of the people. I'm there to help redress the wrongs that were done to the victims."

Strangely, Adriana felt herself warm to his words. There was a little prickle along her backbone, a stirring in her chest. She, too, believed in principles, in helping victims, in right and wrong, and it was rare and wonderful to hear someone espouse such simple, honest beliefs. But she shook off the feeling, reminding herself that winning people over with words was James Marshall's specialty. He knew how to use his eyes and rich, deep voice, how to pull up emotions from people with words. She had seen it during his opening speech at the trial.

Adriana sternly shook off the spell of his words. "How noble of you. But, frankly, there weren't exactly any victims in my father's case." Except her mother.

"There are always victims. If nothing else, a crime attacks our system of laws, the very foundation of our nation. It's a direct blow against all the citizens who have set up the laws as a protection."

"That's an awfully nebulous concept."

"I'm sure you can understand it. The fact that it's something intangible doesn't make it less important. The securities laws are there to protect everyone from fraud, to keep people who deal with stocks honest. If you can break those laws with impunity, then they have no force, and people have no protection. Anyway, in your father's case there were real victims. For one thing, there was his company."

"A corporation is the victim?"

"A business can't be victimized? Because it's big? Because it has money? Are you saying that it's okay to steal as long as you're taking money from a corporation?"

"No, of course not. Don't twist my words. I simply mean that it's difficult to picture some big company as a 'victim.' It's hardly the same as a person getting attacked or robbed or killed."

"I agree. But that doesn't make it an okay thing to do. It's still a crime, and there is a victim who needs protection. Anyway, the vague entity of the corporation isn't all that suffers. Lots and lots of ordinary people own stock in that company, and each and every one of them was hurt financially by what Jack Larson did. He had an obligation to his company and to the shareholders, and he betrayed that trust. And what about the stockholders of the other company, the one that was going to be merged with Contelco? They sold their stock for a much lower price than it would have brought when the merger took place. Every one of them lost money. Is that enough victims for you?"

"Yes!" Tears sprang into Adriana's eyes, and pain squeezed her heart. "My father was wrong! I can't deny it. And no doubt he had to be tried and punished for it. But, damn it, I can't like it, and I can't like the people who did it to him!"

James looked at her for a moment, then sighed and stepped back. "I know. I knew it the instant I saw you in that courtroom. It was bad luck. Bad timing. If we hadn't already gone to trial, I would have withdrawn from the case."

Adriana's eyes widened with surprise. "You would have?"

"Yeah." He paused and looked away, carefully choosing his words. "I'm not used to... feeling the way I did when I met you." He looked back at her. In the darkness, his eyes were black instead of their usual light blue, but they were as intense as ever, boring into her. "I've been told that I'm a cold son of a bitch. But the way I feel about you is anything but cold."

Adriana's chest tightened. Suddenly it was difficult to breathe, and her heart began to beat a hundred miles an hour. She curled her fingers into her palms, digging in her nails. The effect he could have on her with his eyes, his voice, scared her. She could imagine how easy it would be to fall completely under this man's sway. The power in James Marshall didn't come from external things like his job or his family's position and wealth. It came from deep inside him, an intrinsic, natural force that propelled him and drew people to him. If he hadn't been a Marshall, he still would have been someone to be reckoned with, a man who people obeyed and followed. He could pull secrets from inside you, she thought, and it made her shiver. How easily could he reach inside her mind and see what she thought? Did he have any idea that when he was near, despite her dislike and distrust of him, she still felt the tingling prickles of desire?

Adriana sincerely hoped not. It was bad enough having to be around him; it would be awful if he knew that he could still arouse her physically. She suspected that James wouldn't hesitate to use her own emotions against her.

Abruptly she turned away, afraid that her face might give away some of the turmoil inside her. "I see no point in going into any of this. It's over and done with."

"It doesn't have to be."

"It does!" She whirled back around, her eyes blazing now with the emotions that bubbled inside her. "There wasn't anything between us, and there won't ever be. There can't."

He shrugged slightly. "Why can't there be?"

"Because I don't want it! Whatever we felt that night at the country club was something removed from reality. What *is* real is the trial and what happened and the way I feel about that. I can't say, 'Let's start over fresh, as if nothing ever happened.' I'm not that big a person. I'm not that generous. Whatever the rights and wrongs of the case, I could never feel anything for the man who sent my father to prison."

"I'd say that's clear enough." James glanced away, and when he looked back, his face showed nothing of what he was thinking. "I understand that you are . . . not particularly fond of me at the present. Perhaps we can't have back what we had that evening. But don't you think that we can manage to at least be in the same room together without getting into a fight? Can't we be polite? Put aside our differences long enough to do something for the women's center? I don't ask that we be lovers—or even friends. Simply that we not be enemies."

Adriana hesitated for a moment, then said, "Yes," trying to match his coolness. "I'm sure that I can overlook my personal feelings about you enough to be on the same committee. I'm willing to try, at any rate."

He nodded. "Good. Then I'll see you at the first committee meeting."

"Yes." Adriana turned away and bent to insert her key in the lock of her door. Behind her, James remained where he was. She opened the door and shot an inquisitive glance back at him. Why was he still standing there?

"Just waiting to make sure you got in," he said, answering her unspoken question. "Good night, Adriana."

"Good night."

He walked away toward his own car. Adriana got into hers and started the engine, careful not to glance toward him again. She felt strangely empty inside. The vague sense of loneliness persisted as she drove home, and when she unlocked the door and stepped into her little house, its quiet only emphasized her loneliness.

She walked through to the kitchen, turning on the lights as she went and leaving them on, as if the blaze of electricity could banish the blues lurking inside her. She opened the refrigerator but realized that she was neither hungry nor thirsty, so she closed the door and flopped down on a chair, propping her elbows on the table and glumly setting her chin in her hands. She was at loose ends, trying to find something to do so that she could drive away the emptiness of her house. Her life.

Up until now, she had been content here, even happy sometimes, especially when she was working. But now she thought about how little she had gone out since she'd left her mother's house. Almost all her friends from high school had long since moved away, and she had drifted away from the ones who had not. It had been over ten years since she'd lived in this city, and except for her mother, she was no longer close to anyone here. The nature of her work enforced a solitary life-style. To get anything done she had to stay home alone, and there was almost nothing about her work that brought her into contact with anyone, except the clerks in the stores where she bought her materials. It wasn't like Taos where the artists had run into each other on the street and in the shops, where they had had so much in common, making it easy to get together.

She had hardly even gotten to know her neighbors, who all worked in offices during the day and returned home at night, tired and weary of the public, in no mood to socialize. Of course, she had been a little leery herself about trying to establish contact with them, afraid that they would recognize her or her name and start to ask questions about the trial.

It was no wonder she was lonely. Going to the meeting tonight and being around a lot of people again had probably made her realize it. She should get out more, see someone besides her mother. Maybe she ought to call up one or two of the girls she used to know. Women, now, of course. It might be fun to catch up.

Or it might be miserable. Anyone who knew her would have been very aware of her father's trial and probably quite curious about it. Could she stand their questions, their sympathy—or, worst of all, that quickly covered, faintly horrified look, as if she had some disease that might also rub off on them? She had encountered all three when she'd happened to run into old acquaintances. She wanted to think that a former friend wouldn't have such a reaction, but she was growing cynical through experience. One of her mother's supposedly bosom buddies had dropped her like a hot potato after the trial, and there were several other golf or tennis or bridge partners who had become aloof.

It would be easier, she thought, to make new friends. And that was what she was doing. Now that she was settled and Millie was better, she was taking steps to reach out to find other people. After all, she had started by going to the Women's Center offices and volunteering. It had been bad luck that her favorite charity was one favored by James Marshall, too—and even worse luck that she'd wound up on a committee with him. But, still, it was the right thing to do. She would help, and she would meet people with similar interests. Gradually she would form friendships this way. Perhaps she would join an aerobics group instead of taking her usual long daily walks. Or even take a course in something she was interested in.

It would work out. This was only a little hump to be gotten over, that was all. Before long, she would have friends, perhaps even start to date, and then this loneliness would be gone. In time, even the thought of James Marshall might no longer bother her.

Adriana sighed and stood up. That day couldn't come soon enough for her.

The first committee meeting was the following week, and Adriana waited for it to arrive with trepidation. She thought of a dozen excuses for staying home and almost called twice to say that she wouldn't be able to make it. However, she was determined not to let James think she was a coward, and she was sure that was exactly what he would think if she didn't show up. He would be right, too, which was even more galling. So she talked herself out of the telephone calls, and on Tuesday night she was at the Women's Center for the meeting, even arriving slightly early.

After all her fears, the meeting was anticlimactic. There were four other people besides her and James. They soon had her talking about the shelter where she'd worked in New Mexico, so her nervousness quickly fled. James arrived after everyone else and left early, and during the meeting he hardly glanced at her. He was made the chairman of the committee, and he moved the meeting along quickly and efficiently. They agreed on the architectural firms from which they would accept proposals, which led them into a discussion of exactly what they were looking for, which led to a realization that they weren't sure exactly what they did want.

"Why don't we visit the house they have now?" the gray-haired woman beside Adriana suggested. Adriana had learned that she was a doctor and a grandmother—not necessarily in order of importance, Adriana discovered quickly—and she had a dry wit and a quick understanding. She was brisk and no-nonsense and treated

James without any of the deference that people usually used toward him, much the way Adriana would imagine an old elementary teacher might regard one of her pupils, now grown up, even famous or powerful, but always a child with paint-stained fingers to her. "We could look the place over, see what they have that they want to keep, ask the residents and workers what sort of changes they'd make. I mean, we're working in the dark here. We have the size and other specifications that Lynn gave us but, frankly, I don't think that's sufficient."

"You're right. We need to know more before we can evaluate an architect's plan," a man Adriana did not know added.

"Or even explain to him what we want."

Everyone agreed that meeting to tour the safe house was in order, and James agreed to call Lynn and set up a time and date for the tour. After that, he turned the meeting over to the others and left for an appointment.

Strangely, Adriana found that she felt almost dissatisfied when she left the meeting. She hadn't wanted another confrontation with James, yet, somehow, something seemed to be missing.

She went through the following days in a bored, restless mood, unable to stick with her work, yet unable or unwilling to do anything else, either. It annoyed her, but she couldn't seem to shake her vague dissatisfaction. She was glad when Lynn called and told her that the committee had been set up to tour the present facilities the following Monday evening. At least that would give her something interesting to do; perhaps it would shake her out of her strange ennui.

Lynn told her the location of the house, first binding her to secrecy, and the next Monday Adriana drove out to it, arriving a little early. It was an older house in a quiet, tree-lined neighborhood, with nothing to mark it as anything unusual. She parked in front and walked up to the door. She rang the doorbell and heard the sound of someone walking inside, but it was some time before the door finally opened. A tall woman in a trim slacks suit smiled at her politely.

"Yes?"

"I'm Adriana Cummings."

"Yes. Ms. Cummings. I've been looking forward to meeting you." She opened the door wide to let Adriana in and stuck out her hand. "I'm Joy Cupperman. I'm a counselor here at the shelter."

"It's nice to meet you." Adriana shook her hand and followed the woman inside.

"Why don't we wait in my office? You're the first to arrive. A few of the committee members were unable to make it, but I am expecting a couple more of you. We can start the tour when they get here."

James Marshall's busy schedule had probably kept him from coming, Adriana thought. It didn't surprise her; she had suspected that he was more interested in having his name involved in a worthwhile charity than in the actual work. But that was good; she would be more comfortable without him there.

Joy Cupperman offered her a glass of iced tea, and they chatted while they waited for the others. A few minutes later the doorbell rang again, and Joy excused herself to answer it. When she returned, she was followed by James Marshall. Adriana's eyes widened in surprise. Knowing how busy and rushed he always seemed, she had been certain that he was one of the committee members who wasn't coming. Seeing him set up the familiar jangling of her nerves that occurred when he was around. But adding to it now was the panicky realization that if two or three people weren't coming, and James was one of the people who was there, she would be almost alone with him!

Chapter 7

Adriana jumped to her feet as James stepped into the small office, then realized that she must look as if she were about to flee. She blushed, embarrassed.

He didn't seem to notice. He smiled at her, his face lightening with pleasure. "Adriana. When Ms. Cupperman said only one person had shown up, I was afraid that you wouldn't be here."

"I thought the same about you," she replied, though she didn't add that she was anything but glad to discover that he was not one of the missing members.

Joy brought James some iced tea and freshened Adriana's glass, and the three of them sat and waited, talking sporadically. Minutes crept by. The palms of Adriana's hands were sweating, she realized, and she wiped them surreptitiously down her skirt. All the while James was talking to Joy, but his eyes kept coming back to Adriana. She realized that she, too, was glancing at him far more than was either necessary or normal.

She found herself looking at his hands, spread out on his legs. They were strong, capable hands, the fingers a little blunt, the palms wide, with a light sprinkling of black hairs across the backs. They were the sort of hands she could imagine fixing things, lifting, pulling, holding—very masculine hands. She didn't have to imagine to know how they would feel holding her; she had been held by them. She had known their strength and heat.

She glanced away, embarrassed at the turn her thoughts had taken. She would hate to think that James could see in her eyes what she had been thinking about.

"Ms. Cummings?" Adriana realized with a start that Joy was speaking to her and judging by her puzzled expression, apparently had asked her a question.

"I'm sorry. What did you say?" Adriana gave her an apologetic smile. "I'm afraid my mind wandered."

"I was saying that it might be best if we got started. I have a therapy group to lead in thirty minutes."

"Oh. Of course. That sounds best."

"Good." Joy smiled and stood up. "Let's start in the kitchen, shall we?"

She took them through the downstairs, pointing out the strengths and weaknesses of the facilities. "We're drastically, dangerously short of space. That's our main problem. Of course, you're already aware of that. But it shows up in all sorts of ways, not just the lack of bedrooms to accommodate the women who come to us, looking for shelter. For instance, here in the kitchen. It's just an ordinary old kitchen, made to serve a family. The equipment simply isn't enough. We need commercial equipment, not residential. A commercial refrigerator and freezer, for example, and a far larger pantry, capable of storing food for the number of women and children we feed every day. A commercial size stove—we can't cook enough food at one time. We use the dining room and the kitchen for eating, and we still can't seat everyone at once.''

Adriana took a pad and pen from her purse and began to scribble down notes. She noticed that James was carrying a pocket tape recorder, switching it on to catch Joy's words.

''As you can see,'' Joy continued as they walked through the first floor, ''we've used all the available space as extra bedrooms and baths. The formal living room, the den, even a very small sewing room. The result is that we have only the one large rec room at the rear of the house for the residents to gather in. There is no separate facility for our group meetings or for a play space for the children, no quiet room where the women can get away from the noise and read or think or just enjoy being alone. And here's our utility room. You can see that it's too small, and the single washer and dryer we have are constantly in use. We need more than one set. When these break down, as they often do because they're not made for such heavy use, we're really in a fix.''

She led them upstairs, showing them the various bedrooms, most furnished with two twin beds and only a single chest and chair, the larger ones containing a twin bed and a set of bunk beds. ''The twin beds are all trundle beds,'' Joy pointed out. ''We often need an extra bed or two for children. For instance, in this room, we have a mother and her four children. The baby sleeps on a pallet on the floor.''

Adriana tried to imagine living in a single room with four children. ''How do they manage?''

Joy shrugged. ''It's better than living at home. At least it's safe, even if it is cramped. It would be far preferable, of course, to have bigger quarters. But we're so desperate for space that until we have another, larger building, the only way we can have more space here is to turn down even more women. That's why we've just kept squeezing more and more people into the same space. It's heartrending to have to turn them away."

"I know." Adriana had seen it at other shelters she had visited, as well as the one where she had worked. It seemed that no matter how much space was added, there was never enough. Every place had had to turn away women who needed its services.

After the tour Joy discussed the changes that she and the other counselors would like to see made in the building; then Adriana and James sat down with several of the residents to ask what they would like done differently in the new house. Adriana was amazed at James's patience and calm with the women. Almost every time she had seen him, he had been rushed, arriving late or leaving early or both, always walking in a rapid, no-nonsense way, his eyes focused inward, thinking. Yet as they sat talking to the women, there was nothing about him to suggest that his time was limited, that he had to hurry. He had a way of sitting silent and utterly still, his eyes intent on a woman's face, that encouraged her to talk.

By the time they left the house, it had gotten dark. As he had done after the board meeting, James walked with Adriana to her car. She shot him a dry glance. "You really don't need to do this."

"Do what?"

"See me to my car. I'm quite capable of making it on my own."

"Mm. No doubt. But you see, it was the way I was brought up. Old habits are hard to lose."

Adriana rolled her eyes.

"I think it was a useful meeting, don't you?" he went on cheerfully, chatting as if they were friends.

"Yes."

"We learned quite a bit. Or, at least, I did. You may have already known it." Adriana shook her head without saying anything. "It's appalling, isn't it, the lack of proper facilities? Having to turn away women who desperately need help. It seems there ought to be more we should do."

"I'm sure there is. I imagine that you could give up your life to it and still not be able to make a dent in the situation."

"You're probably right. There are times when I think about the tragic situations that so many people are in, what needs to be done and how difficult it is to change anything, and I feel overwhelmed. Sometimes I wonder if what I do makes any difference."

Adriana was surprised to hear such an admission from James. He seemed so confident and in control; she wouldn't have suspected that he ever felt overwhelmed or had a moment's doubt.

He glanced down at her and raised his eyebrows. "What's that look for?"

"What look?"

"The one you were giving me. Like I'd shocked you, or you didn't believe me, or something."

Adriana shrugged. "It's nothing. There are simply times when I'm not sure what to make of you."

"I'm afraid I'm not terribly complex. In fact, certain members of my family have accused me of being simplistic." He paused, as though weighing what he'd said. "Actually, I don't think it's simplicity. It's more…single-mindedness. I latch on to something, and I can't seem to let it go."

They reached her car, and Adriana turned to face him. She had intended to say good-bye and thank him for walking with her, but as she turned, he stepped closer, so that he was only inches away. Her words flew out of her head, and she could only look at him.

"That's what I've done with you," he told her softly. "I can't seem to let go of you."

Adriana pulled herself up as straight as she could and edged backwards. She bumped into her car and stopped. James dropped his briefcase, and his arms came up on either side of her, effectively trapping her between them. She drew a quick, shallow breath. Her heart was suddenly going like a jackhammer.

"I don't think you ever had me," she told him, but the effect of the brave statement was marred by the breathlessness in her voice.

"Maybe not physically. But my mind refuses to give you up."

"Perhaps you need to take charge of your mind, then."

"Perhaps." A small smile played about his lips. "But I find I enjoy thinking about you."

"I can't think why, since I dislike you thoroughly."

"Not thoroughly. I can't believe that." He moved closer, so that their bodies were almost touching. "There must be some speck inside you of what you felt for me the night we met. It was too strong to lose entirely."

"Maybe what I felt wasn't as great as you think."

This time the smile completely captured his mouth. "You're lying now."

"James...this is a pointless conversation. I don't want to talk to you. I don't even want to—"

"I don't want to talk, either." His arms slid around her, and his hard body pinned her against the side of her car. Adriana saw the dark glitter of his eyes before she closed her own. Then his mouth was on hers, and everything exploded within her, just as it had that first night.

For an instant she stiffened against the tumult of sensation inside her; then, with a little groan she gave in. Her arms slid up around his neck, and she clung to him, returning his kiss. His mouth ground into hers, and her lips opened, admitting his seeking tongue. Adriana could feel the whole hard length of his body pressing into hers, all muscle and bone against her softness, as though he were crushing out her feeble resistance. She didn't want to enjoy it, didn't want to welcome his passion, yet she couldn't stop her body from responding.

Her hands clenched the material of his shirt as his kiss delved deeper. A heat as fierce as an open flame was roaring through her now, combining with the heat of his body so that she felt surrounded by fire, consumed and yet more alive than she had ever felt.

James groaned, changing the slant of his lips and kissing her even more hungrily. He rubbed his body against hers erotically, and electricity sizzled through her. He tore his mouth from hers and moved down her neck, murmuring her name over and over in a gravelly voice. Adriana arched her head back, exposing the soft white skin of her throat to his predatory lips.

Under cover of darkness, his hands went to her hips and moved slowly up her body, coming to rest at last on her breasts. He cupped the full orbs through the material of her dress, gently caressing them, the soft movement a delicious counterpoint to the almost savage heat of his mouth on her skin. A long shudder ran through Adriana, and a low, throbbing ache started between her legs. She wanted him in a deep primal way, without reason or thought, and it was only with the last remnant of her control that she was able to keep from ripping at his shirt to get to the skin beneath. She wanted to touch him, taste him, to dig her fingers into his firm flesh, to make him want her so badly that he was almost in pain.

Had she known it, desire was already clawing at James like a wounded animal. All he could think of was pulling her to the ground and taking her right there. The intelligence and practicality on which he prided himself had fled as soon as he kissed her, burned up in the flashfire of passion that had consumed his body. He felt panting and desperate, all animal hunger, his body trembling under the force of his desire.

His lips burned their way to the tops of her lush breasts, thwarted by the edge of her blouse. He curled his fingers around the gathered top of the scoop-necked blouse and pulled it down. His fingers slid over the smooth skin of her breasts, and he realized that her flesh was bare beneath his touch, with no brassiere to hinder him, and desire stabbed him all afresh.

"Adriana," he breathed, and his mouth moved greedily down the slope of her breast. He murmured inarticulate words of passion and praise, stunned by the soft beauty of her flesh and the force of the hunger it aroused in him. For the first time in his life, he felt as if he would die if he could not possess this woman right now. His world had narrowed to nothing but her and this moment, and these feelings rushed through him like a storm.

"Please..." Adriana's word was almost a sob, but she had no idea what she was pleading for. She moved her hips against James in wordless invitation, and her answer came in his muffled groan as he pressed her even more tightly against the car.

His hand moved down her leg, bunching her full skirt, and slipped up beneath it, caressing the smooth flesh of her leg. His fingers seared her skin, and she began to tremble. She wanted him to possess her, wanted to feel him buried deep within her, to conquer him with her own submission. Her hands moved frantically over his shoulders and chest, and she shoved her fingers between the edges of his shirt, popping a button in her haste. James shuddered at the touch of her fingers on his bare skin, and it was all he could do to keep from thundering to the completion of his desire.

Only the frustration of their clothing and their position prevented him from making love to her right there. Almost growling, James jerked away and cursed expressively. Adriana leaned limply back against her car, unable to speak or even think, and her face and body were so clearly melting with desire that it sent another stab of passion through him. He reached around her and grabbed the door handle, opening it.

"Let's go," he said quickly, fighting the fog of desire in his brain as he tried to arrange the mechanics of what he so desperately wanted.

He took her arm, steering her into the car.

"What? No." Her eyes were vague and confused, still soft and shining with arousal, and her hands went out to his chest, sliding around him under his suit jacket. She moved into him, lifting her lips to his.

James's heart slammed inside his chest, and he couldn't keep from meeting her mouth with his. They kissed until both of them were about to explode, and only then was he able to tear his lips away.

"God! Adriana! Please." He hardly recognized his roughened voice. "Let me—we have to—" He shoved his hands back into his hair, struggling to collect his scattered thoughts enough to make a coherent plea. "Get in," he growled finally, almost shoving her down into the car, and started to follow.

Just as he was bending down to get inside, headlights flashed over them, and a car pulled up behind them. James turned, startled, and let out a heartfelt curse when the driver's side of the car opened and Claire Lawrence, the gray-haired doctor who was on the building committee, got out of the car.

"I'm sorry!" she called. "Is it over already? Are you leaving? I got held up at the hospital, blast it."

James closed his eyes, sucking in a breath, and struggled to regain some semblance of normality. Inside the car he heard Adriana gasp as she realized what was going on. He turned to face the new arrival, instinctively positioning himself between Adriana and Dr. Lawrence.

"Hello, Claire." His voice came out hoarsely, and he cleared his throat. He combed his hand back through his hair and straightened his suit jacket to cover the missing button on his shirt. Thank heavens it was dark and therefore more difficult for the woman to witness the disarray their swift moment of passion had left them in. "Yes, I'm afraid you missed the tour."

James bent and picked up his briefcase from where he had dropped it on the ground, holding it strategically over the most obvious hallmark of their passionate encounter as he faced the approaching woman. Plastering what he hoped looked like a smile on his face, he continued, "But I imagine Mrs. Cupperman would be happy to show you around now. She's still there."

Claire Lawrence glanced at her watch doubtfully. "Well, it is awfully late."

"I don't think it would be a problem. Really." James concentrated on injecting sincerity into his voice. Frankly, at the moment he didn't give a damn whether

Claire toured the shelter or got in her car and drove away or disappeared in a puff of smoke. He simply wanted her gone, and as rapidly as possible.

"Well…" Dr. Lawrence stopped a few feet away from him and glanced toward the house, then back to him.

James continued to smile, hoping he didn't look like he was trying to cover something up and wondering why Claire had to choose this moment to be so uncharacteristically indecisive.

Claire nodded her head once briskly. "All right. I believe I will. It would be almost impossible for me to reschedule for another night this week, and I'd like to be able to discuss it intelligently at our next meeting."

"I think you're right. You ought to do it now."

"All right." She smiled and stepped forward to shake his hand. "It was nice to see you, James. Sorry it was so brief." She bent around him to peer into the car. "Oh, hello, Ms. Cummings. Sorry to have missed the tour." Adriana's mumbled reply was unintelligible, but Claire paid no attention. "Well, good night, all."

She strode away toward the house. James turned back to Adriana. She sat slumped in the driver's seat, her forehead resting against the steering wheel.

She had returned to reality with a thump as soon as she heard Claire Lawrence's voice. *Good Lord, what had she been doing? Been about to do?* Shame had flooded through her, dousing the fire in her blood, and she had quickly straightened her clothing and hair, wondering miserably how she would be able to face Claire Lawrence. Even worse, how could she face James, knowing how wantonly, how easily, she had melted in his arms?

Now that Dr. Lawrence was gone, Adriana knew that James was looking at her, but she couldn't raise her head to meet his gaze. After what she'd done, he would think that he could have her anytime he wanted, that all he had to do was touch her or kiss her, and she would turn into a mindless panting creature.

Because she had! Hot tears of humiliation sprang into her eyes. She couldn't deny it. She had been lost to everything except passion for the last few minutes. All she had wanted was to make love with James, and her desire had been quite obvious. She thought about the way she had practically ripped at his shirt because she wanted to feel his skin against her hand. Why, she'd even torn a button off! She flushed with embarrassment at the memory. *How was she going to live with herself?* Never in her whole life would she have believed that she could be so utterly carried away by passion. Quite frankly, she wouldn't have thought she had that much passion inside her. She hated the man, yet her body was still hot and aching, yearning for his touch!

"Adriana."

Some chord trembled deep within her at the low, husky sound of his voice. She shivered and wrapped her arms around herself, wishing desperately that she could make herself invulnerable to him.

James reached down and lightly touched her arm. Adriana flinched away from him. "Don't."

He sighed and sagged against the car. The moment was gone, and Adriana had returned to normal. She despised him again—and now she probably despised herself, as well, for responding to him.

"Adriana, please..." His voice was low, and he fumbled uncustomarily for the right words. "Please don't turn away from me."

"No. Stop." She straightened, thrusting back her tousled hair, and turned tear-bright eyes to him. "I don't want to hear it. I won't listen."

"You have to." He leaned down, bracing his arms between the car and the open door, so that it was impossible for her to slam the door and drive off. "I can't simply let you go."

"You don't have any choice!"

"The hell I don't! If you think that I'm going to let you waltz out of my life after what just happened—"

"Please!" Adriana's voice was choked, and she looked up at him pleadingly, tears streaming down her cheeks. "Please don't make me humiliate myself any further."

James wanted to yell, to grab her and shake her, to kiss her until she was as hot and willing as she had been earlier. But he couldn't hold out against the tear-streaked appeal in her face. With a sigh, he stepped back. Adriana jerked the door shut and started the car. She darted out into the street with a squeal of tires, flipping on her lights belatedly. James stood, watching the red taillights of her car until they were lost in the distance. Then, wearily, he started toward his own car, wondering how the hell he was ever going to get to sleep tonight.

She would resign from the building committee, Adriana decided. There was no way she could attend another meeting with James, not with what she had revealed to him about herself. She felt stripped and vulnerable before him. Far worse, she had lost confidence in herself. She had lost control, been completely overwhelmed by physical desire. It was something that had never happened to her before, that she could not even have imagined happening. No matter how much her heart had been engaged or how much a man might have made her pulse flutter, her brain had remained active. She had always been able to subdue an errant attraction when she had known that it wasn't right. After all, hadn't she once been attracted momentarily to another artist while she was still married—however unhappily—to Alan? She had nipped that in the bud without any problem.

But this . . .

She couldn't bear to even think about it. Yet, at the same time, her mind wouldn't leave it alone. Her thoughts kept going back to that moment when James had pressed her back against the car and kissed her. It made her burn with humiliation to remember it; it was even worse knowing that just the memory of those kisses and caresses was enough to make her breath catch in her throat and a fire start up in her loins. How could she hate him and feel contempt for herself for responding to him, and yet still feel the ache of passion on merely recalling the touch of his mouth and fingers? It was debasing. Horrifying.

She hated to admit that James Marshall had such power over her. Quitting the committee would be an admission of his power, an acknowledgement of defeat, and that galled her. But she was also practical enough to realize that if she did stay on the committee, she would probably face the same situation again, and she had proved that she couldn't trust herself not to give in to him. It would be even worse if, next time, nothing interrupted them and she wound up in the bed of the man who had sent her father to prison.

She refused to allow herself to be a slave to her own desires, and the only way she could ensure that that wouldn't happen was to stay away from James Marshall entirely.

He called her the day after their tour of the shelter, but she hung up on him as soon as she recognized his voice. On Saturday he showed up on her doorstep, but she was wary enough to look out the peephole in her front door before she answered the bell, so she didn't open the door. For a few long minutes she stood at the door, her forehead resting against the smooth wood, palms pressed flat against it, waiting for him to leave. On the other side, James stood interminably, almost as though he knew that she was on the inside and he wanted to force her to open it with the strength of his will. But, finally, he turned and walked back to his car, and Adriana had slid down to a sitting position on the floor, limp with relief. She felt as if she'd passed some test, though she wasn't sure what.

She went to the Women's Center for her volunteer afternoon the next week. She could still do that without having to face James, and she felt even more compelled to do the work because of the guilt at thinking about dropping out of the committee.

It was a relief to do the routine work given to her at the center. Mailing, copying, filing and answering the phone were all things she could do mechanically, with only part of her attention. Her own work had suffered all week because she had been unable to keep her mind from wandering to James.

Late in the afternoon, she was seated at the receptionist's desk while the receptionist took her coffee break when the door opened, and a woman stepped timidly inside. It was all Adriana could do not to gasp, even though she'd seen sights as bad and worse during the time she'd volunteered in the battered women's shelter in New Mexico. The woman who stood inside the door had a black eye and swollen lips, and a livid bruise stood out against her cheek. Adriana was willing to bet that beneath the long-sleeved, high-necked blouse were probably several other bruises, as well. She held the hand of a little girl, a dark-eyed, solemn-faced creature, and Adriana could see that the woman's hand was trembling around the child's. Pity welled in Adriana, and she stood up quickly.

"Please, come in. Can I help you?"

The woman glanced around uncertainly and wet her lips. "Uh . . . I'm not sure."

"Would you like to see Lynn? She's the woman who runs this place. I'm sure she'd be happy to talk to you."

"Yeah. I—guess so."

Adriana crossed the room to Lynn's closed door and opened it, sticking her head inside. "There's someone here to see you."

Lynn looked up, and understanding touched her face as soon as she saw Adriana's. She immediately set aside the paperwork she was doing. "Sure. Send her in."

A few moments later the receptionist returned, and Adriana went back to her job at the file cabinets against the far walls. When she heard the sound of a door opening again, she glanced back, expecting to see the battered woman and her child emerging from Lynn's office. Instead she saw that it was the outer door that had opened again, and this time it was no pitiful woman who walked in, but James Marshall.

"Hey, Carrie. Did Mrs. Gunderson come in? My secretary, Dana, was going to come with her, but she got tied up and couldn't. I'm supposed to meet Mrs. Gunderson here."

"Gunderson?" The receptionist wrinkled up her nose, thinking, and slowly shook her head. "I don't remember anyone by that name." She turned toward Adriana. "Adriana? Did anyone named Gunderson come in while I was out?"

Startled, James turned to follow the direction of Carrie's gaze. He stared at Adriana for a long moment, and she felt herself go hot, then cold, then hot again. She felt foolish and embarrassed, and she wished she could magically disappear. She'd never dreamed that James might come to the center other than for meetings.

"Adriana." His eyes never left hers. "I'm sorry. I didn't see you there."

She swallowed. She didn't like the way his gaze made her feel. Damn him. Why did he have to have such intense blue eyes? She struggled to keep her tone impersonal. "A woman did come in a few minutes ago, but she didn't give me her name. I took her in to see Lynn."

"Did she have a little girl with her? Dark-haired woman, thirty-ish?"

Adriana nodded.

James relaxed. "Good. That sounds like her. I was afraid she'd lose her nerve without her sister Dana there to buck her up." He cast the receptionist a smile, and she beamed back at him, clearly dazzled. "I'll wait for her out here."

James turned back toward Adriana, and she quickly swung around to face the cabinet again. She thumbed through the files, trying to look busy, although she hadn't the faintest idea what name was on the folder in her hand. James came over to her, and she ignored him, continuing to go through the files. He stood for a moment, watching her.

"Why won't you talk to me?" he asked.

Adriana cast an anxious glance over her shoulder at the receptionist. His words hadn't been loud, but it made her nervous to have him discussing the matter so openly. Fortunately, the receptionist was intent on the letter she was typing, apparently oblivious to them. Adriana swiveled back around and gave James a brief look.

"There's nothing to talk about."

His eyebrows rose lazily. "I wouldn't call it exactly nothing."

"I would."

A tiny smile touched the corners of his lips. "Now you're being cruel."

She flashed an exasperated glance at him. "Didn't we go through this the other night? I told you how I felt then."

"No. You didn't say how you felt. You said what you wanted—or didn't want—to happen. That's not the same. I think how you felt, how you *feel,* is something else entirely."

Adriana made her face look as cool and amused as she could manage. "So now you know better than I do what I feel?"

"I think you *know.* You just don't want to admit it. Even to yourself."

"The last resort of men—a woman just doesn't know what she needs. She won't admit it. Of course, it always follows that what she needs has to be that man. Right?"

"I don't know. I'm afraid I can't speak for women, or men, in general. Only for myself."

"Oh, pardon me." Adriana closed the file drawer firmly and stepped over to the next filing cabinet, jerking open the top drawer. "For some reason I got the impression you were speaking for me." She turned her back to him and peered into the drawer, flipping through folders.

"Perhaps I was." James circled around her and stopped on the other side of the drawer, facing her. "I apologize. Let me speak for myself, then. I liked what happened the other night. More than liked it, in fact. I want it to happen again."

"There's no likelihood of that." Adriana struggled to keep her breathing steady. She couldn't let him see that even being around him shook her.

"Why not? Adriana, I understand your reluctance, your resistance to me because of the trial. But when you feel something that powerful, it overcomes other problems. That kind of passion is overwhelming."

Adriana kept her eyes on her fingers, frantically running through the file folders. "Perhaps what I felt wasn't the same."

He made an exasperated noise. "Try another one. I was there, remember? I felt your response. It was my skin you touched, my mouth you kissed, my body you—"

"Shh!" Red flamed in Adriana's cheeks, and she looked toward the receptionist. "Be quiet. This is no place to talk about something like that."

"I agree. But I can't get you to see me or listen to me anyplace else. This is my only choice."

Adriana pressed her lips together. She wasn't going to get caught in *that* trap. She refused to agree to meet him at another time and place in order to get him to shut up now. "You could stop talking about it altogether," she told him with asperity. "That's another alternative."

"Not one I like."

Adriana shot him a fulminating glance. "Not everything in the world is done according to your likes and dislikes."

James rubbed his hand wearily across his face. "Why is every conversation with you another battle?"

"Because you won't leave me alone!" She shoved the drawer in and turned, starting toward the door.

James grabbed her wrist and held her there. Adriana gave a tug, then stopped. She didn't want to draw the receptionist's attention to them by struggling with James.

She clenched her jaw and closed her eyes, struggling to rein in her wild emotions.

Exaggerating a sigh, she said, "What are you planning to do, restrain me by force? Are you going to continue to squeeze all the blood out of my hand until I agree with you?"

James opened his hand, releasing her arm and took a step back. "Sorry. I usually don't come on so strong." He leaned back against the filing cabinet and crossed his arms over his chest. "Okay. I'm not touching you. I'm at a safe distance. Will you agree to talk to me?"

"This is neither the time nor the place."

"Name them, and I'll be there."

"I don't want to talk to you. I don't even want to see you again."

"You'll have to. There's no way you can escape me completely. You have to face me and your feelings about me sooner or later."

"I plan to resign from the building committee." She looked away, unable to meet his eyes.

"You're running out on that because you can't control how you feel about me?"

"No!" Her eyes flashed with anger, though if she had spoken out of thought instead of frustration, she would have had to answer yes. If she had despised James Marshall as much as she wanted to, as she claimed to, she wouldn't have had any problem being on the committee with him. It was because she couldn't trust herself around him that she had to stay away from him.

"Yes, you are. It won't work, anyway. You can't run far enough to get away from me."

"Why are you so obsessed?" she hissed. "Why the hell do you have to chase me? I'm sure there are umpteen other women in this city who would love to go to bed with you.''

''You flatter me. But I don't want one other woman, let alone umpteen. All I want is you.''

''But why?''

''Because I've never before experienced what I felt the other night with you, that's why. No other woman has ever shaken me like that. No one else has ever made me feel so hot and hungry, so wild for her, that I can hardly remember my name.''

Adriana sucked in her breath. Why had she asked? His words had been like a physical touch, turning her loins suddenly heavy and aching. How could he do this to her when he was standing at least two feet away?

''I can't stop thinking about you,'' he went on in a low voice. ''My work's shot to hell. I want you all the time. I even dream about you. If you had any idea what I imagine about you, about us...''

Heat rose in her, and she was afraid the warmth showed in her face. She took a step backward, shaking her head as if she could deny his words out of existence. ''No...''

''Yes.'' He didn't raise his voice or come closer to her or even change expression, but his eyes bored into hers, holding her captive, and his words flowed around her like a caress. ''I've thought about making love to you in every conceivable way. Hard, fast, slow, gentle. Hell, I've even fantasized about handcuffing you to my bed so you couldn't run from me anymore.''

Adriana's eyes widened at his words. She should be shocked at his confession, she knew. His words should make her skin crawl, not send shivers of arousal through her. If any other man had said such things, she knew she would have been repulsed. The difference was that she wanted to be in James's bed.

Her breasts felt heavier, more tender, the nipples tightening as if he had brushed his hand across them, and the ache in her abdomen pulsed. Adriana fought to ignore the traitorous reactions of her body.

"That's purely physical. That's all there was between us, a simple physical attraction. It's easily forgotten."

"You're lying to yourself if you think that. I won't forget it, and I don't think you will, either. I've been attracted to women before, and believe me, this is a whole hell of a lot more. No simple physical attraction has ever turned me inside out."

"There can't be anything else. We don't even know each other, except as someone to dislike."

"I've never disliked you. And we do know each other. Maybe not all the facts of each other's lives. But the essential you—I know that."

Adriana felt the pull of his eyes and voice, the seduction of his words, and it was all she could do to keep from going to him.

"You don't know me," she whispered.

"Try me."

Adriana looked at him. James's eyes never wavered from hers. She felt her fingers begin to tremble. In another moment, she thought, she would be shaking all over. If he reached out and touched her, she might crumble into a million pieces. Never in her life had she felt so torn, so desperate, so hopeless and yet so eager.

As she stood there, trapped in her indecision, the inner office door opened, and Lynn came out with the woman and child who had gone in earlier. "James!" Lynn boomed out delightedly. "How nice to see you."

Adriana jumped and turned. The moment was broken. Gratefully she walked away and flopped down in a chair, avoiding James's eyes.

Chapter 8

Time passed before Adriana began to emerge from her own shaken thoughts and hear the conversation that was going on. James and Lynn were talking intently, while the small woman and her child stood to one side, watching.

"Dammit, Lynn," James was saying. "You can't just turn her away. She needs help." He looked disgusted, one hand on his hip, pushing back his suit coat, the other waving eloquently as he spoke.

The director of the center, on the other hand, looked apologetic but calm. Adriana realized with amazement that someone was at last getting the better of James Marshall in an argument. Surely that was worth paying attention to.

"James..." Lynn shook her head sadly. "I realize how terrible it seems. No, how terrible it is. But we have to face reality. I can't let Mrs. Gunderson into the shelter, however much I'd like to. There are several women ahead of her on the waiting list, and each of them needs our help as much."

"She just got out of the hospital. If she goes back to him, the next time you see her, she may be in the morgue instead."

Adriana shivered.

"I know. I know. That's why we so desperately need more space. But until we have the new shelter, we're limited to the one house we have, and there simply isn't any more room in it. The best I can do is offer very temporary space—only for a night or two—in the one dorm room at the shelter. It's only for emergencies, and she would have to arrange something else after that. We don't allow anyone to stay there longer than three days. We always need that space for women who have no place to go for the night."

James sighed. "Well, that's better than nothing."

"Oh, no!" Mrs. Gunderson spoke up for the first time. She looked horrified. "I can't do that. Where would I go afterwards? If I don't go home tonight, he'll know I left him, and then when I have to go home..."

"She's right," Lynn commented. "The situation will be even worse. She'd be safer staying home and pretending she's not planning to leave."

Mrs. Gunderson nodded emphatically. Adriana was washed with sympathy for her. Poor woman! What a terrible thing to have to face: going home to the husband who had already beaten you up, probably more than once, and pretending that you were going to stay, waiting all the while for a phone call from the shelter saying you could leave him and take refuge there—and the whole time hoping and praying that he wouldn't beat you to death or injure your daughter before that call came.

"That's awful!" Adriana exclaimed without thinking, and the others turned to look at her.

"It certainly is," James agreed. "In some cases, it's like sending someone back to certain death."

"My best suggestion is that she stay with us for a night or two and in the meantime try to find a relative or friend with whom she can stay for a longer period of time," Lynn said.

"I don't have anyone that he doesn't know about!" There were fear and desperation in the small woman's voice.

"Her sister is my secretary," James put in. "He'll go to her first thing. He knows she's always trying to get Ellen to leave him."

"He'll figure you helped, too," Mrs. Gunderson said in a small voice.

James shrugged. "That's no problem. I've dealt with worse than your husband." He turned toward Lynn. "I've talked to the D.A.'s office about her case. We think there's a good chance of a conviction, provided Mrs. Gunderson will testify against him. But obviously they can't begin proceedings against him while the key witness is still under his control." His voice turned persuasive. "All we need is a few months, Lynn. Just until they put him away."

"I'd give it to you if I could. But I can't. Every woman who comes in here needs our help. We simply don't have the room to take them all in. The only fair way we can do it is by using a waiting list."

James raked a hand through his coal-black hair, grimacing as he thought. "Use the shelter emergency room." He looked at Mrs. Gunderson. "The best thing to do is to get you and your daughter away from him immediately. When the three nights are up, I'll put you into a motel room for a while.''

"I couldn't do that. I don't have the money."

James waved the objection aside. "Forget the money. Consider it a favor for a good secretary."

"No. That's not right. You're very kind, but you shouldn't have to pay for that." Tears welled up in Mrs. Gunderson's eyes.

"I don't *have* to. I want to."

"It's too much..." she protested feebly, looking toward Lynn, then back at James. "And besides, what—what will happen later? You can't go on paying for a motel forever."

"I'll work something out. I have a kind and intelligent sister-in-law. My guess is that she can come up with a place for you to stay."

Adriana came forward. "That's all right. You don't need to. Mrs. Gunderson can stay with me."

All three of them swung around to stare at her again. "What?"

"I said she can stay with me. I just moved into a house recently. I'm all alone, and there's an extra bedroom. As long as she and her daughter don't mind bunking together."

"Oh, no." Tears spilled out of Mrs. Gunderson's eyes and coursed down her cheeks. "But you are too kind."

"Oh, I'm not that kind. But why don't you help me pretend I am this time?"

James looked at Adriana assessingly. Something glowed briefly in his eyes, and he said, "It sounds like a good idea to me. She has no connection to you, Ellen, so your husband will never guess where you are. You'll be safe."

"And you can stay until you're back on your feet," Adriana put in. "It won't be any problem."

"Good." James smiled. "That's settled." He walked over to Mrs. Gunderson and patted her shoulder gently. "You'll like Ms. Cummings. I promise." He squatted down so that he was eye-level with the little girl. "You will, too, punkin'. Ms. Cummings strikes me as the type of woman who really likes little girls."

"Really?" The child's eyes widened, and a smile touched her lips. Adriana was amazed at how easily she smiled at James, obviously liking and trusting him. She would have thought the girl would have been frightened of a man, particularly one as powerful and stern-looking as James. Yet Mrs. Gunderson's daughter seemed at ease with him.

"Really. And I'll tell you something else."

"What?"

"Sometime I'll come over to see you, and maybe we'll go to McDonald's. Would you like that?"

The little girl nodded eagerly. "Oh, yes. That'd be nice."

James straightened and turned. Adriana was looking at him, and when he caught her at it, she was embarrassed and glanced quickly away.

"All right, then," James said. "Lynn, put Mrs. Gunderson on your waiting list, and in the meantime she'll have a safe place to stay with Adriana." He looked at Adriana. "Thank you."

She was quick to shrug off his thanks. "No problem."

"I hope I'll see you at the next meeting of the building committee." His words were as much a question as a statement.

Adriana said nothing, just crossed her arms and avoided his eyes. There was no way she was going to let him talk her into that. Not after the way she'd practically melted at his feet today just listening to him talk. She had to stay away from him, and if that meant breaking her commitment to the building committee, well, then that was just the way it would have to be.

"Come on," Adriana said to Mrs. Gunderson, ignoring James. "I was about to leave. Let me take you home."

Mrs. Gunderson smiled her thanks and, taking her daughter by the hand, followed Adriana out of the office. Adriana was careful not to glance back at James.

"My name is Ellen," Mrs. Gunderson said in a soft voice as she got into the passenger side of Adriana's car. "And this is Tonya." She nodded toward her daughter in the backseat.

"I'm Adriana Cummings. I'm happy to meet both of you."

"Wow!" Tonya's voice sounded awed. "Mommy, look at this car. Isn't it pretty?" She bounced experimentally on the seat a few times.

Ellen smiled a little apologetically at Adriana. "Yes, it's lovely, sweetheart. But don't bounce. And fasten your seat belt."

"How old are you, Tonya?" Adriana asked as she started the car and pulled out into the street.

"Seven. I'm almost eight."

"My goodness, I didn't realize how big you were. You'll be in third grade next year, won't you?"

"Yes, ma'am."

"It's awfully kind of you to do this," Ellen told Adriana. "I'm so grateful."

"Don't worry about it. I'm happy to do it. It'll be fun for me. It gets lonely living all by myself. I moved back to Winston-Salem recently, and I don't know many people yet."

Adriana was glad to see that her comment relieved some of the anxiety on Ellen Gunderson's face. The poor woman had enough problems without having to worry that she was being a burden on someone.

In fact, as it turned out, Ellen and her daughter could hardly have been less of a burden. They were both quiet and unobtrusive, and neither of them disturbed Adriana while she was working in her studio. She was also amazed to see, the first time she came out of her workroom at the end of the day, that Ellen had gone through the house, picking up and cleaning.

"Why, Ellen, you didn't need to do this!" Adriana cried.

"I don't mind." Ellen turned and smiled at her shyly.

"But it's not necessary. I don't want you to think you have to pay me back by cleaning the house. There aren't any strings attached to your staying here."

"I couldn't begin to pay you back for what you're doing for Tonya and me." Ellen's brown eyes shone. "And I know you did it out of the kindness of your heart, not because I could do some work for you. But it makes me feel better to do something for you. You know, like not such a moocher. Besides, I can't sit around with nothing to do. I'm not used to it. I've always kept a real clean home."

Adriana smiled at her. She was finding that she liked Ellen Gunderson. She was a sweet, shy person, and Adriana had already seen that she had flashes of unexpected humor. But she desperately needed some confidence in herself. Adriana could see that it would make her feel as if she were contributing, not living off someone else's generosity, if she helped clean the house. Anything she could do that would raise her self-esteem was fine with Adriana. So she ignored the fact that, with her cleaning lady coming in one day a week, much of what Ellen did was unnecessary and said, ''Well, thank you very much. You've done a wonderful job. I certainly appreciate it.''

When Ellen beamed at her, Adriana was glad she had decided to simply accept the gift she had given her without any further protestations.

More and more every day, Adriana enjoyed having Ellen and Tonya there. Having someone around helped to keep her mind off James Marshall, and that was worth a lot. She had the awful feeling that if Ellen hadn't come home with her, she would have spent every minute mooning around over him.

James called a couple of times during the following weeks, each time ostensibly to check on Adriana's guests. She could hardly hang up on him when he wanted to ask about Ellen, but she suspected that he stretched his conversation with her far longer than was necessary, and she found it irritating. Even more annoying was the fact that when she heard his voice, her pulse speeded up and she felt immediately more alive and excited.

About a week after Ellen came to stay with her, Adriana took her and Tonya downtown to the tall, blue-glass Allied Central Bank building, where Ellen was supposed to meet with her attorney. Adriana had heard the attorney's name. He was generally regarded as one of the best divorce lawyers in the state, and he worked for Marshall, Pierson, Tidroe and Sommers, the premier law firm in town. It was also the law firm in which James

Marshall's father and brother were partners, and James had arranged for Lyle Benningfield to represent Ellen.

Adriana wasn't sure whether Benningfield was simply doing a favor for one of his partners or if James was paying the large fee out of his own pocket. Whichever it was, Adriana couldn't help but be amazed at his generosity. Granted, Ellen was his secretary's sister and he would probably feel some obligation toward her, but surely that had been satisfied simply by sending her to the Women's Center. Yet he had come down to the center personally to try to get her in, had urged the D.A. to pursue the criminal case, and arranged for her to have an excellent divorce attorney.

It made Adriana feel a little guilty for the way she had assumed that he was on the board of the Women's Center simply to make political hay. Yet here he was, obviously concerned and caring about one individual woman who could do him little political good.

Doing one kind thing didn't make him a saint, Adriana reminded herself frequently, and of course it didn't change what he had done to her father and family. Still, she couldn't escape the fact that she had been unfair to him. Nor could she deny that the anger she felt toward him was caused more by the situation than by the individual. She would have hated anyone who had been in his position. She knew that everything she thought or felt about him was colored by her feelings about her father and her family and what had happened to them. Had she met James at another time, under other circumstances, she might have liked him; it was obvious that she would have desired him. There were even moments of weakness when she wondered if there might not be a chance that they could get past all this, work through what had happened, or ignore it and build a relationship together.

But that was a subject she didn't like to let herself think about. It would never happen, and she knew she was crazy to even wish that it could. What James had done for Ellen Gunderson didn't matter; there was still a barrier as solid as a brick wall between herself and him.

Adriana accompanied Ellen to her appointment at the attorney's to watch Tonya while Ellen was with her attorney. Ellen was very nervous about seeing him. It was a huge step into the unknown. She was a shy, timid person, and it was obvious that she didn't feel worthy of the favors that James had done her. Adriana hoped that Ellen's self-esteem would improve now that she was no longer living with her abusive husband. But right now she needed support.

So Adriana rode up to the sixteenth floor of the Allied Central Building and stepped off the elevator with Ellen into the small, wood-paneled, plushly carpeted lobby of the law firm of Marshall, Pierson, etc. Next to her, Ellen was gazing around in awe and more than a little apprehension. It was a reception area designed to intimidate and impress, Adriana thought, with its expensive leather wing-back chairs and mahogany furnishings. Adriana gave Ellen's name to the receptionist and then they sat down to wait.

As they sat there, a pair of men came out of the hallway into the reception room, and they stopped when they saw Adriana and Ellen. One of them was a tall, dark man whom Adriana didn't know. The other man was James Marshall.

"Adriana!" A smile flashed across James's face. "I didn't realize that you would be here with Ellen." He crossed the room to shake hands with them.

Ellen bounced up nervously to greet him, and Adriana rose, too. She hoped that her face hid the tumult of feelings inside her. If she had known that she would meet James here, she would have refused to accompany Ellen. Yet at the same time her stomach was knotting in excitement at seeing him. She wished she didn't always have this sort of reaction to James, so confused and upsetting.

"I'm surprised to see *you* here." She was proud that she managed to keep her voice even and rather uninterested.

"I came to go out to lunch with my brother. My secretary told me that Ellen's appointment was today at one, so I thought I'd see how she was doing." He pulled his eyes away from Adriana and smiled at the other woman. "How are you, Ellen?"

"Just fine, Mr. Marshall. Thank you for arranging my appointment with this lawyer. Dana told me how unusual it was for him to take on someone like me."

"Nonsense. I'm sure he's very interested in the case." He reached out and gently squeezed Ellen's arm. "And don't be nervous. Lyle's a nice guy. A real old-fashioned Southern gentleman from Georgia."

"Thank you. He couldn't possibly be any nicer than you."

James chuckled. "Well, thank *you*. Say, I like the thought of having someone in my corner with Adriana."

"Oh, Mr. Marshall." Ellen grinned. "You don't need that, I'm sure."

"I wish I had your confidence in my charms." He looked at Adriana. "Well, which one of us is right? Do I need a friend in your camp?"

"I'm not sure it would be any use," she answered coolly.

"Shot down again." His tone was bantering, without any real concern in it, and Adriana reflected with irritation that James was disagreeably confident that she would someday give in to him. He would not accept that there were any real barriers between them; as far as he was concerned, it was only a matter of time.

"Let me introduce you to my brother. Adam would love to meet you." He turned toward the man who had walked into the lobby with him and motioned for him to come over. "This is my brother," James said as the man joined their group. "Adam Marshall. Adam, this is Ellen Gunderson. And Adriana Cummings."

"Ms. Gunderson. Ms. Cummings." Adam smiled at them both. "It's nice to meet you."

Adriana nodded at him briefly. "Mr. Marshall."

It wasn't difficult to see that they were brothers, she thought. Adam was a trifle taller, and his body was leaner than James's broad-shouldered build. He was also more conventionally handsome than James, without the hardness around his mouth. But there was a similarity in their features, and Adam had the same thick black hair and dark-lashed blue eyes.

Ellen overcame some of her habitual shyness at meeting James's brother. "Hello, Mr. Marshall. It's nice to meet you. Your brother is a wonderful man. He's been so kind to me."

Adam cast an amused glance at James. "How much did you pay her?"

James grimaced. "You're just jealous. You know what they say—a great man is never recognized in his own family."

Adam groaned. "That's because they know him too well."

Ellen's attorney appeared in the lobby, smiling, and whisked her away to his office. Tonya, watching her mother disappear down the hall with the strange man, frowned anxiously. She glanced up at Adriana, and it was clear that she was concerned.

"Where'd they go?"

"He needs to talk to your mom for a while," Adriana reassured the child. She had noticed in the time that they had been staying with her that Tonya began to grow panicky whenever her mother left her sight.

"Why can't I go?"

The girl's frowning little face tugged at Adriana's heart. She knew that Tonya, young as she was, worried about her mother and was afraid to let her out of her sight not because she was afraid of what would happen to herself if her mother wasn't there to protect her but because she was afraid of what might happen to her mother if Tonya wasn't there to protect her. It wasn't the first time Adriana had seen such worries and assumption of responsibility in a child. Many children felt that it was their duty—somehow within their power—to protect their mothers from the men who hurt them.

"It's for grown-ups, honey," Adriana tried to explain. "In fact, it's only for your mom and her attorney. See, the rest of us didn't go with her. But don't worry. She'll be fine."

"That's right," James was quick to agree. "That man's a friend of mine. He won't let anything happen to your mother."

Tonya looked a little uncertain, but she didn't protest.

"I'm staying here with you so you won't be lonely," Adriana added. "You and I can look at a magazine. How does that sound?"

Having caught a glimpse of the magazines sitting on the low coffee table in front of the sofa, Adriana doubted that they would have anything in them to interest Tonya. But she had to say something to distract the little girl from her worry.

Tonya nodded a little reluctantly. Adriana could tell from the wry expression on Adam Marshall's face that she had been right about the magazines. She sighed inwardly, wishing that she had thought to bring some crayons and a coloring book. Well, she would simply have to do her best. She took Tonya's hand and started toward the couch, but Adam interrupted them.

"Say, before you start looking at the magazines, I have something that might interest you even more."

Tonya looked up at him shyly. "You do?"

"Sure do. There's a soft drink machine down that hall. Would you like a soda?"

The girl's face brightened. "Yeah! That'd be great."

"You want to walk down there with me and choose it?" She nodded and released Adriana's hand, walking over to Adam. He smiled down at her. "Are you hungry? You know, we even have popcorn and a microwave to cook it in."

"Really? Can I work it?"

"Sure," he promised with a smile, starting off down the hall with Tonya walking along beside him.

Adriana smiled at the picture they made, then realized self-consciously that James was watching her. "Your brother's good with children," she said.

"I hope so, since he's going to have one before too long." James came a step closer to her.

"His wife's expecting? That's nice. I mean, I guess it's nice."

"Yeah. They're excited about it."

Adriana felt awkward, standing there, virtually alone with James. How had it happened? She had intended never to be caught alone with him again. She glanced away, searching for something else impersonal to use as a barrier between them.

But before she could think of anything, James said softly, "You know, you've surprised me."

"Surprised you?" She looked at him, startled. "What do you mean? What did I do that surprised you?"

He shrugged. "Lots of things. You aren't exactly...what I thought you were."

Adriana scowled. She didn't like the way this sounded. "You mean I'm not as bad as you thought? Is that what you're saying?"

"No. I didn't think you were bad. I just assumed, meeting you at the country club, being Larson's daughter, I figured you for a society type. Junior League, ex-debutante."

"Frivolous and brainless. Is that what you're trying to say?"

"No. Not frivolous and brainless." He grimaced, looking exasperated. "You're the hardest woman to pay a compliment to."

"Well, it doesn't sound exactly like a compliment to me."

"Look, I liked you the minute I saw you—you know that. But I'd never...well, I'd never fallen that hard or that fast for a woman. I'd never been quite so wiped out by a gorgeous face. Usually I'm attracted to a different sort of woman."

"Let me guess. You go for doctors and lawyers, right? Power brokers, maybe?"

"I like substance. Is there something wrong with that?"

"And you thought I didn't have any."

"No. I didn't think that. But I don't think I've ever even known an artist, let alone been interested in one. And society women are not my style. Okay. I didn't know you, and I admit I made assumptions. Wrong ones, no doubt. That's the problem with assumptions."

"And with prejudices."

His eyes narrowed. "Okay. Maybe I deserved that. But you might remember that I'm not the only one here with prejudices—not based on reason, I might add."

Adriana rolled her eyes.

"Anyway, it didn't surprise me to find out that you were involved with a charity. But I never thought that you would get personally involved. That you would take somebody like Ellen into your house, that you would help her so much. I'm trying to tell you that you impress me. You're a good and generous person. Sensitive."

"Artists should be sensitive."

He shook his head. "You couldn't even get through a confession without fighting with me, could you? I simply wanted to tell you that I've realized that I was wrong about you. And I understand much better why you draw me so."

Adriana took a step backward; the intensity of his blue eyes boring into hers was suddenly too much for her.

"I never thought I'd hear myself saying something as illogical and idiotic-sounding as this, but—somehow I think I sensed what you were. I knew what you were like in a completely unthinking way. The way I wanted you was primitive and basic. It took my brain a while to catch up, that's all. But what I felt for you was right."

Adriana wanted to take another step backward; she felt almost as if he had her in a physical grip. But she kept herself from doing it; she was determined not to let him know how much he affected her. "It wasn't right," she said firmly. "It's absolutely wrong. You're trying to make up justifications for a perfectly natural, perfectly meaningless physical attraction. We don't connect in whatever mystical way you're talking about. You don't 'know' me."

Something dark and turbulent flashed in his eyes. "Don't you ever get tired of lying to yourself?"

Adriana's mouth tightened, and she started to answer him furiously, but at that moment she caught sight of Adam and Tonya returning, and she clamped her lips shut on her reply. The last thing she wanted to give Tonya was a glimpse of another man and woman fighting in any way. She simply whirled and stalked over to the couch, ignoring him thoroughly as she sat down and waited for the little girl.

James sighed and turned away. He walked across the lobby to join his brother as Tonya went to the couch and bounced down on the seat beside Adriana.

"Look, Dree! Look what that nice man got me!" Tonya said, holding up her soft drink and a bag of microwave popcorn like trophies.

"Yes, sweetheart, I see. That's wonderful. Do you think I could have a bite of your popcorn?" Adriana forced a smile onto her face and concentrated on not looking up to watch James leave. She heard the ping of the elevator as it stopped on their floor, followed by the sound of the door closing, and only then did she look up. The two men were gone. She let out a sigh, feeling the pent-up energy and anger drain out of her. Adriana told herself she was relieved that he was gone; every time she was around him, she was upset.

And every time he left, she felt as if she'd lost something.

Chapter 9

Adam Marshall thrust his hands into his trouser pockets, disturbing the sophisticated lines of his suit, and leaned back against the side of the elevator, studying his brother. James looked back at him with a studied blankness, as if he had no idea what was on his brother's mind. Adam wasn't fooled by the pose. He'd seen it too many times.

"Well," he said, "that was a beautiful woman with your client."

"Not my client," James countered. "I'm just helping her out a little. She's my secretary's sister, and she's in a bad situation."

"I know. You told me the other day about Lyle representing her." Adam grinned devilishly. "But I'm not following that red herring. It's the woman with your secretary's sister that *I* want to know about."

"Ellen's staying with her. Adriana volunteers at the Women's Center, and she happened to be there the day

Ellen came in. She offered to let Ellen and her little girl stay with her until the shelter has an opening for them."

"Sounds like a nice person. Adriana. Unusual name." He paused. "Pretty." When James still said nothing, he chuckled. "Come on, Jimmy, you're worse than a clam. Who is she? What's going on between you two?"

"Nothing." James's reply was short and laced with bitterness.

"Ah. I see. *That's* the problem."

"Oh, hell," James said as the elevator bounced to a stop on the ground floor. "The problem is she's Jack Larson's daughter."

The doors of the elevator opened, and he strode out, leaving his brother staring after him for a stunned moment. Then Adam came to life and hurried after James, catching up with him at the revolving door. "What?"

Adam continued to follow his brother out into the cold January air and across the wide terrace in front of the bank. "Did you say she was Jack Larson's daughter?"

"Yes." James hunched his shoulders against the chill and trotted down the steps to the sidewalk. Neither brother bothered to wear a coat for the short walk down the block and across the street to the restaurant, preferring the few moments of cold to the bother of a coat.

"Are you crazy?" Adam asked, striding along beside him.

"Yes. I think I am."

They walked across the street in silence, Adam trying to absorb the startling news. "How did all this come about?"

James sighed and shook his head. "She's the woman I went over to meet the night of that party at the country club—you know, the one you and Emily dragged me to right before the Larson trial started."

"Oh, my Lord, I remember now. I didn't recognize her. It's been so long."

"I didn't know who she was then, of course. She's divorced, and she kept her married name, so I didn't even get tipped off when we were introduced. I found out on Monday when she walked into the trial with Millie Larson and the other daughter."

"Wow." Adam raised his eyebrows expressively. Nothing he could think of to say seemed adequate.

They reached the restaurant and went inside, and a hostess led them through the crowd to a small booth near the rear. Though it was hardly a private place, the sheer hub-bub of movement and people talking all around lent them some degree of privacy. They ordered quickly, and when the waiter had moved away, Adam leaned back in his seat and studied his brother.

"You've finally bitten the dust, haven't you?"

James grimaced. "You're so full of brotherly concern, I can hardly believe it." He shrugged and looked down at his water glass, turning it around slowly. "Yeah. I think I have."

"I should have known you'd pick the most difficult way to find a wife. Have you ever thought of doing something the way most people would?"

James gave him a rueful smile. "A wife? Aren't you getting ahead of yourself? We haven't even gone out on a date. Hell, she'll hardly speak to me."

"I've known you for thirty-four years, and I have never seen you bent out of shape about a woman before. I've never seen that look on your face when you look at her. When you talk about her. You've fallen for Adriana Larson like a rock, and you aren't the kind of guy who falls in and out of love frequently."

James leaned forward, resting his elbows on the table and dropped his head, raking his fingers through his hair. "How can I possibly be in love? I hardly know her. After that first night, we haven't exchanged six sentences except in argument. She's beautiful. She's sexy as hell. I'd like to whisk her back to my bed and spend about six months there with her. I don't think that's necessarily love."

"What is it, then?"

"A crazy obsession."

"How many things have you been obsessed with in your life?"

James glanced up at him quizzically. "I don't know. My job, I guess. Certain cases in particular."

"And?"

James shrugged. "Not much else that I can think of."

"Mmm. We all know how quickly you lost that obsession with law."

James looked at him disgustedly. "Okay. So maybe my obsessions tend to be permanent."

"Tend to be?" Adam rolled his eyes heavenward.

"All right. All right. But the way I feel about Adriana isn't necessarily the same. I mean, she's right. We don't have anything in common. There's nothing drawing us together except physical attraction. And my stubbornness—you know I can't stand to lose. If we ever got together, I'd probably lose interest in her."

"James, James." Adam shook his head in mock disbelief. "I think you're lying to yourself on a major scale. You don't know anything about what she's really like? You have nothing in common with her?"

"Okay, well, we are both working on the same charity. That's not exactly something to base a lifetime on."

"Not even when it indicates a similar compassion? A similar interest in helping people? A similar method of taking direct action against something you dislike? I don't suppose that in the course of this working together you've seen any qualities in her that you like."

"Of course I have. She's strong, she's loyal. I could see that at the trial. She's all the things you just said—compassionate, willing to act on her beliefs, kind and generous. Do you know that she opened up her house to Ellen when she heard that Ellen had no place to go, even though she knew nothing about her?" He smiled, remembering, unaware of the pride that showed on his face. "She didn't hesitate or worry about the consequences. She's capable, too. She knows her stuff. Better than I do, really, when it comes to the shelter and the women who go there. The other night, when they showed us through the shelter, she asked lots of intelligent questions and made good suggestions."

He paused. Adam said nothing, simply looked at him expressively. James sighed. "Okay. Maybe I know more than I thought about her. But it's from observation. We haven't spent time together. We haven't tried to get along. For all I know she may have dozens of annoying habits that would drive me crazy. Or she's too careless. Or she's sanctimonious. Lord, I don't know. How can I possibly tell if she's the woman I'll want to marry?"

"I suppose you can't. If there's one thing I don't understand, it's love. Sometimes it kind of grows on you. Other times it simply explodes inside you immediately." He gave a self-deprecating smile. "Somehow it seemed to happen both ways with Emily and me. Suddenly she was driving me crazy. I knew I couldn't live without her. Yet I realized, too, that I must have been falling in love with her for years and was simply too unaware to know it. But

I'll tell you something that even I have learned about love. And that's that you can't understand it or analyze it, either into or out of existence. It's simply there, and you have to deal with it as best you can. All the brains and money and power in the world can't do anything about it."

James's mouth twisted wryly. "You're really making me feel a lot better about this."

Adam made an amused noise. "Sorry. I'm just trying to tell you that it's no use fighting it. It happens to all of us, even you." He smiled reflectively. "And it can be the most wonderful thing ever."

"Can it also be the worst?" James retorted. "I'll tell you, it's driving me half-crazy."

"Don't tell me. Let me guess. It's even affected your work."

"God, yes. I'm sure half the office is wondering what's the matter with me. The worst thing is, I feel—I don't know, *lonely,* I guess. Like I've lost something. In the evenings at home, I'm no longer content by myself. I used to enjoy being away from people and the noise and the telephone ringing all the time. It was a blessed relief at the end of the day, a time when I could get a lot of work done or do some serious thinking or regenerate my batteries. Now..." He shrugged expressively.

Adam nodded sympathetically. "I understand. But you can still have that. In a way, it's even better when you share it with someone."

"Yeah, but what about when you *can't* share it with someone? You know me—I'm not exactly lacking in self-confidence."

Adam hooted. "I think you could safely say that."

James shot him a quelling glance. "But I'm beginning to wonder. What if I can't overcome the obstacles this time? What if this is something I can't beat? This is not my field. You can't reason someone into loving you. You can't prove it. Hell, you can't even force it down her throat.''

Adam frowned uneasily. ''Do you think there's no way you can win her over? Is she completely indifferent to you?''

''Indifferent? Hardly. She hates my guts. That's probably putting it mildly. In her eyes, I'm the man who sent her father to prison, who made her whole family suffer, who held her mother up to public ridicule and humiliation. It doesn't matter that Jack Larson was guilty as sin, or that he was really the one responsible for what happened to them. It doesn't matter that he was so weak he sold out everyone who trusted him because he had the hots for a woman. Oh, no, that's entirely beside the point. *I* was one of the men who exposed his guilt, *I* forced the world to see it. I'm inextricably tied up with Adriana's bad feelings about her father and the trial and the press. She wants to forget all of it, including me. How do you convince a woman in that situation to fall in love with you?''

''I don't know. I don't know if you can convince anyone to fall in love with you, frankly. But there is one thing—I'm certain that dislike, even hatred, is better than indifference. It's emotion, at least.''

''Yeah. The wrong emotion.'' James sighed. ''Oh, I've told myself that. I know the old clichés, too. But sometimes it's hard to remain convinced of them when you get shot down for the fourth or fifth time... or the twentieth.''

''I think I'm hearing things. Is James Marshall really talking about giving up?''

James shot Adam a dark look. ''I'm serious.''

"So am I. Is that what you're ready to do? Give up on this woman?"

James simply gazed at him for a long moment. Finally he said slowly, "No. I'm not. I don't know if I could ever give up on Adriana." He paused. "You know, I think you may be right. It's crazy, but I think I've actually fallen in love, and we've never even gone out on a date. I must have lost my mind."

Adam smiled faintly. "Well, it's about time. Welcome to the human race, little brother."

Both Adriana and Ellen were quiet on the ride home from the attorney's office. When they reached the house, Ellen and Tonya disappeared into their room, and Adriana went to her studio to vent her frustration in her work. It was a method that had always worked for her in the past, even through her divorce and her father's trial. She could get lost in the precision and beauty of her craft, so that everything else disappeared like mist in the sun.

But this afternoon, she couldn't shake the grumpy, gloomy irritation that had dogged her from the moment James Marshall had left her in the lobby of Marshall, Pierson. She felt at loose ends, unable to concentrate, and she quickly botched the piece she was weaving and had to pull out three rows of yarn. With a sigh, she laid down her shuttle and worked instead on sketches for future patterns, reasoning that at least they were easier to correct if she did mess them up. But nothing came to her except the usual circling, unending, useless thoughts about James, and finally she wound up snapping a perfectly good pencil in two and hurling it across the room.

Damn him! Was she never to have any peace again? Now he had invaded the one area she had always managed to keep free and personal. Why couldn't she get rid of him? Why couldn't she root out the physical attraction she felt for him and get on with her life?

That was all it was, physical attraction. She was convinced of that. He was handsome and sexually appealing to her in a way that no other man had ever been. There was something sensual and stimulating about him, and her body automatically responded, even though her mind and heart knew better. That wasn't a crime; she didn't mind admitting that she had physical desires, even for someone like James Marshall, as long as she didn't let them run away with her. But *this* was one she seemed to be unable to control. She had never known an attraction this sharp, this strong. Or this wrong.

Sometimes she wondered if perhaps its very impossibility was part of the appeal. She knew she couldn't have him, could not satisfy the passion that he aroused in her. And she knew enough about human nature to suspect that knowing that only heightened her desire. It was like trying to convince yourself that you didn't want a certain thing to eat. The more you thought about it, the more you wanted it. She had discovered that it was often easier simply to eat whatever it was she craved and after that the desire for it diminished.

She wondered if it was possible to do that with sex. What if she went to James and admitted that she wanted him? What if she asked him to make love to her, and he did? Once she had satisfied this...this *craving* she had for him, then she might be free of it. She wouldn't have to keep thinking about him and the times he had kissed her, always fighting her own instincts, struggling to deny her desire for him. She would know what it was like to be in his arms, and she would be rid of the hunger. That made sense.

But Adriana knew she could never do it. She wasn't bold enough to go to him and ask him to take her, and even if she was, she knew she couldn't live with herself afterward. Her desire might be satisfied, but she would have slept with the man who had sent her father to prison, and she would never be able to forget that. She would feel cheap and sleazy, so ruled by base physical desires that she would go to bed even with a man she despised. She refused to allow herself to become that kind of person.

The only thing she could do was stay away from him and hope that, without seeing him, she would be able to forget him. With some reluctance, because she hated to give up the project that she had started on, she called Lynn and resigned from the building committee. Lynn was shocked and unhappy, and she tried to talk Adriana into staying with the committee at least until they had the preliminary plans set and the bids in. But Adriana held firm, and finally Lynn was forced to accept her decision.

The following Tuesday was the next meeting of the committee, and Adriana was very aware of when the time for the meeting arrived and then passed by. She sat watching television with little interest and playing a game of solitaire on the coffee table. Ellen and Tonya had gone to visit Ellen's sister, Dana, so Adriana didn't have any company to help pass the time. Eight o'clock passed, then nine, then ten. Adriana couldn't have said what had happened on any of the shows that had taken up the TV screen. She couldn't remember the names of them or who the stars were. The eleven o'clock news was rolling on and she was shuffling her cards again when there was a thunderous knock on her front door.

Adriana's heart leaped into her mouth. Her first terrified thought was that it was Ellen's husband and he had somehow located her here. She sprang up from the couch and tiptoed into the tiny entryway, leaning lightly against the door to peer out the peephole. The face she saw on the porch in front of her door, faintly distorted by the security lens, was not that of a violent stranger but of someone she knew all too well. James Marshall.

Adriana sighed and leaned her forehead against the door. What was she going to do? Even as she thought, James's fist thudded against the door again, and she jumped back.

"Damn it, Adriana, open the door! I know you're in there, and I'm not going away until I see you. Unless you'd like all the neighbors to start staring out their windows, I suggest that you—"

He broke off as Adriana turned the knob and jerked the door open. She planted her hand on her hip and faced him squarely, her chin slightly lifted. "Exactly what do you think you're doing?"

"Forcing you to face me, that's what." He shoved the door open wider with one hand and walked in, then slammed the door behind him.

Adriana crossed her arms and cocked an eyebrow in what she hoped was an unimpressed, derisive way. "Am I to be treated to a display of your temper tonight?"

"Cut out the smart-mouthed crap. You know why I'm here."

"I do?"

"Yes, you certainly do. The committee meeting was tonight." She waited, not saying anything, and the lines bit deeper around his mouth. "One thing I never figured you for was a coward. But apparently that's exactly what you are."

"A coward?" she repeated, her hackles rising.

"Yes. A coward. I don't know what else you'd call it when you drop your favorite charity flat and leave an entire committee in the lurch, not to mention the women in that shelter and all the ones waiting to get into it—just because you're scared to be around me."

"I'm not scared."

"No? Then what are you? A dilettante who got bored with her latest project? Weren't there enough eligible bachelors there for you? Or not enough media coverage?"

"You know that's not true." Anger sizzled through her, and she had to clench her teeth to restrain her temper.

"Yes, I do know it. Because I know that the truth was what I said the first time—you're afraid to see me again. Why are you so scared, Adriana? Surely you can't seriously believe that I might hurt you."

"Of course not! I'm not frightened of you."

"Then that must mean you're frightened of yourself. Who else is left?"

"Frightened of myself? Don't be absurd."

"I'm not. I'm being honest, which is a hell of a lot more than I can say about you at the moment. You're lying to me, and, what's worse, you're lying to yourself. You're scared that if you're around me too much, you won't be able to retain that precious control of yours. Your body and your heart might take over and kick out all the dead baggage of your resentment. You're scared of falling in love with me, afraid that your own desires will be too strong for you. Isn't that it?"

Adriana wanted to scream. His surmise was too close to the truth, and it was galling that she had so little control over her own senses and passions. It was even more annoying and humiliating to find out that James knew exactly what effect he had on her. She couldn't admit to him that he was right. Yet she found it impossibly hard to lie, either.

"Get out," she grated. "I don't want you here. I don't want to see you or hear from you. Can't you understand that? The very sight of you makes me furious."

"Maybe. But that's not all it makes you." He moved in close to her, and she took a stumbling step backward, coming up against the unyielding wood of the door. He planted his hands on either side of her head and bent down until his face was only inches from hers. "It makes you nervous...and hot...and so itchy you feel like you're about to jump out of your skin. Just like it does me."

"That's not true." She winced inwardly at how feebly her voice came out.

"Like hell." James's eyes bored into hers. "Give in to yourself, Adriana. Just once. Forget who I am and who you are, and let your desire take you where you want to go."

Adriana couldn't speak, could only stare up at him, mesmerized, her breath coming in short pants. Her fingers pressed into the wood behind her, as if she could dig into it and hold on.

"Let me make love to you," he whispered, and he was so close she could feel the touch of his breath against her face, hot and soft and sensual as a caress. His hands left the door and went to her waist. Slowly they moved upward, spread wide over her flesh, until they reached her breasts. Adriana's eyelids fluttered closed as his fingers gently curved over the soft mounds, cupping them. "Let me..."

Adriana sagged against the door, feeling too heavy and shaky to stand upright anymore. His hands were like fire on her body, burning through the cloth of her blouse and seemingly down into her very soul. He was right, she thought; she was too weak to resist him. Her own body betrayed her every time he was around. Tears gathered in her eyes. "Please . . . don't do this to me."

James looked down at the moisture dampening her eyelashes, and his mouth tightened. He let out a soft curse. "Dammit, Adriana, I'm not trying to hurt you. I only want to give us both pleasure. Why do you act as if I'm torturing you?"

"Because you are!" she flared, her eyes opening.

James looked angry and torn . . . and smoldering with desire. Adriana had a sudden urge to move into him, pressing her body against his, and heat seared her at the thought. She wanted to feel his response, wanted to hear the intake of breath that betokened his fraying control and feel the immediate flaming of his skin, to know that his desire for her was every bit as strong as hers for him.

"God, Adriana," he said in a breathless voice. "If you don't want me to make love to you, don't look at me like that."

"I'm sorry." She glanced away, biting her lip. She couldn't even keep her thoughts from showing instantly on her face.

"You can't tell me that you don't want me."

"No." Her voice shook slightly. "You know I do."

He drew a deep breath. "Then what is it? Am I that terrible? Do you really despise me so much?"

Adriana found that she couldn't lie in response to the stark hurt in his words, couldn't even smudge the truth. "I don't despise you," she admitted. "I don't think you're terrible." No matter how many times she told herself that she did, she knew it wasn't true; it was only one of the ways she tried to hold herself in line against the desire she felt for him.

She felt his body relax, and he leaned his forehead against the door beside her, his body cradling hers without actually touching her anywhere. She felt enveloped by his strength and heat, and yearned to crawl inside the cocoon he offered, to let him enfold her, take her. Make her happy again.

"Then what is it?"

"I can't," she moaned. "Don't you see? I just can't! Whatever he's done, however I feel about it, I can't betray my father like that! My mother, my whole family. I'm not that cheap, that easy."

He chuckled, a sound that held as much raw ache as amusement. "Ah, sweetheart, let me assure you—you don't come cheap. Or easy. I've paid for every second with you with a hundred sleepless hours. A thousand painful thoughts."

"Stop it. You know that's not what I mean."

"I know." James nuzzled her hair, his hand coming up on the other side to cup her face. "Don't be so hard on yourself," he murmured. "You wouldn't be betraying your father or the rest of your family."

"No?" Adriana wanted to melt into him, to let him comfort her. She loved the feel of his lips against her hair, his hand curved over her cheek. Because it was so inviting, she jerked away. "How do you figure that?"

"You don't owe them the rest of your live. You don't have to sacrifice your happiness, your future, because they don't like me."

"It's more than that, and you know it. They don't just dislike you. You're their enemy. You ruined them."

"No." His eyes blazed. "I didn't ruin them. Your father did that all by himself. He was the one who committed the crime. He was the one who was fooling around on your mother. You put the two of those together, and it guarantees maximum publicity. I feel sorry for your mother and you and your sister, but not guilty. I wasn't the one who put any of you in that position. It was Jack Larson.''

''I can't help but love him.''

''No one's asking you to stop.''

''How can I love him and sleep with you? You may not call it betrayal, but I can't imagine Daddy feeling the same way. I can't imagine a man I could find who would hurt him worse or make him angrier.''

''Maybe that's true. But if you can accept what he did and still love him, don't you think he should be able to accept your choice in men without cutting you out of his life?''

Adriana shrugged. ''You always sound so reasonable. . . .''

''That's because I am.'' He grinned.

Adriana rolled her eyes and turned away. ''Oh, James . . .''

Why did the man have to be so appealing? It wasn't fair.

''Will you promise me one thing, at least? Will you tell Lynn that you've changed your mind and stay on the building committee? We really need you.'' He paused. ''I don't want to think that I chased you away. I— My main goal in life is not to make you miserable. However much you may think otherwise.''

''I know.'' He was being unusually kind. Especially after the way he'd come storming in here shouting that she was a coward. But she knew the frustration that had built up inside him; she felt it, too. It was enough to make you want to yell, even throw things. In some ways it must be even worse for James, wanting her and not feeling the reluctance she did, only thwarted by her refusal. ''I realize that, but I don't think I can go on being on the committee. It's . . . too difficult.''

James gazed at her for a long moment. Then he shook his head, and his face looked ineffably sad. ''You know, all my life, I knew that I could get whatever I wanted if I just worked at it. There's not much that money or brains or sheer persistence and hard work won't take care of. I guess I've always been a little arrogant, thinking that other people were simply lazy, unwilling to do what it took to make it. But I've finally met up with something I can't have no matter how much I struggle for it. No matter how much I want it.''

Tears sprang into Adriana's eyes. One thing she had never experienced with James was a feeling of pity for him. It seemed at odds with a man so capable and certain of himself. But now, looking at the sadness in his eyes, her heart ached within her. She wanted to comfort him, but she couldn't choke out any words.

James sighed. ''You won't change the way you feel about me. It's emotion, and all the reasoning in the world won't change it. To you I'm an enemy, and I always will be. All I do by keeping after you is cause you pain. Maybe it's time I quit beating my head against the wall.'' He paused and looked away for a moment. ''Come back to the committee, Adriana. I'll resign. That way you won't have to worry about running into me there. And I'll leave you alone. I won't come around again harassing you.''

''What?''

''I don't want to make your life a misery. I can see that's what I'm doing. As usual, I've been too intent on what *I* wanted to realize what I was doing to you. There's no reason why you should have to forego your friends or your activities because of me.''

He reached for the door handle. Adriana stared at him, dumbstruck. It was difficult to absorb what was happening. James had actually given up on her. He was quitting the building committee so she wouldn't have to see him again; he was promising to stay away from her. She would no longer have to struggle to keep her passions under control when he was around. She would be free to forget about him. He was leaving her life.

Desolation swept through her.

James opened the front door and stepped through it.

Adriana took an involuntary step after him. "James! No. James, wait."

Chapter 10

James froze. A long beat passed; then slowly he turned back toward her. His voice was carefully neutral. "Yes?"

Adriana swallowed. She didn't know what she wanted to say to him. She only knew that she couldn't let him disappear from her life like this. "I—I'm sorry."

He made a dismissive gesture. "Don't worry about it."

"No, please!" She moved a step forward, clenching her hands together. "I mean, I—I don't want you to go."

Something flared in his eyes and was quickly brought under control. "What are you saying?"

"I'm not sure exactly. But I—" Tears sprang into her eyes, and she had to blink them away. "It hurts to think I might never see you again. I don't want that."

He jammed his hands into his pockets, as if that was the only way he could restrain them, and his jaw tightened. It took him a moment to speak, and when he did, his voice was low and husky. "You know it's not what I want, either."

"I don't know what to do!" Adriana's face twisted, and the tears began to spill from her eyes.

He came to her then and took her head in his hands, wiping away the tears from her cheeks with his thumbs. He stared down into her eyes. "Okay. You've told me what you don't want. Now tell me what you *do* want."

"You." Her word was the merest breath.

James's eyes darkened. The skin of his hands was suddenly fiery against her cheeks. He bent and kissed her. His mouth was hot and demanding, pressing her lips apart, his tongue filling her. Adriana shivered and clutched the front of his shirt, intoxicated by the taste and scent of him. She had never felt so lost, so mindless and primitive in her desire. There was no thought in her mind any longer, only the sensations he aroused in her and the hunger to have more.

She kissed him back desperately, her tongue twining around his, and she pressed herself into him, as though she could somehow meld them together. His arms went around her hard, almost squeezing the breath from her, and he lifted her off the floor.

He wanted to consume her fully, to taste and touch every part of her. *To know her.* It was heaven to kiss her, yet it wasn't nearly enough. His mouth ground into hers, changing the angle of their kiss, and he let her slide down him back to the ground, throbbingly aware of every inch of her body as it rubbed against his. His hands roamed over her with restless, eager hunger, frustrated by the impediment of her clothes. He wanted to feel her naked flesh against his, to see her and touch her. He groaned deep in his throat, his fingers digging into her blouse, and he had to fight the urge to simply rip the clothing off her.

James broke off their kiss and straightened, panting. His face was flushed, his eyes glittering. What he saw when he looked at Adriana did nothing to decrease the desire that was raging through his veins. Her head was still tilted back, her cheeks aflame with color, her mouth soft and moist and dark rose from his kisses. Her eyes fluttered open in surprise at the loss of his mouth, and they were glowing, alive with pleasure and desire. Disappointment flickered across her features.

"What—why—" She swayed toward him in an instinctively seductive movement.

Another bolt of desire plunged down through him, nearly shaking him from his control. James drew a deep breath. "I'm at the end of my rope," he confessed huskily. "I don't think you want this to happen here, do you?"

"What? Oh." Adriana stepped back. "No. I—" She shouldn't have wanted it to happen anywhere, she knew, but she was past reason now. Her nerves were sizzling, her blood thrumming, and there was no way in the world that she was going to send him away tonight. She slipped her hand into his and led him into her bedroom.

James paid no attention to the house through which they walked; he wouldn't have noticed if it had been completely unfurnished or filled with the finest antiques. The only thing his mind could concentrate on was closing the door of that bedroom and pulling Adriana into his arms again, undressing her and feasting his eyes on her luscious body, pulling her down onto the bed with him and sheathing himself inside her satiny warmth.

He swallowed. He was already hard as a rock and aching for her, and his thoughts weren't helping that state one bit. But he found it impossible to think of anything else. He wanted to take it slowly, to seize every last bit of pleasure from the lovemaking that he'd been yearning for for months. He wanted to explore Adriana, to learn every response of her body, every touch that pleased her; he wanted to stoke her desire, to build it almost to the breaking point. He wanted to make theirs the most shattering lovemaking either of them had ever experienced. Yet he was so eager and had waited for so long that he wasn't sure he could last for even a fraction of the time that would take. He wanted almost as badly to plunge into her immediately and soothe the ache in his loins, to satisfy the hunger that had been there so long.

Adriana walked into the large master bedroom of the house and stopped. She turned toward James, feeling suddenly hesitant and embarrassed. Her hand fell away from his, and she watched him, her mouth dry. He reached back and closed the door, then turned the lock.

The click of the lock sounded all through her. She felt its finality, its promise, deep inside her. This was it; there was no turning back now. No place for fear or regrets. She was about to go to bed with James Marshall, and even though she felt a little awkward, a little uneasy, she was far more eager and excited.

James walked to her slowly, his eyes never leaving her as he stopped and reached out to take the first button of her blouse between his fingers. Adriana drew a sharp breath. She had expected him to kiss her, not begin in quite this blunt way. And yet . . . there was something decidedly sexy about his directness, an honesty and urgency that spoke of his intense passion.

Adriana looked into his eyes, held by his steady gaze. His fingers undid one button, then slid down to the next, and the next, until her blouse fell open. He slid his hands beneath the two sides of the garment, high up, so that his palms rested flat against her chest above her breasts. Slowly, his eyes glowing ever more hotly, he pushed the fabric up and back, caressing her skin as he shoved the blouse down her arms. The fabric whispered into a pile at her feet, leaving her clad in her brassiere. James unsnapped the front clasp and hooked his fingers through the straps, sliding it down to join the blouse on the floor.

The color rose in Adriana's face. James's eyes left hers finally and traveled downward. For a long moment he gazed at her naked breasts, and Adriana saw the quickened rise and fall of his chest, the fuller, slacker set of his lips. The faint embarrassment she felt fled before the evident passion on his face, and the coil of desire in her abdomen turned tighter. He started to reach for the fastening of her jeans but she stopped him, taking his hands and pulling them back down to his sides.

"No," she murmured. "It's my turn now."

His eyes darkened, and he sucked in a breath, and she knew that her words had aroused him further. He kicked off his shoes and opened his arms wide, as though inviting her to go to him. A faint smile played about her mouth as she began to unfasten his shirt, starting with the cuffs, then going up to the top and working downward. When she was finished, she placed her hands under his shirt and pushed it up and off his shoulders, just as he had done with her, except that her hands started at his stomach, not high on his chest, and travelled all the way up his torso, rubbing across his flat nipples as they went. By the time his shirt had joined hers on the floor, James's lips were parted slightly, and she could hear the heavy intake of his breath.

Adriana had loved the feel of his skin, smooth and warm, dotted with the wiry hairs of his chest, and she returned to it as soon as she had sent his shirt tumbling off his arms. She combed her fingers through the dark, curling hairs, drifting in and following the line of hair downward to where it disappeared in the waistband of his trousers. She felt the heavier rise and fall of his chest beneath her hands, and she glanced up at his face. His mouth was heavy and full, his skin flushed. Passion glittered in his eyes, and Adriana wondered how she had ever thought their blueness was cold.

She slid her hands out and upward again, following the lines of his ribcage. James jerked involuntarily as her fingertips moved back in, touching his nipples, and his hands came up. But he did not pull her to him or even grasp her shoulders, only crushed her hair in both hands, letting the fiery silk spill through his fingers. Adriana moved forward and rested her cheek against his chest, curling her arms around him. She leaned against him for a moment, listening to the heavy thud of his heart beneath her ear, caressing the sculptured muscles of his back. Gently she pressed her lips to his skin.

James groaned, and Adriana felt the quiver of his flesh beneath her mouth. She smiled, pleased in a basic feminine way at her effect on him. Not much unsettled the imperturbable James Marshall; it was sweet to know that she could shake him out of his control.

Her lips made their way to one flat masculine nipple, and her tongue flicked out to circle it. James made an inarticulate sound, and his fingers clenched even more tightly in her hair, tugging at her scalp. Adriana hardly noticed the prick of pain; she was too preoccupied with the taste of his flesh and the feel of it against her tongue.

"Oh, no," he rasped, taking her shoulders and setting her back from him. "My turn now," he repeated her words.

He bent and lifted her into his arms, carrying her to the bed across the room. Carefully he laid her down upon it and stretched out beside her. His hand came out to cover one of her breasts. With hot eyes he studied the soft movement of his fingers as they caressed the white mound of her breast. He traced the wide circle of her nipple, then the harder, thrusting button in the center. Her nipple puckered and tightened at his touch.

James played with her nipple, rolling and stroking it until Adriana was moaning, arching up to him, lost in passion. With a sigh of satisfaction long-delayed, he lowered his head and took her nipple in his mouth. Adriana gasped, her fingers clutching the bedspread beneath her, as a pleasure so exquisite it was almost pain rippled down through her body and flooded her loins. James sucked her breast, his tongue circling and lashing the hard bud of her nipple. He had dreamed for weeks—no, months—of tasting her flesh, but the reality was far sweeter than anything he had imagined. The sensations darting through him were electric, overwhelming. His mouth widened hungrily over her breast, and he pulled hard and deep.

Adriana almost sobbed as the chord of pleasure thrummed through her. The throbbing between her legs intensified, and she moved restlessly, seeking fulfillment. James's hand slid down her body and between her legs, answering her silent plea, and she shivered, clamping her legs around him.

His control was rapidly dissolving, and he trembled with the effort of holding on to the shreds of it until he could have his fill of touching and tasting her. He felt like a starved man released upon a banquet; he could not get enough of her. His mouth moved to her other breast and began to feast on it, and the pleasure rocketed in him. He murmured her name against her skin, his hand gently rubbing over the denim that enclosed her femininity. He could feel the dampness there, which excited him even more. With trembling fingers, he unzipped her jeans and his fingers slid inside, moving down over the slick material of her panties to the hot, wet place between her legs.

Adriana moaned and moved against his hand. The evidence of her desire almost undid him, and James pulled away from her for a moment, struggling to retain some remnant of control. Adriana slid away from him, startling him, and he almost scrambled after her to pull her back, pierced with a primitive fear that she was escaping him. But she only shoved off the remainder of her clothing, kicking off her shoes and throwing the jeans and panties onto the floor. Then she lay back down on the bed beside him.

She pressed her lips to the inside of his elbow, sending shivers darting through him. Then her mouth began a long trek across his skin, traveling up his arm and over his chest. James rolled onto his back, luxuriating in the pleasant torment of her mouth, arousing him with each brief, soft kiss. She was turning him inside out, and he wasn't sure how much more he could take, even as he quivered under the pleasure of it.

James fumbled at his belt and trousers, unfastening them, then shoving them down. Desire pounded in him, crying for release. Adriana reached over to help him, pulling his trousers and underwear down his legs and off onto the floor, and at last the hard evidence of his desire sprang free. Adriana's hands fell away. Tentatively, she stretched out a hand and let her fingers skim along the hot, throbbing shaft. James groaned and rolled over, pulling Adriana beneath him.

He had reached his limit and was past reason or restraint. Adriana's legs opened to him, and he slid into the dark, hot home his aching flesh craved. He began to thrust, and Adriana matched his movements, sending the desire inside them flaming out of control. Passion consumed them both, and they moved together in a desperate frenzy, until at last the passion exploded deep within them and pulsed out through their bodies in a final wild and enervating pleasure.

Adriana wrapped her arms tightly around him, and James shuddered as his seed poured into her. Gasping for air, he collapsed against her, drained of all energy and afloat in a haze of passion. Adriana buried her face in his shoulder and held on to him.

It was a long time before either of them was able to pull away, but finally James rolled onto his side, his hand still resting on Adriana's stomach and his other arm pillowing his head. He smiled at her, lazy, exhausted and utterly content. He couldn't remember when he had felt so at peace. He leaned over and lightly kissed the point of her shoulder.

"You're beautiful," he whispered.

Adriana smiled and reached out to smooth a hand over his hair. "So are you."

He grinned. "Sure. Now I know you've gone off the deep end." He paused. "Not that I mind, of course."

Adriana felt deliciously languid and sated, her mind drifting in a rosy haze. She closed her eyes and snuggled back into James, and he curled his body to fit hers like nesting spoons. Reaching behind him, he grabbed the edge of the comforter and pulled it up, rolling the two of them in it like a soft, warm cocoon. Gently they slid into sleep.

Adriana rolled to the left and came up against an unyielding barrier. She grunted and twisted in the other direction, but couldn't move that way, either. Slowly her mind rose from the depths of sleep, pulled up by the frustration of being unable to sleep in another position.

She was tangled up in something, swathed like a mummy, and she pushed against it, freeing one arm. She came to consciousness at the same moment that she realized that the barrier on one side of her was warm and breathing. A man. James Marshall.

Her eyes flew open; she was fully awake now. She was lying in bed with James. They had made love last night and fallen asleep here on top of the bed, wrapped up in the bedspread. It was no wonder she felt like a mummy.

James rolled onto his back, disturbed by her squirming, and she was able to move. Carefully she peeled away the comforter and sat up. She realized that the arm she had been lying on was numb, and she kneaded it unconsciously as she tried to assimilate the situation she was in.

She had been weak for a moment, unable to let James walk away. She had confessed that she wanted him, that she couldn't let him go, and from then on she had been lost. It had been inevitable that they would end up in bed together. She had let herself be ruled by desire; she had tossed away all pride and consideration for her family. What would her father think if he knew what she had done? Or her mother? Millie had gone through so much misery because of the trial; Adriana knew that her sleeping with the prosecution would probably be more than her mother could bear.

For that matter, what must James himself think of her? She had made it plain that she didn't like him, that he was her enemy and that of her family, yet she hadn't been able to let him walk away. She had been so hungry for him that she had tumbled into bed with him. Wouldn't James, even though he'd wanted to make love to her and had obviously enjoyed it, regard her as a weak person, someone whose beliefs could be easily overridden by a roll in the hay?

Adriana grimaced and blinked back the tears that came into her eyes at the thought. Was that really who she was? She had always regarded herself as so strong. Secure in her beliefs and ready to fight for them, if necessary. Wasn't that exactly why she and her first husband had had so many problems, because she had been too strong, overwhelming him? Alan had certainly told her so, many times.

Yet now here she was, in bed with a man she had sworn she despised, ruled by her passions instead of her head or her heart. Where was the strength in that? Adriana couldn't see any. She jackknifed her knees and folded her arms atop them, leaning her forehead on her arms in a weary, almost despairing gesture. What in the world was she going to do now?

She jumped a little, startled, when James touched her back with his fingertips, trailing them down her back.

"I never realized before how beautiful a spine could be."

Adriana closed her eyes. His touch was soft and loving, and it warmed her all through. No matter how much she might condemn herself for what she had allowed to happen—no, admit it, *encouraged*—she couldn't deny that his touch made her go all warm and gooey inside. It made her heart swell with happiness to hear him utter soft compliments. He was such a hard, even stern, man so much of the time; she had seen him be unbending, sharp, unrelenting. It made his gentle words and touch even more special. For a moment she was seized with the desire to lie back down, snuggle into his arms, and indulge in sweet words and lazy caresses.

"Oh, James . . ." Her words were almost a groan.

"What?" He had reached the base of her spine and now his thumb was making its way up the knobby outcroppings of her backbone.

Adriana shivered and slid just beyond his reach, wrapping the comforter around her as much as she could.

Behind her, James frowned, his eyes narrowing. "What's the matter?"

"Nothing." She shook her head in an impatient, annoyed way. "Everything. Oh, hell…why can't things ever be clean and simple? Why is life always so messy?"

"I don't know. I used to think that was what my life was. Clean and simple, I mean. Until I met you."

Adriana twisted around to send him a disgusted look. "Meaning *I* messed up your life?"

"Complicated it." He smiled faintly. "I wouldn't say messed up. But it's definitely more interesting lately. Less predictable. I'm not used to having to worry about my private life. Frankly, I'm not used to having much of a private life."

"I'm sure not. You're always the prosecutor."

James sighed and linked his hands behind his head. "Okay. Obviously this isn't going to be a morning of sweet nothings and renewed lust. What's the crux of the matter? You're regretting going to bed with me?"

Tears filled Adriana's eyes. "It was a stupid thing to do."

"You'll pardon me, I hope, if my opinion differs from yours."

"Don't joke about it. Please."

"I wasn't joking." He sat up, too, running one hand back through his tousled hair. "Good Lord, Adriana, what do you expect me to do? Say 'I'm sorry, what a mistake,' and slink out of your life? That's not what I think. What I feel. I don't regret last night. In fact, I'd like for it to continue. I'd like to do something really daring and take you out to dinner or a movie."

"Stop it! You're making fun of me."

He sighed heavily. "Sorry. I guess I am. I'm not used to being rejected, at least, not so summarily or so quickly. It usually takes a woman a while to realize what a thoroughly difficult man I am."

Adriana whipped around and glared at him. "Well, that's certainly what you're being right now. Couldn't you even try to understand?"

"To understand what?" James returned heatedly. "That you feel guilty for making love with a man your father would disapprove of? For following your heart instead of your family's expectations of you?"

"That's not true! I'm not upset because I did something my family didn't 'expect' of me!"

"No? They why don't you tell me exactly what it is that *is* upsetting you? Because I'm having a hell of a hard time understanding your anger over something that made me—"

He broke off, his mouth twisting into a grimace.

"Made you what?"

He shook his head. "I'm not sure. Happy, I guess, though that's too mundane. Content. At peace. Grounded." He glanced away. "I don't know how to express it. I feel like an idiot saying it, given the way you feel about what happened. But it was something of importance to my life. It shook me." He looked back at her, his eyes gleaming with even more intensity than usual. "I've never been so... I don't know, taken out of myself. When we made love, it stunned me. I..." His voice roughened with emotion, and he broke off. "Oh, hell, this is pointless. It isn't something I can argue you into feeling."

He swung off the bed and began grabbing up his clothing and putting it on, moving with quick, impatient jerks, not looking at her.

Adriana drew in her breath at the sharp pain that stabbed her heart at his words. In her guilt and anxiety she had been thinking only of herself, but the realization that she had hurt James flooded her with remorse. She couldn't bear the set, guarded look on his face or the flash of pain she had seen in his eyes. She was disturbed and confused, roiling with guilt and remorse, yet also undeniably warmed by the intensity with which he had spoken. James was not an emotional man, or, at least, not one who readily showed his feelings. Adriana would have staked her life on that. Yet he had told her without reserve how much their lovemaking had affected him, how deep his longing for her ran. His words had almost been an admission of love. He had exposed his deepest emotions to her, and she couldn't allow him to leave thinking that what they had shared last night meant nothing to her, that she felt only guilt and regret over it.

"No, wait!" She reached out a hand toward him.

He hesitated and turned. All the defenses were up in his face. "Don't do this to me again," he said flatly. "I can't go on with all this up-and-down, now-you-want-me-now-you-don't stuff. I'm a simple, straightforward kind of guy."

"I'm sorry." She was close to tears. "I don't mean to be contradictory. I don't want to cause you any pain. Oh, God, I'm so confused."

"About what?"

"I don't like the way I feel about you. I don't *want* to feel this way!"

He waited silently, watching her.

"I—I want you to know that last night wasn't meaningless for me, either. It was . . . special." She swallowed and linked her hands tightly together, looking down at them as if she could find there the right words to say, the right way to feel. "I've never been carried away like that by my passions. I've never felt so out-of-control. So out of myself! It was scary. And it was wonderful, too. I don't want to lose that!" She looked up at him again, her eyes shining with unshed tears. "I don't want to lose *you*. But how can I continue? I feel so guilty and wrong! Whenever I look at you, it hurts, because I feel so much, and it all clashes against each other. I'm torn apart, James. I can't bear to cause you pain. I can't bear to cause my parents pain."

She began to cry, the dry little racking sobs of someone for whom tears didn't come easily, and shoved her fingers back into her hair, clenching them. "I don't know what to do! I'm so sorry."

James's face softened, and his taut body relaxed. "Ah, sweetheart, no. Don't cry." He went to her, one large hand reaching out to smooth over her hair.

Without thought Adriana went up on her knees on the bed and into his arms. She wrapped her arms around him and leaned her head against his solid chest and cried out all her frustration and confusion.

"Shh. It's all right. It's all right." Soothingly, James's hand traveled over her head and back while the other held her tightly to him. He curled down over her protectively, resting his cheek against her hair. "I promise. We'll make it right."

"How?" Adriana sobbed, her hands digging into his shirtback.

"I don't know. We'll figure it out later. Trust me. I'm great at working out strategies. That's my specialty." He smiled and kissed her head. "Just don't shut me out. Don't turn me away."

"I don't think I can!"

Adriana pulled away and looked up at him. Her face was wet and softened by crying, and her eyes looked soft and huge, framed by starry damp lashes. Quietly she went on, "I've tried, and I never manage to do it. I don't think I'm strong enough."

"You're strong enough for anything. Too strong, I think, to throw away your own happiness because of what someone else might think."

Adriana sighed and leaned against him again. "Oh, James, what am I going to do?"

When she spoke, her breath caressed the bare strip of skin between the open sides of James's shirt. Suddenly he was very aware of his partially clad state and Adriana's nudity. The comforter she had wrapped around her had slipped off when she rose to her knees to hold him, and her body pressed against his was utterly naked. He could feel the nipple of one breast pressing into the bare flesh of his stomach. Perhaps even more titillating was the heat and softness of her flesh through the barrier of his clothes.

Adriana, now that her spate of tears had subsided, was also growing acutely aware of her state of undress. She moved a fraction, and the cloth of his shirt and trousers rubbed her skin. Her mouth was only a breath away from his chest; she could easily turn and press her lips to it. She shivered at the thought.

Suddenly his hands were on her shoulders, digging into them and pulling her up. Adriana lifted her face, and James buried his mouth in hers. They kissed passionately, their tongues seeking and hot, and Adriana reached up and peeled back his shirt, pulling it down off his shoulders and arms. It dropped to the floor, followed moments later by the remainder of his clothes, and they tumbled back onto the bed, locked in an embrace.

This time their lovemaking was sweet and slow. They took the time to explore and taste, to satisfy their curiosity and arouse their passion to the fullest. And when at last they reached the blazing peak of their fulfillment together and came softly floating down to rest on the other side, each of them knew that stopping their affair was no longer possible.

Chapter 11

It was a long time before either James or Adriana had the energy or will to move. They lay together in peaceful satiety, now and then murmuring something to each other, but most of the time savoring what had happened in silence. Adriana knew that she could not push James out of her life now; there was no point in trying. All she could do was continue seeing him and hope that word of it didn't get back to her mother or father. Right at the moment, she wasn't interested in worrying how she was going to keep such a secret and for how long.

She wanted only to float in the haze of her pleasure, with the warmth and security of James's arms around her. For the first time in weeks, even months, she felt deeply comforted, no longer confused or torn. Whatever happened in the future, at least she had this now. At least she had faced up to her overwhelming desire for James; no longer would she have to suffer through the frustration of struggling to deny it to both him and herself. He might have been her family's enemy, perhaps it was a betrayal of her family to make love with him, but it was what she had to do. She realized that now. It was the only way that she could find any ease or happiness for herself. She had been miserable the entire time that she had been fighting her attraction for him.

Finally James rolled up onto an elbow and glanced over at her bedside clock. He sighed. "I have to go. I'm already half an hour late to the office." He looked back down at her and smiled. "I don't want to leave you."

"Then don't." Adriana linked her hands behind his head and grinned at him flirtatiously.

"Don't you know that you aren't supposed to tempt me? I'm an officer of the court, and I have my duty."

Adriana rolled her eyes. It felt delightful to tease like this with him, although she suspected that she would feel guilty about it later. She rose up and kissed him lightly on the lips. "Well, never let it be said that I interfered with an officer of the court going about his duty."

"Too bad." He kissed her again, then broke away with a groan of regret and rolled out of bed. He walked into her bathroom, grabbing up his clothes from the floor.

A few minutes later he came out again, showered and dressed, though somewhat rumpled and in need of a shave. Adriana, who had gotten up and put on a robe and returned to sit on the bed, grinned impishly. "Don't you think you're going to raise a few eyebrows going into the office like that?"

James chuckled and cast a rueful glance down at his suit and shirt. "I don't think my wardrobe improved from spending the night in a heap on the floor—or from being dumped there a second time." He looked back up at her, and there was a devilish gleam in his eyes.

"I'd suggest you drop by home first for a change and a shave."

"I think you're right. This is one morning that Justice will have to wait." He strolled across the room and sat down beside her on the bed. "I had more important things to attend to."

He bent and kissed her thoroughly. When at last he pulled back, Adriana tried to gather her scattered wits enough to make a retort, but she couldn't. James gave her another, more platonic, kiss on the forehead and stood up. "I'll call you later. You going back to sleep?"

"Mmm-hmm. One of the advantages of being a self-employed artist."

"Must be the life."

He walked toward the door into the hallway, and Adriana stiffened, unconsciously sucking in a gasp. James turned, surprised. "What is it?" He saw the look of trepidation on Adriana's face, and he frowned. "What's the matter?"

"Ellen will see you. She'll know you spent the night here."

He looked at her quizzically. "So? She's a grown woman. I don't think it will shock her out of her shoes." He continued to gaze at her, his expression turning thoughtful. "You're ashamed for her to know that you slept with me, aren't you?" His tone hardened. "In short, you're ashamed of me."

"I'm not. I'm simply a little embarrassed by the situation. There's no crime in that. Not all women are at ease with other people knowing they've spent the night with a man."

"I don't think it's 'a man.' I think it's me."

Adriana tightened, waiting for the quarrel to grow between them again. Why had she been so careless as to admit to her embarrassment? Now he would be angry and hurt again. But, to her surprise, James simply shrugged.

"Okay." He gave her a brief smile. "I'll try to sneak out."

Adriana could almost see the gears of his brain whirring into action. No doubt he was already working on some kind of brilliant, logical strategy to make her come around to his way of thinking. Well, he'd find out soon enough that the messy realities of human emotions didn't bend too easily to logical strategies.

"I'll call you later."

Adriana nodded. Then he was gone, closing the door behind him. After a moment, she heard the rumble of James's voice in the distance and a higher pitched squeal that could only be Tonya, followed by an adult female voice. Well, so much for his sneaking out. She sighed and lay back against her pillow.

Later she would have to address the problem, try to figure out what she was going to do about James and the way she felt about him, about the affair sitting on the horizon waiting for them. *But not right now.*

A smile touched her lips, and her eyes turned starry. Right now all she was going to think about was what had happened last night. Smiling, she closed her eyes, and minutes later she slid into a contented sleep.

Adriana was embarrassed a couple of hours later when she walked out of her bedroom and down the hall into the kitchen. In the den, the television was running, and she assumed that both Ellen and Tonya were there. But when she stepped into the kitchen, she found Ellen seated at the small table, going through the employment ads as she sipped a cup of coffee. Adriana hesitated; she hadn't really prepared herself to face Ellen this morning. She had headed straight for the coffee after she had showered and dressed, assuming that she wouldn't have to face the situation before she had consumed a little caffeine, at least.

Ellen glanced up from the table and smiled at her cheerily. "Hi. How are you?" Then she rolled her eyes. "Sorry. Stupid question."

Adriana felt a blush rising along her cheekbones. She hated that; it was the curse of her redhead's fair skin, and it made her feel like a teenager. She turned away abruptly, unable to come up with a response, and went to the coffeemaker as a refuge. "I'm fine," she answered Ellen's question, ignoring the following comment. "How about you?"

Ellen shrugged. "Want some breakfast? I could whip up some eggs real quick."

Adriana shook her head. She wasn't much of a breakfast eater, but it had been difficult to convince Ellen of that fact. "I'll have some toast in a little bit."

Ellen was grinning at her like a Cheshire cat. Adriana turned away, pouring her coffee and diluting it with milk. When she turned back toward the table, she found Ellen still grinning. Inwardly she sighed. She might as well get it over with. It was obvious that Ellen was going to do nothing but think about James's visit last night.

"Okay. You might as well say it."

"Say what?" Ellen looked at her with round, innocent eyes.

"Whatever it is you're going to say about James Marshall. I know you saw him leaving this morning. I heard you all talking."

Ellen's grin grew broader, if that was possible. "I don't have anything to say. I'm just so happy for both of you that I can't stop smiling. I think it's wonderful that you and he are in love.''

"In love?" Adriana stopped with her coffee cup halfway to her lips. "Wait a minute. I think you're assuming more than was indicated..."

Ellen chuckled. "Yeah. Right. I've seen the way he looks at you—and the way you look back at him. If that isn't love, I don't know what is.''

"I think it's something a lot more basic.''

"Oh, you don't mean that.'' Ellen's eyes glistened with romantic fervor.

Adriana regarded the other woman a little sourly. She couldn't imagine how a woman who had been through what Ellen had in her marriage could retain such a rosy outlook on love. "You are an incurable romantic.''

"I know. And you wonder why I am,'' Ellen replied astutely. "But I can't give up on love just because I had a bad marriage. I don't want to. How can a person go on living if she doesn't believe deep down inside that there really is love and it really can work for two people? Otherwise, what's the point? I can't bear to live in all that gloom and doom.''

Adriana smiled. She liked Ellen. She didn't think that she would have retained nearly the hope and enthusiasm for life that Ellen had if she had been in her position. "I think that, too. My marriage didn't turn out very well, either, but I always thought I was bound to meet and fall in love with a different kind of man, someone dependable and loving and strong. I just knew that there had to be men like that, because my father was—''

She broke off, remembering with a faintly sick feeling in the pit of her stomach that Jack Larson had turned out not to be the man she had believed him to be, either. Was she always wrong when it came to men?

Ellen didn't even notice the abortive reference to Adriana's father. She leaned forward, the employment ads forgotten, and planted her elbows on the table, leaning her chin on her hands. "But that's exactly the kind of man James Marshall is."

Her words startled Adriana a little. She wasn't used to thinking of James in those terms. She realized that all she could ever see were the things that separated them. Dependable and strong? James was certainly those. Adriana couldn't imagine him shying away from anything, no matter what it cost him. Loving? He seemed too hard a man to be loving, but then she remembered his gentle touch last night and this morning, the soft, caressing words he had spoken to her. A delicious shiver ran through her. Yes, surprisingly, she thought James could be a very loving man, for all his sometimes stern exterior. Would he be loving to her? Could he love her? Did he already?

And how did she feel about him? She had been so busy denying and fighting her feelings, concentrating on the impossibility of anything happening between them, that she hadn't really examined her feelings toward James, at least not in a rational, unbiased way. For weeks she had been telling herself that it was simply bald, unmitigated lust that she felt for him, nothing deep or true or fine. But what was it that pulled her so strongly toward him? Was it simply that he was handsome? That he had charisma? Had she really fallen for a man because he had sexy hands and a sensual mouth?

Surely she hadn't become that shallow. James was appealing, but Adriana knew that much of his appeal came from his personality. He was compelling because he was so strong and committed. He was powerful and challenging, and it was those qualities that gave life to his good looks, that made him not merely handsome, but a man she couldn't keep from being drawn to.

It wasn't only his looks or the melting way he kissed her that made her forget her resolution not to sleep with him. Adriana was too honest not to admit that what she felt for James was far more than mere physical attraction. But it wasn't love, either; it couldn't be that.

"Maybe James is those things," Adriana agreed reluctantly. "But that's not all there is to it. It's a strange situation."

Ellen looked puzzled, and Adriana launched into an explanation about her father's trial and imprisonment and the role that James Marshall had played in it. Ellen watched, her eyes growing wider by the minute as Adriana talked. When Adriana finished her story, she let out her breath in a long sigh.

"Oh, my... I didn't know. I had no idea."

"There wasn't any reason for you to. As you might guess, it's not something I talk about readily."

"But then how did you two start working together?"

"We didn't," Adriana replied shortly. "I mean, we didn't start out to work with each other. Somehow we just wound up on the same committee. I should have gotten off it as soon as I learned that he was on it, but for some reason I didn't."

"I imagine I know what that reason is." Ellen paused. "I just can't believe that you started out as enemies. I mean, every time I've seen him look at you, it's plain as day what he feels about you."

A breathless excitement rose in Adriana's throat, and she struggled to push it down. "I think you must be seeing things."

Ellen snorted. "Yeah. Right."

It was obvious that Ellen didn't believe her. Frankly, Adriana couldn't blame her. She wasn't sure that she believed it herself.

Adriana found it difficult to concentrate on her work that day. She kept listening for the sound of the phone. She told herself that it was stupid. There was no reason for James to call her. What was there to say? What had happened, had happened. They would probably see each other again before too long, but that didn't mean that James would be calling her all the time. He was a very busy man, and there wasn't room in his schedule for social calls. Nor was there any reason for her to want him to call. She wasn't some college girl to sit around waiting for the right boy to call and ask her out. There was work that needed to be done, and the time taken out for a telephone call would simply be a waste. It was even more of a waste to sit idly by, the shuttle of yarn lying still in her hand, while she daydreamed about James Marshall.

But no matter how much she talked to herself, she still couldn't seem to get any work done, and she jumped for the phone each time it rang. Once it was her mother and another time an old friend from New Mexico; twice it was someone trying to sell her something. But late in the afternoon, when she picked up the phone once again, her heart beginning to thud in anticipation, it was James Marshall's voice that answered her hello.

"Hey. It's me." His voice was low, and she could hear noises in the background, as if he were calling from a public phone.

"Hi." Her own voice softened, and Adriana leaned against the wall, her body feeling suddenly like warm clay.

"I've been in court all day. I wanted to call you earlier, but I couldn't get away."

"That's okay."

"Not for me, it wasn't." There was a chuckle in his voice, but it was warm and ripe with sexuality, as well. "I kept thinking about you. I couldn't concentrate."

A grin spread across Adriana's face. "You too?"

"Yeah. Were you the same?" He sounded a little hopeful, almost boyish.

Adriana realized how much she'd given away with her words. But she didn't care. Why not admit it? "Yes. I've hardly gotten anything done."

"Good."

"Why good? I'm supposed to be working."

"I'm glad I'm not the only one."

"You're not." Her eyes were closed, picturing James in her mind. He must still be in the courthouse from the sound of voices in the background. He was probably at one of the pay phones in the hall, leaning, as she was, against the wall, hunched around the receiver to give himself whatever small amount of privacy he could.

"I want to see you tonight."

"All right." The brief answer was all she could manage. His husky words, obviously laden with longing, sent chills all through her.

She heard the release of his breath and realized that he'd been uncertain of her response, hoping that she would say yes. It was a little amazing—and warming—to think that the confident James Marshall was anxious about whether or not she would want to see him again.

"Good," he said. "I have to run back to the office and clean up some stuff there. Give me a couple of hours. Say, seven o'clock?"

"Fine."

"Would you like to go out to eat? Or what?"

"I don't care." Absently Adriana twirled the phone cord around her finger as she rested against the wall, thinking about James's arms around her. Their heat, their strength. With her eyes closed she could almost imagine that he was there. "I just want to be with you."

There was an instant of silence; then James said quickly, "I'll be right there."

Almost before she knew what was happening, he hung up. Adriana lowered the receiver and cast an amused glance at it. As the import of his words hit her, heat sprang up low in her abdomen and spread through her. Her admission of her desire to be with him had stirred him so that he was coming running to her, even though it meant throwing aside his work and his schedule.

When he arrived at her door little more than thirty minutes later, Adriana was waiting for him, freshly made up and dressed in slacks and a soft turquoise sweater, her hair falling in casual waves over her shoulders. As soon as she opened the door, James reached out and grasped her shoulders, pulling her to him and wrapping his arms around her.

"Mmmm," he groaned. "You feel good. Smell good, too." He turned his face into her hair, breathing in her scent. Then he kissed her, a long, searching kiss that left no doubt as to his intentions. He raised his head and looked down into her face. He brushed his fingertips over her cheek. "You're so beautiful. Sometimes I didn't think I was going to make it through today without seeing you." A smile lightened his sensual mouth. "My secretary thinks I've lost my mind."

"Maybe you have."

"Maybe so. But I'm discovering that insanity has its pleasures."

Adriana chuckled, and James bent toward her as if to kiss her again. Then, in the back of the house, Tonya chuckled. James stiffened, his face filling with the awful realization that they were not alone in the house.

"I forgot . . . Ellen and Tonya are here?"

Adriana nodded and grinned. "Otherwise I would have met you at the door dressed in something . . . ah, a little different."

James sucked in his breath sharply and his eyes darkened. "What are you trying to do, torture me?"

Adriana shook her head. "Nope. Trying to wangle an invitation to your place."

He grinned. "You got it, lady." He curled an arm around her shoulders and propelled her outside.

James drove to his house at a rate that was somewhat faster than was safe, and the moment they stepped inside the front door, he pulled Adriana into his arms again and began to kiss her. But she pulled away.

"No, wait." She smiled at him, her eyes dancing. "I want a tour of your house."

James groaned. "Are you kidding?"

Adriana shook her head. "No, I've never seen it, you know." She did a slow pivot, looking all around her, her hands linked behind her back.

James watched her, enjoying the way her stance thrust her breasts out against the soft sweater. "I'll show it to you later," he promised hoarsely.

"Now what kind of hospitality is that?" She made a playful little pout.

Her lips looked soft and utterly kissable that way. James knew that she was teasing him, and he liked the electric fingers of anticipation that shot through him in response. There was a relaxed intimacy in such sexual teasing that he'd never known with Adriana before.

She walked away from him, her hips swinging in a way that heated his blood. At the doorway into the dining room, she paused and glanced back at him over her shoulder. "Well, are you coming?"

She kicked off her shoes and sauntered into the room. James quickly followed her. Adriana glanced around the room, reaching out to stroke her hand down the length of the polished mahogany table. James watched her, feeling the caress all through him. She walked toward the kitchen door, unfastening her watch as she went. She laid it down on the gleaming sideboard and pushed open the swinging door into the kitchen.

James followed her and leaned against the refrigerator, watching her walk around the kitchen, looking at everything, pulling the gold earrings from her ears as she did so. She laid them down on the kitchen island. "Nice place," she commented, turning to face him.

"There's lots more." His eyes gleamed wickedly.

"How nice." She continued into the large living area. As she walked around it, her hands went to the little round buttons down the front of her sweater, unfastening them desultorily. James crossed his arms, clamping his hands beneath the opposite arms, and his eyes never left her. When she reached the far end of the room, she looked back at him and let the sweater fall back, sliding down her arms and off onto the floor. Then she slipped through the door into the bedroom wing. James followed her.

In the guestroom Adriana peeled off her slacks. In his study, she reached behind her and unfastened her brassiere, slowly pulling off the lacy scrap and freeing her luscious breasts. The blood pounded in James's temples, and his breath was short and fast. He had to clench his hands to keep from reaching out to her, but he wasn't about to. Not now.

The boldness that had impelled Adriana at first had ebbed away with each succeeding garment, so that when she slipped down the hall into his bedroom, there was a faint flush of embarrassment on her cheeks, and she kept her face turned shyly away from him. But she finished what she had begun; her own blood was surging too heatedly in her veins for her not to.

"This must be the master bedroom," she said softly, her fingertips sliding beneath the lace band of her panties.

"Yes." The word came out as almost a croak. He could see the pink of her painted fingernails through the lace. He felt her fingers on her satiny flesh as if they were his own.

Adriana looked up at him, her courage failing her for a moment. When she saw the expression on his face, taut and heavy-lidded, heat surged through her, and she swept the flimsy triangle of material down her legs and off onto the floor.

He stood still for a heartbeat longer, just watching her, and then he strode across the room, yanking off his suit jacket as he came and tossing it heedlessly on the floor. The lawyer tie came off, too, so hastily it was still a loop when he pulled it off over his head and dropped it. But that was all he took the time for before he grabbed her by the shoulders and started kissing her. His mouth was as voracious on hers as if he'd never kissed a woman before, but far more expert. His fingers kneaded the smooth flesh of her shoulders and back. He slid his hands down her as he kissed her over and over, hardly seeming to draw a breath.

His fingers pressed her hips into him, silently proving his burning hunger. Then his hands trailed upward again and around in front until they touched her breasts. His breath came out in a ragged gust against Adriana's cheek as his fingertips curved around her flesh. James made a noise deep in his throat, and she could feel his faint trembling where his fingers touched her breasts.

She moved up into him, kissing him back fervently, and her fingers curled into his shirtfront, clinging tightly. Her heart hammered in her chest, so hard that she thought that he must surely feel it.

James thrust one hand into her hair, wrapping it around his fist. Pulling her head back, he trailed kisses down her exposed throat, gently nibbling at the soft white flesh. His mouth moved over her chest and down onto the quivering top of one white breast.

He jerked away from her, tearing at his clothes. His face was flushed, his eyes glittering, and he stared at her with an intent hunger all the time he skinned out of his clothes. When he was naked at last, they moved together again, kissing and caressing wildly, and they tumbled back onto his bed, lost in the mad rush of desire. They rolled across the bed, a tangle of arms and legs, their bodies slick with sweat, as they kissed greedily.

James explored her with his mouth and hands, rediscovering each luscious inch of her, until Adriana was almost sobbing with frustrated passion, longing for the glorious fulfillment only he could give. Then, at last, he entered her, filling her, and a groan escaped Adriana.

She was tight and hot around him. He was almost mindless with pleasure, trembling under the force of his passion, lost to everything except the honeyed sweetness of her body. He thrust deep into her softness, as though he could pierce the core of her being, plunging into her again and again, driving both of them ever higher until at last the pleasure exploded within them, taking them out of themselves and into the white-hot realm of mindless ecstasy.

Much later, as they lay snuggled in his bed, James lazily stroking through the strands of her hair, he murmured, "You know, I think I'm beginning to understand your father. I never could see it—risking everything that he did just to help out his mistress. But now..." He kissed her hair, and his hand strayed down over the curve of her shoulder. "I can see how a man would do anything to please a certain woman." He bent and kissed the point of her shoulder where his head had just been. "The woman he loved."

Adriana went still. Had James just implied that he loved her, too? It certainly sounded like it. It was quite an admission from the reserved, cool-headed James. Adriana didn't know what to do. Did he expect a response from her? Something in her wanted to turn to him and snuggle into his chest, to tell him that she loved him, too. But her throat closed upon the words. She couldn't say it. Not yet. She wasn't sure whether she would ever be able to.

Adriana's life suddenly seemed to be filled with James. It was a rare night when she didn't see him, and he called her every day at least once. They went to committee meetings together and eagerly pored over the plans for the new shelter. Sometimes they went out to dinner or a movie or a play. Many times they simply sat together at his house or hers, talking and smiling, unable to get their fill of being around each other. There were evenings when James had to work, and he would sit at the desk in his study, briefcase open and papers spread out around him, making notes in his almost illegible scrawl across the pages of a yellow legal pad. Adriana would curl up in the easy chair in his study, reading or sketching an idea for a design, or often simply watching James as he bent over his work, his forehead knotted in concentration.

It was odd at first to go out in public with James. She felt almost guilty, and she was afraid that someone who knew her mother would see them together and mention it to Millie. That was the last thing in the world that Adriana wanted to happen. Though in general she believed in doing what she wanted to and thought was right, not worrying about others' opinions, in this instance she preferred secrecy. She was certain that her mother would fall apart if she learned that Adriana was dating the man who had sent Jack to prison, and she simply couldn't be responsible for that. Millie's life was tough enough as it was, and she had finally gotten back to where she was enjoying herself again. Adriana was determined not to destroy that happiness for her.

James guessed Adriana's concerns and was irritated by her desire to keep their relationship a secret. However, he kept his silence on the matter, revealing his annoyance with only a twitch of his lips or a raised eyebrow.

As time went by, she relaxed more and more. Her mother didn't find out about her relationship with James. Neither of them was inclined to hang around with the country club set, so they ran into few people that knew their families. And the longer she was with James, the more her uneasy guilt evaporated, like mist in the sun.

James helped Ellen get a temporary job with a small local law firm whose receptionist was out on maternity leave. A room opened up at the women's shelter, and Ellen and Tonya moved into it. When her divorce became final, she planned to move out of state with the child. "I don't care where I go," she told Adriana. "I just want to get as far away as I can from *him*."

With her houseguests gone, James and Adriana spent more and more time at her place. It was a warmer, more welcoming and comfortable house than James's rather austere bachelor's quarters. Once, when they were sitting cozily together in the huge, overstuffed chair in her den, watching an old movie on TV and munching on popcorn, James glanced around the room, frowning thoughtfully, and commented, "You know, it seems a lot more…pleasant here. I mean, it's more comfortable than my place, or something."

Adriana smothered a giggle at his puzzled expression. "I wonder why that is?"

"Do I detect a note of sarcasm in your voice?" He scowled at her playfully.

"Mm. You might."

"All right. What's wrong with my house?"

"Nothing. It just looks a little…unlived in."

"How do you mean?"

"Well, for one thing, look around at your walls next time you go in there. I think you have one picture in your whole house."

"Yeah. I meant to look for some pictures, but I haven't had the time."

"How long have you lived there?"

He paused. "Two years."

Adriana cocked one eyebrow.

"Okay. I get your point. All right, I admit I'm not much of a decorator."

"I think it's more that you never spend enough time there. Your office is more your home than that house. Why'd you buy it?"

"I needed the deduction. Interest on a house is one of the few things left under the new tax laws that—" He caught sight of Adriana's meaningful look and broke off.

"My point exactly. It has all the personal warmth and charm of a tax deduction. The furniture is expensive. Some of it's comfortable. It's a perfectly functional place. But there's nothing of you in it. It needs color, personality."

He tilted his head, as if considering her words. Then he glanced around the room. "I think I like it better here." He grinned. "I spend more time here than at home, anyway."

That was true. He had gradually been making inroads into her bedroom and bathroom, leaving a toothbrush, a shirt, a pair of shoes, until now there were several inches of his clothes hung at one end of her closet, a jumble of his masculine toilet articles on the counter in the bathroom, and a drawer in her dresser reserved for him. Last week she had even had a key made for him so that he could get in when she wasn't there or was busy in her studio. With a start, Adriana realized just how much he had been moving in. Why, it wasn't much of a step between what they were doing now and actually living together!

She glanced at him and found him watching her. Was that why he had brought this subject up? Did he want them to live together?

A warmth spread through her at the thought of sharing a house with James, of his coming home every evening to her, of their eating together, laughing, talking, sleeping together every night. It seemed wonderful, and yet . . . how could she? She was already in over her head with him. She couldn't let the relationship get more serious. She would never be able to keep it from her mother if James was living with her.

"I was wondering..." James began, and Adriana stiffened, afraid of what he was going to say. "I'd like for you to go somewhere with me for a weekend."

His request was so far removed from what she had been thinking about that she stared at him, blinking. "What? What are you talking about?"

"My younger brother's getting married in a few weeks. In Texas. The whole family's flying out for the wedding. I'd like for you to go with me."

"But...I mean, that's a private family occasion. They wouldn't want me there."

"Why not? I'm allowed to bring a guest. I don't think anyone will be shocked or annoyed."

"But it's so..." She didn't know exactly what she meant. But somehow a family wedding seemed too intimate. He wouldn't invite a casual girlfriend to fly to Texas for a wedding; his doing so implied an intimacy and commitment that made Adriana nervous.

"So what?"

"I'm not sure. It just doesn't seem the place for someone who's a stranger to the family."

"You're not a stranger."

"Not to you."

"To any of them. They've heard a lot about you."

Her eyebrows went up. "They've heard about me? From you?"

He nodded. "Of course. Mother's exceedingly curious, too. I've barely managed to avoid taking you to some incredibly boring dinner at the Marshalls so that she can look you over. But this wedding'll do it. They'll all get a chance to gawk at you."

"You're making this sound terribly inviting," Adriana commented dryly.

James smiled. "It won't be as bad as it sounds. You'll like Tag."

"Tag?"

"My brother. The one who's getting married. And the girl he's marrying is nice. We Marshalls specialize in women with pleasant personalities, as well as stunning looks."

Adriana groaned comically. "Laying it on a bit thick, there, Marshall."

"Just telling the truth. Ask anyone."

Adriana sighed. She had the feeling she was going to regret going. But she couldn't resist, either. "Okay," she agreed. "I'll go."

Chapter 12

James was on the floor of Adriana's living room, leaning back against a chair, his briefcase open beside him and papers spread out around him. He had been working, using the coffee table for a work space, but Adriana had brought him a cup of coffee a few minutes ago and stretched out on the couch facing him to talk, and he had abandoned his files. He had changed from his suit into khaki pants when he'd gotten home from the office earlier, and he wore his shirt hanging outside the trousers, the sleeves unbuttoned and rolled up. He looked relaxed and happy and very much at home there in her house, and Adriana enjoyed looking at him.

He was telling her about Adam getting a motor home for the trip to Texas for Tag's wedding, and he gesticulated widely as he described how big it was. "And they're leaving this morning, even though the wedding is six days away. He says he wants to be able to take it in easy stages, so Emily won't get too tired."

"Is she having trouble with her pregnancy?" Adriana had never met Emily, but James had mentioned her several times, and she knew that Emily was expecting her first child soon.

"Nah." James rolled his eyes. "Adam's just being paranoid. The doctor said she shouldn't fly, because the flight would entail sitting too long in a cramped position. She's less than a month away from her due date. But Emily insisted on going to Tag's wedding. She's known him for years and is fond of him. So Adam came up with this brainstorm about driving to Texas in a motor home so Emily could lie down if she wanted, or get up and move around every few minutes."

Adriana smiled. "He sounds like a wonderfully concerned husband."

James chuckled. "I think he's driving Emily nuts."

The doorbell rang. Adriana sighed and got up to answer it. She was enjoying being with James all alone, just talking, and she didn't want anyone interrupting. Of course, it was probably somebody selling something, and that would make it doubly irritating.

But it was no salesman. Just as she stepped out of the living room into the entryway, the front door opened and her mother came in. "Adriana? Oh, there you are, dear. You really shouldn't leave your door unlocked like that."

Millie smiled at her daughter, and her eyes travelled past her into the living room. She saw James. Her eyes widened in shock, and she stopped speaking. Adriana stood between them stiffly. She didn't know what to do. It was obvious that James was comfortable and at home in her house, not only from the way his tie and suit jacket were tossed across the back of the chair, but also because his slacks couldn't possibly have gone with the jacket. Then there was the easy, relaxed way he was sitting there. Adriana could imagine what her mother was thinking.

"Mama, I—" She took another step toward Millie, her hand going out a little toward the older woman. She stopped, unable to think of anything she could say that would explain the situation away.

"I—I'm sorry. I didn't mean to intrude," Millie said a little stiffly. "I didn't realize you had a guest."

James rose to his feet and walked toward them. "Mrs. Larson. How are you? I'm James Marshall."

"Yes. I recognize you, Mr. Marshall." Millie's smile was plastic.

Adriana's stomach twisted inside her. What her mother must be going through! What she must think about Adriana! She couldn't imagine Millie seeing this situation as anything but a betrayal. "James and I work together on a committee for the Women's Center," Adriana put in hurriedly, trying to smooth things over. "He's on the board."

"I see. Well, I don't want to interrupt you. I just came to, uh, drop this off." She glanced down at the book in her hand as if she couldn't remember what it was or why it was there. "I—you'd mentioned you wanted to read it, and I was out eating with Gwen, and—well, anyway, here it is."

"Thank you." Adriana took the book from her quickly. "Would you like to come in? Have some coffee?"

That was ridiculous, of course. She could just imagine her mother sitting down to sip coffee with her father's prosecutor. But she couldn't act as if she wanted her to leave, either.

"No, dear, thank you." Again the plastic smile. "It's getting late, and I should go home." She turned toward James. "Good-bye, Mr. Marshall."

"Good-bye."

Millie turned and walked to the front door, Adriana trailing awkwardly behind her. Her mother left, and Adriana closed the door, turning and leaning back against it with a groan. She turned toward James. He was watching her, and his face looked chiseled out of granite. He turned and began picking up his papers, stuffing them into the briefcase. Adriana watched him, and the knot of anxiety in her stomach grew.

"What are you doing?"

"Leaving," he replied shortly, not looking at her. "I'm sorry I embarrassed you."

"James…you didn't embarrass me. I— It was just an awkward situation."

His head snapped up. "It wouldn't have been awkward if you had told your mother you were seeing me. Instead, you've been trying to hide me from her, like I was some socially unacceptable disease you'd picked up somewhere."

"I wasn't trying to hide you!" Adriana snapped.

"No? Then what would you call not telling her about us? Making sure that we never meet?"

"I call it being sensitive toward my mother's feelings. I don't have to shove our affair in her face. I knew it would upset her. I knew it would be humiliating to her. I didn't want to do that to her if I could avoid it."

"What about me? You think it's not humiliating to *me* that you try to pretend I don't exist? That you keep our relationship a secret from your family and friends? Sometimes I'm surprised you'll even go out with me in public."

"You're being ridiculous." His words stung, doubly so because she couldn't deny that they had some truth to them.

"Do you have any idea how it feels, knowing that you're ashamed of me? That you think I'm good enough to sleep with, but not good enough to be with you in any other way?"

"James!" She was shocked by his words. "That's not true!" Had she made him feel that way? "That's not it at all. It's not that I don't think you're good enough or that I'm ashamed of you."

"No? Then what is it? I have trouble telling the difference when you don't even let your mother know you're seeing me. That says a lot about the permanence of our relationship, doesn't it? 'Well, this guy won't be around long, and Mama wouldn't like him, so I won't tell her about him.'"

"It's not like that! You're putting the wrong interpretation on everything." Adriana felt panic rising within her. James was furious. He was taking it all wrong. "I'm not ashamed of you. I— This is a special situation. I didn't want to hurt my mother. She's been through so much the past year, and she's just getting back to having a normal life. Or sort of a normal life. I didn't want to bring up all the bad memories for her again. Damn it, I owe her something! She's my mother. I couldn't selfishly say, 'Well, I want to see him, and to hell with what it does to you!' You saw her face. She was stunned."

"Of course she was. But she wouldn't have been if you had told her about us."

"She would have been just as hurt then. It would have been at a different time, that's all. I was trying to avoid it, at least for a while. I wanted to give her time to get over the trial, to get some perspective."

"I think you're the one who needs some perspective. It's your life, yet all you can see is how it's going to affect your mother."

"I can't hurt her again!" Adriana burst out, and her words ended on a choked sob. Tears were streaming out of her eyes; she couldn't hold them back any longer. "She's had enough of that. I can't betray her, not after what Dad did to her."

"So you're going to try to make up to her for your father's betrayal? Adriana..." His face softened at the sight of her distress, and he sighed with mingled pity and exasperation. He came toward her, reaching out to take her arms. "Don't you know you can't put back what your father destroyed? *He's* the one who hurt her, not you. It's not your responsibility to make her happy or to protect her from anything upsetting. No matter how much you love her or want to help her, it simply isn't possible."

Adriana couldn't hold back the sobs. "But he's my father. And he hurt her so."

"Shhh." James took Adriana tenderly in his arms, the anger draining out of him. He smoothed his hand down over her hair. "It's okay. I think your mother wasn't the only one he hurt."

She clung to him as the sobs racked her body. "How could he have done it? How could he have done it?"

James bent and kissed the top of her head. "I don't know, sweetheart."

He held her as she cried. Later, when her tears had stopped, they went to bed, and he cuddled her in his arms until she fell asleep. James lay awake for a long time after that, listening to the even sound of Adriana's breathing and treasuring the feel of her body in his arms. He wondered if the specter of her father would always be between them.

* * *

James was already gone the next morning when Adriana awoke. She showered and dressed quickly and hurried over to her mother's house, not even bothering to eat breakfast or put on makeup. Her mother was still in her gown and bathrobe when she got there, sitting in the den and sipping a cup of coffee while she read the newspaper. She looked up when Adriana appeared in the doorway, then stood up quickly, setting the newspaper aside.

"Hello, darling. I didn't hear you come in."

"I used my key."

"Would you like some coffee? Breakfast, maybe? Have you eaten?"

"No, but I'm not hungry. Mama, I have to talk to you about last night."

Her mother sighed, and her face looked suddenly older. Adriana suspected from the puffy look around Millie's eyes that she was not the only one who had been crying.

"Oh, Mama, I'm sorry! I'm so sorry!"

"Why didn't you tell me? When did this happen? I was so flabbergasted. I know I must have looked like an idiot."

"No. I was the one who did that. I should have told you. Prepared you. It was just that I hoped I could keep you from finding out somehow, at least for a few more months."

Her mother looked bewildered and hurt. "But, sweetheart, why didn't you want me to know?"

Adriana blinked. "Why didn't I want you to know! Mama—I—isn't it obvious? I didn't want to hurt you. I was afraid you'd think I was a traitor, that I was selfish and didn't care about your feelings, but only about what I wanted to do. I didn't want anything to happen between James and me! I truly didn't. But I couldn't seem to stop it. I kept seeing him at the committee meetings, and every time it was like being hit with a sledgehammer. The first time I didn't know who he was—I met him at that party I went to at the club before the trial—but even when I knew, after the trial, I couldn't shake the feelings I had for him, no matter how hard I tried. You probably think I'm utterly lacking in control and ethics and—and good taste! But I couldn't stop the way I felt about him.''

Millie chuckled. ''Of course I don't think any of those things about you. I know you too well—apparently better than you know yourself. I'm sure you fought your attraction to him tooth and nail. Unfortunately, we can't necessarily control our hearts.'' Her smile turned a little sad.

Adriana knew she was referring to her own love for Jack Larson, and her heart ached for her mother. ''I'm sorry, Mama,'' she whispered. ''I wanted so much not to hurt you.''

''You haven't hurt me, dear. You mustn't think that.''

Adriana cast a disbelieving look at her. ''You can't be happy to learn that I'm dating James Marshall.''

''I have to admit that he's certainly not the man I would most like to see you with. When I saw him last night, it did hurt. All the way home, I kept thinking about the trial, remembering the pain. It wasn't pleasant.'' Her eyes grew vague, as if she were looking inward instead of out upon the world. ''Particularly remembering the denial I went through, the lying I did to myself and everyone else. It hurt to face up to the truth, but at least that was better than those months of pretending I didn't believe what I knew deep down inside was the truth.'' She shrugged. ''I can't deny that seeing James Marshall reminds me of a time I'd rather forget. But I think after a while I could get used to seeing him. That fresh reminder wouldn't be there. I'd come to see him for himself and not for the trial.''

Adriana stared. It was all she could do to keep her jaw from flopping open. ''Mama! Surely it's more than that! He's the man who put Daddy away. He's one of the men who prosecuted him, who put you through the agony of the trial. Daddy didn't deserve the pain and humiliation that trial subjected him to, and God knows you certainly didn't. You must think of James as your enemy. Don't you? Don't you feel as if I've betrayed you and the rest of the family by being with him?''

Millie looked at her gravely for a moment. ''I think that's more of a problem for you than it is for me. I won't pretend that I ever felt any liking for James Marshall or either of those other prosecutors. But once I got over the need to pretend that Jack was innocent, I knew none of them was really my enemy. Prosecuting your father for his crime doesn't make James a bad man. It was Jack who committed the crime, not James. And it was Jack who was the cause of my pain and humiliation. I can't put your father's sins off on James Marshall, much as I'd like to. Certainly I'm not going to have a fit about my daughter dating him just because he did his job, because he upheld the law.''

Adriana shook her head in disbelief. ''I'm sure I could never be as forgiving or generous as you.''

''It's not generosity. I'm simply realistic. It took me a while to get there, but . . . I mean, honestly, what good does it do me to hate James Marshall?''

''I did,'' Adriana told her honestly. ''Sometimes I feel so guilty and bad for liking him. He was my family's enemy. How could I feel this way about him? I *ought* to hate him. He's a sanctimonious, ambitious, rigid—'' She broke off and looked at her mother. She sighed. "Charming, sexy, even tender man. How can I feel so confused, so split up, over him? I don't want to feel anything for him, yet I do, more and more every day. I'm afraid I'm falling in love with him. And I don't want to. I—you know, before all this, if I had met James, I would have thought, now there's a man with the strength I need. Someone good and honest, full of integrity, powerful, intelligent. Someone like Daddy." Her voice wavered, and she stopped, swallowing. She looked away.

"And now you worry about whether he really *is* like your father?"

Adriana's head snapped back toward Millie.

"Whether he's deceitful?" Her mother went on. "Unfaithful? Likely to let you down when you need him the most? Not really strong, but weak at the core?"

Adriana drew in her breath sharply. "I love Daddy."

"I know you do, dear. But I think you hate him a little, as well. It's only natural. You put him up on a pedestal. You were his little girl, his darling. He was the man against whom you measured all other men, and they usually came up short. It must have hurt terribly when you found out he wasn't the perfect man you had envisioned him to be. You must have felt betrayed and abandoned, just like I did. He didn't cheat on you in the same way he cheated on me, but he revealed his very real feet of clay."

"Of course it hurt." Adriana kept her eyes turned down, watching her fingertips as they picked at her slacks. "But I still love him. I've had to accept the fact that he's human and has weaknesses just like everyone else. I don't guess falling in love with someone and doing whatever you can to help her is the greatest sin in the world."

"No." Tears glittered in Millie's eyes. "But what he did isn't exactly admirable, either. I wonder... I wonder if you've really accepted it. Accepted him."

Adriana shrugged.

"He told me you haven't been to visit him even once."

"I can't bear the thought of seeing him locked up. What good is it to talk to him through one of those little phones, with people all around you?"

"It that really what it is? Is that enough to keep you from visiting someone you love? Sometimes I think you're holding in a lot of bad feelings about your father, that you're furious with him. There's nothing wrong with that. You have every right to be angry with him. He hurt you very much. He hurt all of us, and because of what he did, our whole family was held up to public scorn."

Adriana sat with her elbows on her knees, her hands shoved into her hair. She couldn't bring herself to look at her mother. It hurt to hear her mother say these things about her father.

"But I think that because you love him you can't bear to say how you feel about him. Particularly *to* him. I wonder if you might not be turning your feelings about your father into anger and resistance toward James Marshall. He's a much safer target. It's a lot easier to blame James. It's also a lot safer to keep your heart to yourself and not give it to a man. He might turn out not to be all he seemed. He might deceive you, hurt you, bring your world down around your ears again."

Adriana made an impatient sound and turned away from her mother, rising and walking a few steps away. "I think you're carrying this psychoanalysis bit too far, don't you?"

"Maybe. But I've been seeing a therapist since the trial, and it's helped me. She's opened my eyes to a lot of things, including how I laid the blame for your father's trial off on everyone else—the prosecutor, Patricia Dayton, even myself. Everyone but the person on whom the blame obviously rested."

"That's not what I'm doing."

"I'm not so sure. Honey, all I want is for you to be happy. If James Marshall can make you happy, if he's the man you could love with all your heart, then how I feel about him or how your father feels about him doesn't matter. And what your father did shouldn't keep you from falling in love with a man. I don't want you to be scared and defensive. I don't want you to push James away because of your hurt or your anger over Jack."

"Mama, this is silly. My being angry at Dad wouldn't make me angry at James. I think it would be the opposite, if anything. I'm not trying to hold him off because I'm scared he'll betray me like Dad. I told you—I simply felt disloyal for liking him. I was afraid of hurting you. I never dreamed that you would accept it so calmly." Adriana was aware of a vague irritation with her mother. It seemed bizarre that Millie could be nonchalant about her having an affair with James Marshall when Adriana herself had had so much conflict over it. Of course, she was glad that her mother *wasn't* terribly hurt by it, but still . . .

Those things she had said about Adriana being angry at Jack and turning it against James, about her being scared of him hurting her as her father had hurt Millie— well, that simply wasn't true. She couldn't deny that she had been terribly disappointed in Jack, but she also knew that she still loved him. He was her father, after all, and nothing could change that. She had accepted what he had done, and the fact that she hated the thought of visiting him in prison didn't mean that she was avoiding him or her feelings about him. Adriana was glad that her mother had managed to find some peace of mind by visiting a therapist, but that hardly made her an expert on the human psyche.

Millie looked at her daughter for a moment longer, then raised her shoulders in an expressive shrug. "Well, it was just a thought. As you can see, I've managed to survive seeing you with James Marshall. I'd like to meet him sometime—under better circumstances, I mean."

"All right. Maybe when we get back from Texas."

"Texas! Why in the world are you going to Texas?"

"We're going to a wedding. James's brother is getting married this Saturday."

"Oh, I see."

"Don't get that look in your eye. Just because James is taking me to his brother's wedding doesn't mean we're about to get engaged ourselves."

"No, of course not. But going to a family wedding fifteen hundred miles across the country does indicate some seriousness, wouldn't you think? He must be in love with you."

Amazingly, Adriana felt heat rising into her face. She was unaware of how her face softened at the thought of James and his feelings for her, but her mother saw the tenderness around her mouth and the glow in her eyes, and it confirmed more than ever her suspicions about the depth of Adriana's affection for him.

"I don't know, Mama," she murmured. "I know he...cares for me."

Wisely, her mother refrained from commenting and steered the conversation in another direction. Millie got coffee for them both, and they chatted for a few more minutes while they drank it. Then Adriana left.

Later, Adriana kept thinking about her mother's words. Could she possibly have been right? Adriana didn't think so; it sounded absurd to her. Yet she found that she couldn't get what her mother had said completely out of her mind. At odd moments the memory would nag at her.

She was glad when Friday arrived and she had to fly to Texas. At least the trip and the wedding would keep her mind occupied.

James picked her up and drove to the airport, where they joined his parents. It was the first time that Adriana had met Leith and Joyce Marshall. Leith was a silver-haired, more dignified version of James's brother Adam, and his mother, Joyce, was calm and reserved, every expensively tinted hair in place, her clothes perfectly coordinated with her accessories. Adriana had trouble believing that, as James had said, Joyce was suffering from any pangs of curiosity regarding Adriana— or anything else, for that matter.

Joyce smiled at Adriana when James introduced her and made gracious small talk as they awaited their plane's departure. Adriana was a little uncomfortable. Did James's mother realize who she was? Would she ask after her mother? Was she hoping and praying inside that her son wouldn't get entangled with a felon's daughter? Though Joyce was nothing but polite, Adriana was relieved when they were able to board the plane and she and James sat behind his parents, out of conversational reach.

In Austin, they rented a car and drove for over an hour to a tiny town southeast of the city. It was a good deal warmer here than it had been in Winston-Salem, and the soft spring that was just budding there had turned into heat here. The landscape reminded Adriana a little of New Mexico, though greener and containing more vegetation, and she felt a pang of homesickness. She would like to take James to Taos, she thought, and show him all the places she had known and loved.

She shook the thought from her mind. Why did she feel this compulsion to share various parts of her life, both past and present, with him? She didn't think it was a good sign. She was being foolish. With every passing day she became more and more involved with him, and she knew that that could only spell disaster for her in the end. They could have no future together. He was a prosecuting attorney with a bright future and an unblemished reputation; there were many who speculated that he could have a very successful political career. Her father was a felon. She could imagine the damage that could do to his career. If nothing else, the situation was so bizarre, with him having been one of the men who prosecuted her father's case, that he would never be free of gossip about it. There might even be speculation about his ethics in regard to her father's case.

The prospect was equally dim on her side. She couldn't marry the man who had sent her father to prison. She couldn't turn against Jack.

It was an impossible situation for any long-term relationship, and she was sure that James must be as aware of that as she was. He, too, was simply being led astray by his emotions and desire, and someday he would come to his senses. The desire would subside, the emotions ebb. And he would leave her.

Adriana blinked the tears out of her eyes. She refused to start bawling right there in the rental car with James's parents in the back seat. She concentrated on the scenery outside the window and ignored the faintly puzzled looks she was getting from James. He sensed that something was wrong; he was annoyingly good at that.

They passed through the small town where the wedding would be held and drove several more miles before James slowed the car and turned into a dirt drive. Adriana gazed around her with interest as they drove toward the big house at the end of the drive. This was obviously a large cattle and horse operation. There were barns, corrals and loading chutes on one side of the driveway, and stables and paddocks on the other.

As James pulled the car to a stop in front of the sprawling ranch house, the front door flew open, and a black-haired man came out, grinning broadly.

"James!" He trotted down the steps and strode across to the car, greeting James with an uninhibited hug as he stepped out of the driver's seat. "Gee, it's great to see you."

"You too." James gave him a wry grin and shook his head. "I never realized how boring life in Winston-Salem would be without you there to stir things up."

"I told you I had my uses."

Adriana got out of her side of the car and leaned against it, unabashedly studying Tag. Knowing James, Adam, and their parents hadn't prepared her for meeting Tag. He was a Marshall, no mistaking that, with the black hair and those blue eyes and the tall, lean build. He was, if anything, even more perfectly handsome than either James or Adam. But in him she saw none of the seriousness, determination and concentration that were obvious in the other Marshall men. His grin spread clear across his face, and his bright blue eyes danced with amusement and good cheer. It was obvious that Tag

Marshall was a man who enjoyed life and everything in it.

He glanced across the top of the car at her, and, if possible, his grin grew broader. "Well, hello. I'm Tag Marshall. And you must be Adriana."

"Yes. Hello. How are you?"

"Great." He cast a joking glance at his brother. "Well, well, Jimmy, my man, your taste is certainly improving. This is somebody I think you'd better hold on to."

"Oh, I intend to." James, too, looked over at Adriana, and the tender smile that he reserved for her softened his face. "I've been telling her that she's stuck with me."

With irritation Adriana realized that heat was creeping into her cheeks as a result of James's words. She glanced away.

"Then we'll have to help convince her that it's inevitable." Tag gave James a brotherly pat on the back. "We can't let a woman like this get away. Have you noticed what a vast improvement the women we marry are making in the Marshall family? Before too long I think they might actually make it almost human."

"You're full of nonsense, as always," Joyce Marshall told her son as she came around the car to greet him, her cool voice tinged with an affection that Adriana hadn't noticed in it before. She placed her hands on Tag's shoulders and stretched up to kiss his cheek.

"Ah, but you love me anyway, don't you?" Tag's unflagging good humor and charming grin were difficult to resist.

The front door opened again, and Adam Marshall and his wife Emily came out.

"How are your feeling, dear?" Leith Marshall asked solicitously as the couple drew near.

Emily, a quietly attractive blonde, smiled. "Wonderful. The trip couldn't have been easier. I took a nap every afternoon, and Adam must have stopped every two hours for me to get out and walk around a little. The only problem I have is keeping him from smothering me."

Adam, who had kept his hand solicitously under his wife's elbow as she walked to the car, grinned a little shamefacedly. "I admit it. I never thought I'd be the anxious father-to-be, but . . ." He shrugged expressively.

Adriana smiled along with the others.

"Well, Adam should take care of Emily." Tag beamed down at his sister-in-law with obvious affection. "I'm just amazed he realizes what a treasure he's got."

"Oh, Tag . . ." Emily swatted playfully at his arm. "Hush, you'll make him worse. Then I won't be able to get up and leave the room without him following me to make sure I'm all right. Do you know what he was asking me last night? If I wanted to move our bedroom downstairs so I wouldn't have to go up and down the stairs! Can you imagine?"

She smiled up at Adam fondly, belying the annoyance of her words. Then she looked over at Adriana. "I'm sorry. You must think we're awful, going on about ourselves, and here I haven't even introduced myself. I'm Emily Marshall."

"Adriana Cummings." Adriana reached out to shake her hand.

"It's going to be nice to have other women here," Emily went on, her warm smile making Adriana feel welcome and at home. "Being around only these two men is enough to drive you completely batty. When they aren't pampering you, they're teasing you to death."

The group strolled back into the ranch house, and Emily guided Adriana to her room. "If you need anything, just let me know," she told her, making a gesture around the comfortably furnished room. "I tried to get the rooms ready for guests. Tag is absolutely hopeless. None of the guest baths even had soap and shampoo when Adam and I arrived. But I'm getting awfully lazy and forgetful these days." She touched her rounded stomach. "Do you suppose having a baby does something to your brain? Anyway, if I forgot anything, just let me know. I've more or less located where everything is here."

"It looks wonderful."

"I like it here. Sometimes back home everything the Marshalls own can be too absolutely perfect. I like things a little plainer."

Adriana grinned. She liked Emily. "I'm pretty plain myself."

"Not in looks," Emily said frankly. "James told us how beautiful you were, but, you know, you make allowances for a man in love."

Adriana's heart leapt crazily. A man in love? She knew he cared for her; he wanted a deeper commitment from her. He had even said that he loved her. But it was different hearing it from someone else; somehow it made it more real, more permanent, not just a fevered desire of the moment. The only thing was, she wasn't sure whether it excited her or scared her. Maybe a little of both.

"Thank you," she murmured, turning away to hide whatever her face revealed.

Later that day she met Tag's fiancée, Julie, a fresh-faced girl with curling reddish-brown hair and bright green eyes. She had a warm smile and an easy, unpretentious way about her that Adriana liked. She came from a large, noisy family, and they lived in an old farmhouse that seemed filled to the brim with music, laughter and pets of all descriptions. The love she and Tag felt for each other shone in their eyes, and, looking at them, Adriana thought that this was the way love was supposed to be. It was natural and easy, without any of the struggle that went on between her and James. These two loved each other without question, without reserve.

She mentioned that opinion to Julie in the evening after the rehearsal, while they were all gathered at Julie's big old house. Julie looked at her, her eyebrows shooting up, and then she began to laugh.

"I'm sorry. I didn't mean to be rude," she apologized, bringing her laughter under control, though the corners of her mouth continued to twitch dangerously. "It was just that when you said that about it being so effortless and easy with Tag and me... well, it was actually so different that I had to laugh. It wasn't easy or natural at all." She shook her head, her eyes dancing with merriment. "Far from it. The fact is, I didn't want to like Tag. When I first met him, I thought he was a spoiled, rich, shallow playboy. I thought he spent all his time partying and drinking and breaking women's hearts. Even after I got to know him and discovered what he was like, I was afraid to let myself fall in love with him. I wouldn't admit it, and once I even broke up with him."

"Really?" Adriana stared. "But you seem so perfectly suited for each other."

"Suited?" Julie chuckled and shook her head. "I guess we are, but I couldn't see it. I had trouble getting past the externals. You know, his being rich and sophisticated, and my being a hick from the sticks. And I had trouble trusting him, believing him. I was scared, frankly. I was afraid to let go and let myself love him."

"I don't think it's ever easy falling in love with a Marshall man," Emily commented, coming around the side of the couch and lowering herself carefully onto the cushion beside Adriana. "Sorry. I was standing behind you and couldn't help overhearing."

"But surely you and Adam...I mean, he worships the ground you walk on."

"Well, I'll admit that I don't mind hearing you say that." Emily grinned. "But it wasn't always that way, I can tell you. Used to be Adam hardly knew I was alive. No, I shouldn't say that. He knew I was the most efficient, hard-working secretary in the firm, and he liked that. But as far as being a person..." She shook her head.

"What changed his mind?"

To her surprise, a flush rose up Emily's neck, and she smiled a small, secret grin. She shook her head. "Oh, that's too complicated to go into. But, anyway, we... started going out. Then I was scared to death that I would lose him. I couldn't believe that he could fall in love with someone like me, or stay in love with me. One thing I learned about the Marshall men, though—they're a tough, faithful bunch. They don't fall in love easily. But once they do fall in love with you, they don't let go."

"Well, Tag is certainly persistent," Julie agreed.

It had to be a family trait, Adriana thought dryly, remembering how dogged James had been in his pursuit of her. She wondered if Emily was right. Were they really utterly faithful? She thought that James probably was, and certainly Adam and Tag gave every indication of being unswerving in their affections. But, then, Adriana couldn't help but remember how firmly she had been convinced of her own father's faithfulness to his wife, family and company. She knew firsthand how much love could blind one to the truth.

Unconsciously she turned and glanced toward James. He was standing beside the fireplace with his brothers, his hands in his pockets, seemingly in grave discussion. Then a grin flashed on Tag's face, and the other two laughed. Adriana's heart squeezed within her chest, watching James. He was so handsome, so solid. Was it crazy to think that she could trust him forever, to have this desire deep inside to put her heart in his hands?

He must have felt her gaze on him, for James turned and looked at Adriana. He smiled across the room at her, and she couldn't have kept an answering smile from spreading across her face for anything. Just his smile made her insides quiver. She had the awful feeling that she no longer had any choice about putting her heart in his keeping. She was afraid it was already there. The question was whether she dared to let it remain.

She thought back to what her mother had said. Was she really holding back from James because of the anger she felt toward her father? Was she afraid to trust James, or any man, because of Jack's betrayal of her mother— and of her own beliefs about him? Had she directed her anger at her father onto James, then continued to keep him at arm's length because she was scared to trust again? Was she holding on to her anger at Jack and keeping it like a buffer between her and James?

She had thought about her mother's words many times since that day. She hadn't wanted to believe them then and she didn't want to now. And yet…she couldn't help but wonder.

Chapter 13

The wedding went off the next day without a hitch. It was a sweet, simple ceremony in the small Baptist church in Brinkman, and Adriana found herself unexpectedly moved, watching it. When Tag and Julie gazed at each other, reciting their vows, such love shone in their faces that it brought tears to Adriana's eyes. She stole a glance at James, sitting beside her. Feeling her eyes on him, he turned to look at her, and he smiled, reaching out to take her hand. Adriana wondered if he, too, had felt the power of the ceremony. Was he also wondering right now what it would be like if it were the two of them up there instead of Tag and his bride?

Afterward they went to the reception, where Adriana met a dizzying array of the local townspeople. She talked to Julie's grandfather, a charming silver-haired man, for a while, then chatted with Julie's younger brother, Riley. She glanced across the crowded hall once or twice and found James. As he talked, he looked around periodically until his gaze fell on her. Then he smiled and returned to his conversation. It warmed Adriana to see how he kept an eye on her, never hovering or possessive, but always aware of where she was and how she was doing.

After Riley drifted away, Adriana moved toward the edge of the room, where there were chairs lined up against the wall. Her shoes hurt her feet—they went beautifully with the dress, but not with her toes—and she wanted a chance to sit down. Seeing Emily sitting by herself in one of the chairs, she angled toward her and plopped down beside her.

"Hi."

Emily's head was leaning back against the wall, and her eyes were closed, but they flew open when Adriana spoke. She smiled a little tightly. "Hi. How are you?"

"I think that's what I should ask you." Adriana straightened and leaned forward. Now that she looked at her carefully, she could see that Emily didn't look good. Her face was pale beneath her makeup, and there was a strained tightness to the skin around her eyes. "Are you all right?"

"I'm sure I'll be fine. I probably overextended myself, that's all."

"Then you *aren't* feeling well."

Emily shook her head a little. "I've been having a few cramps."

Adriana sucked in a breath. "Cramps! Emily!"

"Now, don't get carried away. If you tell Adam, he'll probably have a coronary. That's why I decided I'd sit down for a while and see if they would go away." She paused. "Lots of women have false labor pains early. I've read about it."

Emily's words did nothing to reassure Adriana. Why would she be talking about false labor pains unless she was feeling them—or real ones?

"Why don't I sit and keep you company?" Adriana suggested. "That is, if you don't mind."

"No, I think that would be nice." Emily closed her eyes again, and Adriana saw her face tighten. She watched the other woman, concerned, and after a moment Emily relaxed.

The sat together quietly for several minutes. A couple of times Emily tried to make small talk, but Adriana quickly assured her that she didn't need to make the effort.

"That's right." Emily cast her a sideways glance, her tight mouth relaxing into something almost like a smile. "You'll be family before too long, won't you?"

"Family?" Adriana repeated blankly. Then, as she understood Emily's meaning, her eyes widened. Emily thought she and James were going to marry? How had she gotten that idea? Was it just a wild guess on her part, or had James said something that had made her think so? She would have liked to question her, but it was obvious from the pinched look around Emily's mouth that she didn't feel like answering questions.

Adriana glanced around the room quickly. She spotted James standing near the punch bowl, talking to a man she thought had been introduced as the manager of the Marshalls' ranch here in Brinkman.

"Why don't I get James?" she asked Emily.

"No, please. I'm sure it will go away in a few minutes if I rest. I don't want to alarm Adam."

"He won't tell Adam—unless it's necessary."

When James looked up and caught her gaze, Adriana waved at him as subtly as she could, telling him to come to her. He gave her a slight nod, and a moment later said something to the man with whom he'd been talking, then walked away from him. He came straight to Adriana, and the knot in her chest unwound a little with each step he took toward her. It wasn't that she couldn't have handled the situation by herself, she knew; after all, she hadn't needed anybody to come to her rescue in years. But there was something awfully comforting in knowing that she didn't have to handle it alone—and that James would be able to deal with whatever arose.

Adriana realized, with a startled uprush of feeling, that she trusted James. She had complete faith in him, not just in his cool head and his abilities, but in him as a person. He was solid, through and through; he was a man she could rely on. Whatever doubts she had about him or their future were intellectual only; instinctively, deep inside her, she trusted him. When there wasn't time to worry or think herself out of it, she turned to James for help, somehow knowing that he would be there for her. The realization was so surprising that for a moment she forgot all about the importance of why she had called James over.

"Hey." He stopped in front of them, smiling. "What's up?"

Adriana gazed at him blankly for a moment before she recalled where she was and what was going on. She opened her mouth to explain, but it wasn't necessary. He had looked down at Emily and guessed the situation. Quickly he squatted beside her.

"Em? Are you okay?"

By now Emily's skin had turned ashen, and her forehead was damp. "No," she murmured, opening her eyes and trying to smile at James. "I don't think so."

James swung toward Adriana. "Get Adam. I'll take Emily out to the car. And get Tag, too. We have to find a hospital." He stood and bent over Emily solicitously. "Can you stand up if I help you? Or would you rather I picked you up? I don't want to hurt you."

Emily cast an agonized glance around. "No, please don't carry me out of here."

"Okay, then, let's walk." He put his hands under her elbows and eased her to a standing position. Emily straightened up as much as she could and, leaning against him, began to walk toward the side door.

Adriana hadn't stayed to watch their departure. She moved rapidly through the dwindling crowd. Tag and Julie were the first ones she spotted, and she grabbed Tag urgently by the arm. "Where's a hospital? A good one."

Tag's eyebrows vaulted upwards. "What?"

"I think Emily's going into premature labor. Something's wrong with her, anyway."

Whatever differences had been apparent in Tag, he was still a Marshall through and through. He didn't waste time on doubts or questions. "Austin would be best, I'm sure, for anything out of the ordinary. But it's at least an hour's drive. Better get her to the regional hospital in Wickman. It's only twenty minutes away. From there they can take her by helicopter to Austin or Temple if it's necessary."

"You want me to call an ambulance?" Julie asked, her forehead creased in concern.

"Nah," Tag assured her. "James or I can drive, and it'll be faster than waiting for an ambulance."

"Okay." Julie set down her champagne glass and swept up her voluminous skirts, catching them in one hand. "You go on with Adam and James. We'll follow you all."

"I'll get Adam," Adriana offered. "Have you seen him?"

Tag frowned, glancing around. "I think I saw him go out back with Dad. Dad probably wanted a smoke."

They took off in three different directions, Tag going to help James, while Julie went to change and Adriana headed for the rear of the hall to look for Adam. She found him outside in back with his father, as Tag had predicted. Leith was smoking a small cigar, and Adam was talking to him. Adam looked up curiously as she approached, and his face grew instantly apprehensive. He started toward her quickly, leaving a startled Leith.

"What is it? Is something the matter with Emily?"

Adriana nodded. "James and Tag are with her. They've gone out front."

He didn't wait to hear any more but took off at a run around the side of the building. Adriana followed him, and behind her Leith tossed aside his cigar and came after them.

"Emily!" Adam rounded the corner and came to a stop at the sight of his wife, leaning against James and making her slow way along the sidewalk. Then he broke from his momentary paralysis and ran to them.

"Adam!" Emily looked up at him, relief filling her face.

Tenderly he bent over her, then swooped her up in his arms and started walking rapidly to the street. Tag, who had run to the parking lot for the car, pulled up in front in the tan Mercedes that the family kept at the ranch. James opened the back door for Adam, and he settled Emily gently inside, then crawled in beside her. James glanced back at Adriana, and she motioned him to go on. He nodded and jumped into the front seat, and the car took off.

"What's going on?" Leith Marshall asked, coming up beside Adriana and watching the car drive away.

Adriana was finishing explaining the situation to him when Julie came trotting out the front door, dressed in an elegant silk suit, high heels and purse in hand. Joyce Marshall was right behind her. Julie led the way to a long, bright red pickup truck, the kind with a second seat behind the front, and they all piled into it.

"Sorry. This is the only car I had keys to," she explained.

"Heavens, don't worry about something like that," Mrs. Marshall said in her usual calm voice as she climbed up into the truck, heels, Bill Blass dress and all, and slid into the small rear seat. Adriana noticed that though her voice was as unruffled as ever, Joyce's face was tight, the tiny lines suddenly quite visible, and her hands were clasped together tightly. "All that matters is getting to the hospital."

They did that. From where Adriana sat she could see that Julie kept the speedometer hovering around eighty the entire time, despite the narrow roads, but it seemed to take forever to reach the hospital. When they pulled up at the emergency room door of the small hospital, they saw the Marshall Mercedes parked in front of it. Julie let them out and went off to park the truck while Adriana and the Marshalls went inside.

The three brothers were in the small waiting room. Adam was pacing like a caged tiger, and the other two sat watching him. James jumped up when Adriana entered and came to meet her, pulling her into his arms and hugging her tightly. He kissed the top of her head.

"Are you okay?"

"Of course." She looked up at him. "How about you?"

He shrugged. "I'm fine. Adam's about to wear through the carpet, of course. They wouldn't let him stay with Emily while they examined her."

A doctor came out a moment later and explained that there wasn't enough time to take Emily to Austin, but that as soon as the baby was delivered, both mother and child would be rushed to Breckinridge Hospital in Austin, if necessary. A nurse directed them to the more private obstetrics waiting room on the second floor. The six of them filled the tiny room. Adam couldn't stay still. He kept sitting down, then jumping up and walking, then sitting down again.

Adriana sat with her hand in James's. Though he said nothing, she could feel the tension in his body. It was obvious that Emily was well-loved by everyone in the Marshall family, and they were all worried about her. Adriana noticed that Tag was holding on to Julie's hand, too, and even Leith and Joyce linked their hands, supporting each other. Adriana cast a worried look at Adam. Poor Adam. He must be deathly worried.

It struck her, with some surprise, how much she felt for this family. Until yesterday she hadn't even known any of them except James and, very slightly, Adam. But somehow she already cared for them. Emily was a sweet, kind woman; it would be difficult not to like her or to be scared that something terrible might happen to her or the baby. And Julie... though she was several years younger than Adriana, Adriana had felt an immediate kinship with her. She had an earthiness and practicality about her, a lack of pretense, that were immensely appealing. Tag, Adam, even Leith to some extent, reminded her in various ways of James—a certain look, a smile, a way of tilting the head while he thought. Even Joyce, cool as she seemed, felt affection for Emily; she was quite worried about her. She'd even been a trouper about climbing into the pickup earlier, without a word of complaint or horror, though Adriana was sure that Joyce Marshall had never been inside a pickup truck before in her life.

They were strong people. Likable. Dependable. It should come as no surprise to her, she thought. They were, after all, James's family, the stock from which he had come. But it *did* surprise her. She had never thought about liking James's family or feeling as if she belonged with them. In fact, she had never thought about them at all. She had permitted only James's presence in her life; she had made sure that his background, his family, his work, all stayed in some shadowy netherworld outside. She hadn't wanted to know them, she thought; she hadn't wanted the entanglements. She hadn't wanted to become part of the fabric of James's life or let him become part of the fabric of hers.

Yet here he was. Despite her best intentions he had wormed his way into her heart and soul. She could no longer imagine a life without him. Now he was bringing in his family, too, forcing her to open up her life even more, to break the narrow band of loyalty she had wrapped around the little unit of her family. She suddenly saw with amazing clarity how she had barricaded herself in with only the people she already loved, closing herself off protectively from developing feelings for anyone new.

She hadn't wanted to be hurt.

Strange. She hadn't been able to see that when her mother suggested it to her last week. Or, at least, she had refused to acknowledge it. What else had her mother been right about?

There was a sound at the door, and the same doctor stood there, grinning broadly. "Mrs. Marshall is doing well." He looked at Adam. "And you are the father of a brand new baby boy. Just a hair over five pounds."

The whole waiting room burst into laughter and loud exclamations. The doctor stood there grinning while Adam grabbed his hand and began to pump it enthusiastically.

"A grandson!" Leith looked inordinately proud. "The very first."

Joyce squeezed her husband's arm, smiling happily, and went up on tip-toe to kiss his cheek. He turned and kissed her soundly on the mouth. All around the room couples were kissing while Adam thanked the doctor and quizzed him in minute detail about the state of Emily's health.

"He said I can go in and see her right away," Adam, looking tired, proud and radiant with happiness all at once, told them after the doctor left. "It's a good-size baby for a preemie, he said, and no complications. Emily's doing great. He thinks there was a couple of weeks miscalculation of the due date, and the baby's only two weeks early, or something like that." He chuckled. "He said he 'reckoned that baby just wanted to be able to say he's a Texan.'"

Everyone laughed, glad for a release for their tension.

"Well, of course," Julie teased. "I should have realized that's what it was."

Adam went in to see Emily, and the rest of them strolled down to the nursery to gawk at the newest member of the Marshall clan. James looped an arm around Adriana's shoulders, pulling her tightly to him as he leaned against the glass, grinning foolishly down at the balled-up, fiercely frowning, little red bundle of humanity lying there. Adriana looked at the baby, then up at James, and a lump formed in her throat. She knew at that moment how desperately she loved him.

It was a noisy group that rode home in the pickup, six of them squeezed into the two bench seats, so that they could leave the car with Adam at the hospital. They talked and laughed and exclaimed over the baby. Tag joked about it being an unusual way to start his honeymoon, and Adriana reminded them how strange they must have looked, sitting there in the hospital waiting room, the men in tuxes and the women in their formal dresses. Everyone's spirits were high, and everything they said sounded clever.

Later, much later, the rush of adrenaline faded and the thrumming nerves relaxed. Adriana realized, sagging, how tired she was. By that time she and James and his parents had said good-bye to Tag and Julie, sending them off at last on their honeymoon, and the four of them had returned to the large ranch house. Adriana changed clothes, but then she sank onto the bed to sit and gazed numbly into space.

A knock sounded at her door.

"Yes?"

The door opened, and James stuck his head in. He, too, looked tired, and she could hear weariness threading through his voice. "Hi. What're you doing?"

"Nothing." She shook her head. "I'm kind of wiped out."

"Yeah. Me, too." He paused. "I was going out to sit on the porch."

"It's nice. The weather's warm here for the first of March." Adriana rose and went with him. "Want me to sit with you?"

"Sure. That's what I came to ask." He put his arm around her, and they walked out the door.

Outside, the evening was velvety black and pleasantly cool, with just the faintest of breezes brushing against their skin. There was a country smell in the air, a scent of freshly turned dirt and new flowers and green things beginning to sprout all over.

"Mmm. Nice," Adriana commented as they settled back into the old rockers.

"Mmm-hmm." James's hand rested lightly on hers. His head was back against the tall rocker, and his eyes were closed.

Adriana's chest ached, watching him. She felt almost like crying, though she wasn't sure why. But somehow the rush of tenderness and love inside her was almost too much to hold in.

He opened his eyes and turned his head toward her. He smiled. Adriana swallowed hard and smiled back. James raised her hand to his lips and kissed it.

"I wanted to talk to you about something," he said softly.

"What?"

"Everything that happened today—the wedding, the baby, rushing to the hospital like that—I don't know, they made a lot of feelings come up in me. Ones I usually ignore, I guess. In the past I thought a career was enough for me, that it was all I needed or wanted. I didn't want a wife or a family. I didn't love anybody that much." He paused and looked at her. His eyes were serious. "'Til I met you. Now that's not enough. It's not even number one on my list. You are. I thought to myself, what if it had been *you* who was in danger, who was rushing to the hospital? It gave me cold chills. I'm not sure I could live without you. I know I wouldn't want to.''

He took a deep breath. "I don't want to be in your life part-time anymore, Adriana. I love you. I want to marry you. I want us to be together. I want to have a family with you. To look down at a kid in the nursery like we did at Adam's baby today and think, 'That's mine, mine and Adriana's.'''

Adriana's chest tightened; she could hardly breathe. "You want us to get married?'' Her words came out as almost a squeak.

"Yeah. That's exactly what I want. I don't want to live without you anymore. I want to be a part of you. I want you to be a part of me." He shook his head. "Maybe this sounds stupid and old-fashioned . . .''

"No," Adriana reassured him quickly. "Oh, no, it's not stupid at all. Nor old-fashioned. It's wonderful. Sweet. The best thing anyone's ever said to me.''

He waited for a moment. "Then what's your answer? Will you marry me?''

Adriana hesitated. She looked away, staring out over the dark lawn. "I—I want to,'' she said slowly. Her eyes came back to his. Her face was taut. "More than anything, I want to say yes.''

"What's stopping you?''

She hesitated. "There's something I have to do first. Something I have to clear up.''

He frowned. "What are you talking about?''

Adriana shook her head. "It's— Oh, I can't explain it, really. Just give me a day or two. I promise I'll give you an answer as soon as I can. I have to talk to my father first.''

Irritation spread over James's face. "You have to get his permission?''

"No. But I have to settle something with him. Before I can have a life with anyone."

The next day Adriana flew home to Winston-Salem with James. They said little. She knew that he was curious and uneasy about her talk with her father, but she couldn't explain to him what it was that she needed to do, or why—especially since she wasn't sure herself. She just knew that her mother was right; she had to come to some kind of peace with her father before she could be heartwhole again and free to marry James.

She drove out to the Federal minimum security prison where her father was being held and was ushered into the visiting area by a guard. To her surprise, the visiting area was not a row of booths with glass separating the visitor from the prisoner but simply a large room with several groupings of chairs and sofas, rather like a rec room in a community center. There were two men, each in blue jumpsuits, seated in different parts of the room and talking with someone. Adriana sat down on one of the hard, straight-backed chairs and waited stiffly.

After a few minutes her father entered the room. He, too, was wearing one of the dark blue jumpsuits, and his hair was cut shorter, not with its usual expert styling. He looked older than a mere few months would warrant, Adriana thought, but his face was wreathed in smiles as he came toward her, hands outstretched.

"Adriana!" He grasped her shoulders and pulled her to him for a hug. "It's so good to see you, sweetheart! I was beginning to be afraid that you weren't ever going to come, it's been so long."

"I guess it's taken me a while to work up the courage," she admitted.

"Well, it's great to see you now." He hugged her again for emphasis, and they sat down. Jack retained a hold on her hand, squeezing it now and then. "You look wonderful." He chuckled. "You needn't return the compliment. I know I look like hell."

"No, you don't."

He grimaced and cast a look down at his clothes. "Not exactly elegant attire. But that's only part of it. You age fast in prison, I think, even one of the government's country clubs like this one."

"Daddy, why did you do it?" Adriana's question popped out, surprising even herself. She hadn't planned what she was going to say, but she hadn't thought she would say this, either.

Her father blinked, then smiled a little cynically. "No 'Daddy, I know you're innocent'?"

Adriana sighed and looked him straight in the eye. "Is that what you want me to do? Pretend that I believe you? That I still think you're a great guy, a hero?"

Jack Larson sighed. "No. I guess that's too much to ask."

"Yeah. I think so." Tears sprang into her eyes. "I couldn't believe it, Daddy." Her voice grew smaller. "For the longest time I held on, thinking that somehow it would turn out that you hadn't done it. That they didn't have a case against you."

He rubbed his hands across his face tiredly. "Sometimes you get caught up in something and you do things that you never would have dreamed you could do. Things you're embarrassed to even think about. You hurt people you love. And you're not even sure why." He glanced at her a little shamefacedly. "I suppose you could say I went through a mid-life crisis. I was beginning to feel old. Then I met Patricia.... I felt like a young man again, crazy in love. I would have done anything for her. Have you ever loved somebody like that?''

Adriana nodded. ''Yeah.''

''That's why I gave her the information. I knew it would help her in her career. She'd get ahead in her firm. It would solidify her position with her clients. I wanted to help her. It didn't seem like a horrible thing to do. Contelco wasn't going to go under because of it.''

''But you betrayed their trust in you. Mother's trust. Your whole family's. Didn't that mean anything to you?''

''I didn't figure I would get caught. I guess people never do. I thought no one would know about it.''

''Even if no one knows about it, it's still a betrayal.''

''Yeah. You're right. I knew it was shady. I knew it was hurting your mother. But I was so crazy about her, I wasn't thinking straight.''

''All my life I looked up to you,'' Adriana said softly, and tears glittered in her eyes. ''I thought you were a great man. Smart, kind, strong. As far as I was concerned, you could do anything! When Alan and I got divorced, I kept my faith in men because I knew that some of them had to be good like you. You weren't deceitful and dishonest.''

''I know. You put me on a pedestal, and I certainly wasn't going to disillusion you. I enjoyed knowing that you thought I was the perfect father. It was nice for the old ego. I knew it was wrong. You shouldn't build someone up into something a lot better than he really is. It's only going to hurt you in the end. He can't possibly live up to his superhuman image.''

''I didn't think you were superhuman,'' Adriana snapped. ''I just thought you were a good man. I thought you had ethics. I thought you were loyal. I thought you loved Mama.''

"I did love your mother. I still do."

Adriana sent him a flashing look of disgust. "Yeah. Right. That's why you had an affair—such a torrid affair, such a *deep* love that you committed a crime for her! I can see how much you loved Mama."

"That had nothing to do with your mother. It was all something else."

"You're right. It wasn't anything to do with Mama. It was all to do with you, your weakness, your—your lack of moral fiber! Damn it! How could you have done it?" Her voice cracked, and she pounded her fist on her knee in frustration. "I hated you for doing that! To her! To me! I loved you so much, and I feel as if you betrayed everything there ever was between us. I feel as if our whole relationship, our whole life, has been a lie! I never really knew you. You aren't the man I thought was my father, and I don't know who you are!"

Tears streamed down her face, and she sobbed raggedly.

"I'm sorry, sweetheart," her father said in a low voice. "I'm sorry. I understand why you hate me. I wish to God there was something I could do about it."

Tentatively he reached out and smoothed his hand over her hair. Adriana's sobs grew louder, and instinctively she leaned toward him. He put his arms around her and held her, and she cried against his chest, as she had done when she was a little girl and her heart had been broken by some childish hurt. "Oh, Daddy!"

"I know, sweetheart. I know." He patted her back awkwardly.

Finally her tears stopped, and she pulled back from him. She wiped her tears away and let out a shaky sigh.

Her eyes and head ached, and there was a sadness in her chest, but there was relief, too, spreading through her, and a sense of having finally turned some corner in her life.

"That's why I haven't been to visit you," she told him softly. "I was furious with you, yet I still loved you. I couldn't reveal how hurt and mad I was."

"I'm glad you did. I'd rather that than not seeing you again. I know I hurt you, Dree, and I'm sorry. You have to believe that."

She looked at him, and for the first time in months she felt as if she could look him in the eye again. She didn't feel the nagging resentment and bitter disappointment. "I guess I expected too much of you. I did think you were better than everyone else—stronger, braver, brighter. Maybe I didn't allow you to be human."

"I know it'll never be the same again between us..." He couldn't quite suppress the note of hope in his voice.

"No. I don't think it will."

He nodded, looking down. "But I hope you won't cut me off entirely. I do love you, Dree, whatever you think of me."

"I know you do. And I love you." It was different now; there was no longer the element of hero-worship in their relationship that had once been there, no longer the conviction that her father was the best and could do no wrong. But still, she loved him; she couldn't help but love him. He was, after all, her father.

She offered him a smile and leaned over to kiss his cheek. "Thanks. I—I'm glad I came."

"Me too, sweetheart. Come back. Will you?"

"Yeah. I will." She hesitated. "Dad...I probably ought to tell you. I've been dating James Marshall."

It took an instant for the name to register, and then his eyes almost popped from his head. "Who!"

"James Marshall."

An expletive escaped his lips, and he said bitterly, "Well, that's certainly one way to get back at the old man."

"I didn't do it to get back at you. In fact, I struggled not even to like him for the longest time. But I love him, and it's crazy to pretend I don't just because he had to try your case. I—I hope you can accept it someday."

"And if I don't, then too bad, huh?"

"I won't give up James, if that's what you mean. I don't expect you to be overjoyed. But I hope that in time, well, that we'll come to take each other for what we are."

"I'll be damned." He shook his head. "That's the last thing I ever expected you to say." He sighed and stood up. "But I'll tell you, like you told me, I still love you, honey."

Adriana smiled. "Good."

They parted without another hug, but with no more bitter words or tears, either. Adriana walked out of the prison and across the asphalt lot to her car. She felt released. Free. It was as if the bitterness and anger had flooded out of her with her hot words and tears.

She jumped in her car and turned back to the highway, speeding toward Winston-Salem. Toward home... and James.

But on the way she remembered that James would not be at home yet. He would still be at work. She glanced at the clock in her car. She didn't want to sit at home, passively waiting for him to return. She was too full of excitement and love. She had to see him now; she had to tell him.

She drove to Greensboro and went to the U.S. Attorney's office. It was in the Federal building, and there was a certain eerie feeling about walking back into the same building where she had watched her father's trial. More than one head turned to look at her as she walked through the maze of offices, and she knew that several people probably recognized her from the trial and were agog with curiosity about her presence. Well, let them wonder; she didn't care. All that mattered was finding James.

He wasn't in his office, and his secretary suggested that she try downstairs in one of the conference rooms or in the law library. She glanced into the library, but he wasn't there, either. She continued down the wide, almost deserted hallway, opening door after door.

She found him at last in an empty courtroom. It was not the one in which her father had been tried, but a far smaller one used primarily for less formal hearings. James was seated at one of the tables, bent over an open file, his hand shoved into his thick hair. Adriana paused in the doorway, smiling fondly at the typical picture of intent concentration he presented. She must be far gone, she thought, when a little thing like that could make her throat swell up with love.

She stepped into the room and closed the door behind her. The noise brought James out of his trance, and he turned around. When he saw Adriana standing there, his face registered astonishment, followed quickly by delight, and he stood up and started toward her.

"Adriana! I never expected to see you here. What are you doing?"

"I came to tell you something."

"Good." He kissed her hard and briefly. "I'm glad, if it brought you here."

"I came to give you my answer."

He straightened, his eyes suddenly alert. "Okay."

"It's very simple. My answer's yes. I want to marry you. I love you, and I want to spend at least the rest of my life with you."

"At least?" A broad grin spread across his face. "Well, that's exactly how long I want to be with you, too."

He pulled her to him tightly and kissed her again, this time more thoroughly and more tenderly. "I love you," he murmured as he pulled back a little and gazed down at her.

"I love you, too. I'm sorry I've been so crazy and confused."

He shook his head. "Don't worry about it. All that matters is now. And the future. We've got all the time in the world together."

"Good." Adriana linked her hands behind his neck and smiled up at him.

"You know," he arched an eyebrow speculatively, "I've had this fantasy about you and a courtroom for a long time. . . ."

"James!" Adriana gasped and laughed. "Not here!"

"No? I could lock the door." He began to nibble at her neck.

"Mmm. Well . . . you *are* awfully persuasive."

"My stock in trade," he murmured, and his tongue teased at her ear.

"I think you've made your case," Adriana said weakly, melting against him.

"Best argument I've ever made." He chuckled and bent to kiss her again.

*   *   *   *   *

SILHOUETTE·INTIMATE·MOMENTS®

IT'S TIME TO MEET
THE MARSHALLS!

In 1986, bestselling author Kristin James wrote A VERY SPECIAL FAVOR for the Silhouette Intimate Moments line. Hero Adam Marshall quickly became a reader favorite, and ever since then, readers have been asking for the stories of his two brothers, Tag and James. At last your prayers have been answered!

In August, look for THE LETTER OF THE LAW (IM #393), James Marshall's story. If you missed youngest brother Tag's story, SALT OF THE EARTH (IM #385), you can order it by following the directions below. And, as our very special favor to you, we'll be reprinting A VERY SPECIAL FAVOR this September. Look for it in special displays wherever you buy books.

Take 4 bestselling love stories FREE

Plus get a FREE surprise gift!

Silhouette Special Edition

presents

SONNY'S GIRLS

by Emilie Richards, Celeste Hamilton and Erica Spindler

They had been Sonny's girls, irresistibly drawn to the charismatic high school football hero. Ten years later, none could forget the night that changed their lives forever.

In July—
ALL THOSE YEARS AGO by Emilie Richards (SSE #684)
Meredith Robbins had left town in shame. Could she ever banish the past and reach for love again?

In August—
DON'T LOOK BACK by Celeste Hamilton (SSE #690)
Cyndi Saint was Sonny's steady. Ten years later, she remembered only his hurtful parting words....

In September—
LONGER THAN ... by Erica Spindler (SSE #696)
Bubbly Jennifer Joyce was everybody's friend. But nobody knew the secret longings she felt for bad boy Ryder Hayes....

Coming Soon

Fashion A Whole New You. Win a sensual adventurous trip for two to Hawaii via American Airlines®, a brand-new Ford Explorer 4 × 4 and a $2,000 Fashion Allowance.

Plus, special free gifts* are yours to Fashion A Whole New You.

From September through November, you can take part in this exciting opportunity from Silhouette.

Watch for details in September.

* with proofs-of-purchase, plus postage and handling

Silhouette Books®

SLFW-TS